Praise

"*Winter Light* tugs at your heart, reminding you of what it's like to be a young person growing up, unsure of what to wear, how to behave, who and what to care about. Unsure of anything. The story is a ride through Class V rapids that will keep you hanging on white-knuckled till the end. A great read."
JANA MCBURNEY-LIN, AUTHOR OF *MY HALF OF THE SKY*

"*Winter Light* is the extraordinary and intricate story of Mary Donahue, a teenager from the darker side of life whose struggles, resilience, and courage will be forever seared in your brain and your heart."
JOYLENE NOWELL BUTLER, AUTHOR OF *BROKEN BUT NOT DEAD*, *MATOWAK: WOMAN WHO CRIES,* AND *DEAD WITNESS*

"Martha Engber has crafted a well-paced, thoughtfully structured, insightful novel that draws the readers' compassion for Mary and the motley collection of 'burnout' teens that are Mary's friends. We witness Mary's heartrending struggles to break free of economic and social class boundaries, the effects of careless parenting, and the low expectations of others, subjects the author handles with great skill and subtlety."
PAULETTE BOUDREAUX, AUTHOR OF *MULBERRY*

About the Author

Martha Engber is the author of *The Wind Thief*, a novel, and *Growing Great Characters from the Ground Up*. A journalist by profession, she's written hundreds of articles for *The Chicago Tribune* and other publications. She had a play produced in Hollywood and fiction and poetry published in the *Aurorean*, *Watchword*, and other journals. A workshop facilitator and speaker, she lives in Northern California with her husband, bike, and surfboard.

www.marthaengber.com

Winter
Light

Martha Engber

Vine Leaves Press
Melbourne, Vic, Australia

Print Edition
ISBN: 978-1-925965-44-5
Published by Vine Leaves Press 2020
Melbourne, Victoria, Australia

Cover design by Jessica Bell
Interior design by Amie McCracken

A catalogue record for this book is available from the National Library of Australia

To my mom, who was my Mrs. McCarthy

Chapter 1

Tues., Dec. 12, 1978

Mary lay with her cheek against the school desk, staring into the winter dusk. Bare tree limbs looked black against the ash sky tinged with the orange of a sinking sun. Everyone said this winter would be bad. The worst in recent history. Real scary boogeyman shit. The cold colder than the coldest. The snow deeper than the deepest. The coldest and deepest in years, maybe since the Ice Age. Whistling winds, blizzards, ice-sheet highways, one prediction bleaker than the last. Whatever came would have to be a real whopper of catastrophe, though, because you don't grow up in this old Chicago suburb on the Burlington-Northern Line without knowing the meaning of frigid. And you don't survive fifteen years with three older brothers and a worthless, his-glasses-glaring-all-the-time, alcoholic father without knowing how to dig yourself out from under.

But then she narrowed her eyes because Mother Nature could be a mean bitch, even on days when nothing much happened. Like today. No blizzard, no limb-tearing wind. Yet look at the muted glow of that dying sun, the sky bleeding out slowly, quietly, alone. Like the work of a serial killer.

She didn't bother looking at the clock above the classroom

door. The time always 11:59—forever on the verge—because nobody bothered to fix the thing. Mr. O'Brien had ducked out twenty minutes ago, saying he needed something from the office, when everybody knew he went to have a smoke in the teachers' lounge. The time must be close to three when the bell would ring.

She turned her head and rested her other cheek on the desk. She studied the girl in the next seat over. The same girl who always sat in that same seat, probably even on the days Mary ditched. Though the girl had to be fifteen, too, she looked twelve, what with the skinny body and flat chest. She read with one hand on her forehead and an elbow lodged on a stack of books. She wore a white button-down shirt beneath a dark blue wool sweater with a ring of small whales circling the collar. And how everything matched, too. Jesus. The sweater with the corduroys, the corduroys with the socks, the socks with the ribbon that kept a perfect curl of brown bangs off of her face. But the shoes gave her away. No real prep would be caught dead wearing cheap Oxford knockoffs with a dweeby wedged heel. That made the girl a wannabe, and the only thing worse than a prep was a fucking prep wannabe.

Mary lifted her head and with two fingers, flipped a strand of long, strawberry blonde hair over her shoulder. "You got the time?"

The girl looked up.

Mary counted three Os: two made by the girl's surprised brown eyes, and the third by her prissy lip-glossed mouth.

"The time," Mary said.

The prep looked at her watch. "Five to three."

"Thanks."

The girl returned to reading. Mary looked out the window again. The sinking sun meant the temperature would drop soon, too, probably to near zero. Yet she had no ride waiting for her, so she'd do what she always did and walk home.

She'd cross the street and cut through the hole, a wooded lot good parents forbid their kids to cut through, especially after that girl got murdered there last summer. She'd been a loser with dirty hair and a bad complexion, but even so. Nobody deserved to be strangled.

Mary would continue along 47th Street as the streetlights blinked on and the headlights of oncoming cars flashed across her chest. She'd walk by the same houses she passed every day, middle-class jobs of stucco and brick. While most looked nice, every block had at least one dump like the one where she lived. A place where though you switch on the overhead light in your room, the cold and dark remain inside of you. So you smoke and listen to your favorite album, Pink Floyd's *The Dark Side of the Moon*, a gift from your best older brother, Danny. And somehow you try to stop thinking about death. When you're only fifteen and have your whole life ahead of you, you're not supposed to dwell on strangled dead girls or guys like Terry Kath, the guitarist for Chicago who'd just croaked of an accidental self-inflicted gunshot wound.

Bang!

She jerked, the pulse in her neck throbbing with the sudden race of her heart. The sound she'd heard had been somebody coughing. Just a cough, not a gunshot, and Christ, what was wrong with her? A drop of sweat snaked down her back beneath her black Ted Nugent T-shirt. She thought of taking off her midi-length wool coat with the trampled fake fur collar, but the bell would ring soon. So she'd sit and do nothing and pretend she didn't care. As always. Maybe forever.

But then the wannabe prep cleared her throat, the sound quiet and polite. Mary considered the girl again, though longer this time and without blinking.

"What you reading?" Mary said.

Again the girl looked startled. "Well..." She rotated her wrist to show the cover. Instead, Mary kept her eyes on the girl. Apparently confused, the prep looked down, cleared her throat and said, "*Jane Eyre*."

"What's it about?"

"Um—"

"What's *um*?" Mary said, deadpan.

The girl pressed her lips together.

"Just teasing," But Mary didn't smile.

The girl's right eyebrow dipped. A *yeah, right* look. Yet she answered anyway. "It's just this girl. She's an orphan and has this really hard life."

"Gee, how sad."

"Well, you asked," the girl said with enough edge in her tone to almost make Mary smile. She liked people who could take care of themselves, especially those who didn't look like they could.

Mary propped her head on her hand. "I'm not trying to be a bitch or anything."

Which was true. Nobody wants to be a bitch. That's just how you get tagged sometimes, mostly because other people don't understand. They think you're trying to be a smartass, when really you want to learn what you don't know, but you're not good at asking. Either that or they look you up and down, and after studying your not-so-fancy clothes and not-so-cheery face, decide you're a bitch because you look like one.

So she sugared her tone a tad. And though she couldn't dish up a fake smile, she tried not to look so serious, or whatever had put off this girl who couldn't take a joke.

"I'm just saying," she said, "must be nice not to know about that shit firsthand. You read about it and when it gets too depressing, just close the book."

But apparently she hadn't sweetened her tone enough. The girl dropped her eyes to her book. Jaw tight, shoulders tense, face averted; everything about her slammed shut, barring entry to the Big Bad Bitch, and Jesus, what an impressive reaction.

The bell rang, and the prep stood so fast she knocked her desk sideways. She scooped up her books, and rather than leave the desk askew, as Mary would have, the girl tugged the desk into place and walked toward the door with quick, hipless steps. To choir practice, maybe, or a giggle with the girlfriends.

Mary extended her arm. She cocked her thumb and index finger and pointed at the girl's retreating head. She itched to pull the trigger. Then again, you never know who might save you someday. A good Samaritan. A guardian angel. A stranger just waiting to jump out of nowhere to do saintly deeds.

Too bad she didn't believe such bullshit. Yet she lowered the barrel anyway.

Chapter 2

Wed., Dec. 20

Mary squinted into the blue, late-afternoon sky and inhaled on her cigarette, her ass freezing even as her lungs burned. The six of them—she, her four friends, and a creep hanger-on—were idiots for being here in the forest preserve in this cold. But she didn't want to go home. None of them did. And nobody had any money for Mickey D's, so what else was there to do after school and before she went to work?

Her eyes wandered the preserve; nothing sadder than a winter forest hemmed in by suburbia. Bare trees starving within sight of civilization. But in the summer, Jesus. In the summer, what a place to party, the trees offering shade on those sticky days when hair down your back feels like a wool blanket. And when fully leafed out, the trees provide privacy for you and your boyfriend, or you and your loud crowd, because no neighbors live close enough to call the cops and complain. Yet you still have to watch for the police anyway, cruising their black and whites along the winding entrance road from Ogden Avenue, past this parking lot to where the road ends at the picnic pavilion.

But today the parking lot was empty. The limbs of skeleton trees blew in the wind, two feet of snow at their trunks.

The locked red brick bathroom looked like a windowless fortress and the J-shaped toboggan chute down the side of the hill seemed a silent call to death. Everything closed, hard, the wind a zipper catching your skin. Yet her friends stood around, joking, laughing, shifting from foot to foot. None wore hats or gloves. None had coats worth shit, all of them used to being cold. Used to crowding together either to keep warm or because you're sick of being alone and they are, too. The kind of people who will come get you when you're desperate for a ride or haul you out of your head when you sink too deep, something regular people don't understand, those who live in houses where Christmas cookies get baked. How could you explain to such safe and complacent people that while you might not be popular in the prep or jock sense, among your own kind, you've got status? While advantageous to be known, your actions followed and your input sought, that's no substitute for having a core group that will protect you, all of you doing for the other what you'd do for yourself because no one else will. This group. These friends. Chuck, Lucy, Tina, and Mary's boyfriend, James.

Chuck only ever wore his dead dad's olive, drab Army jacket, a Vietnam treasure beyond that of The Beast, his black Impala that carted their asses everywhere, including here. And Chuck's sister, Lucy, owner of the wide-mouthed smile and dazed, blue-eyed gaze that earned her Airhead of the Year two years running at Danny's annual Char the Weiner BBQ on the last day of school. Then there was Tubby Tina—who'll punch you if you say that to her face—with the shitty hair and bulging hips stuffed into too-small jeans.

Which left James. Sweet James. A junior with light blue eyes, he had the body of Jim Morrison and the energy of a five-year-old on speed. Though the best thing about him was his smile, that of a corrupt choirboy. He worked overtime to keep Mary happy, which countered the *you're nothing* talk of a wasted dad. At least most of the time.

Bob was here, too, but Bob wasn't a friend. He was a hunch-shouldered, lean-bodied freak Chuck invited occasionally, hoping Bob would, out of the generosity of his silent, antisocial heart, score some free shit off of his older brother, who was said to be connected to some real badasses in the city. *Baaaad*, Tina repeated whenever the subject arose.

Mary shook her hair from her face. Her stomach rumbled. She took another drag on her cigarette, because that's what you do when you're so hungry you want to throw up. She'd long ago discovered tobacco did for nausea what Raid did for a cockroach. Kills. It. Dead. Never mind that over the long-term, tobacco's truth would be *kills—you—dead*. Then again, long-term lingered too, too far away to think about.

She glanced sideways. Bob stared at her and probably had been for a while, judging by how still he stood. Not smiling, just staring. Him and his stringy blond hair and half-closed eyes the color of mud, like a psycho dog. She looked away. She listened, sort of, to the conversation around her. When she heard the name of a guy who was supposed to come to the party tonight, she exhaled and said, "He's a douchebag."

James laughed. "Just because he grabbed your ass that one time."

"I'll bet he's grabbed his mother's ass," Mary said.

"I wouldn't doubt it. But man, can he lay hands on some excellent shit," Tina said while hopping from foot to foot in her sneakers, the soles so flat she slipped her way from one step to the next. She pulled a strand of hair from the corner of her mouth. "Once, he let me try some of his blow—"

"In exchange for a blow," Chuck murmured. Everybody but Tina and Bob laughed. Then again, Bob never laughed.

"Fuck you," Tina said to Chuck.

Mary yawned.

"Who's bringing the beer tonight?" Lucy said while huddling against Chuck.

Mary felt James move behind her. He slipped his hands into her front coat pockets and pulled her close, his chest to her back. His hidden fingers wandered farther and farther south until finding her crotch.

In a slinky, cat-like stretch of tone, he whispered in her ear, "You think your brother could help us out again?" He referred to Danny, a senior who possessed a coveted fake ID.

James's touch made her groin tingle. But she didn't feel like feeling like that right now.

"How the fuck should I know? Ask him." She popped her ass back into James's groin. He bent double and groaned dramatically.

"You heartless wench," Chuck said, laughing.

"He's not hurt," she said.

James straightened and socked Chuck in the arm. "You ask Danny then."

"Check it out," Tina said and pointed to a brown station wagon coming toward them. The car parked near the toboggan chute next to the locked restroom, maybe fifteen parking spaces from Mary and her crowd. A girl wearing black ski pants got out. Her pink hat matched her pink mittens, and Christ, where was the unicorn festival? She jogged to the tail of the car. Another kid got out. The back window lowered and both kids pulled out a toboggan that kept coming and coming.

"Holy shit," Tina said. "It's like a never-ending turd."

Younger, shorter, and dressed in blue, the second kid looked like a boy, most likely the girl's little brother. He pulled the toboggan by a rope handle to the chute. The girl talked to the driver through an open window. Then the girl leaned in through the window and kissed the woman on the cheek. A light, fast touch of lips, so easy, so routine. A daughter kissing her mother.

"Shit," Mary murmured.

"What?" James said.

She looked at him. "What?"

"You said *shit*."

"I did not."

"Did too."

"So? Who gives a shit?"

The mom backed up, waved, and drove off. The kids lined up the toboggan at the top of the chute. And Jesus, who would do that? Plunge down a hill, hoping you don't fly out of the wooden trough before shooting out the end into a field of snow?

James scooped Mary around the waist and pulled her toward the chute.

"Have you ever done it?" he said.

"I think not," she said, borrowing Mr. O'Brien's favorite line from some old book.

Lucy jogged past James and Mary toward the kids. The girl sat at the front of the toboggan behind the curled wooden hood. The boy hugged her waist. They scooted their bodies forward three times. The toboggan inched toward the edge with each thrust then disappeared over the edge, the kids' screams trailing.

"Shit!" Lucy yelled from where she'd stopped to watch. Mary and the others walked up just as the kids flew out the bottom of the chute. The toboggan raced across the snow and stopped a few yards from the trees. The kids jumped up, laughing— little bunnies of glee—when only moments ago they'd been yelling like slasher-movie victims. The kids pulled the toboggan toward the stairs.

Chuck walked up behind Lucy and massaged her shoulders. "You want to try?"

"No!" Lucy said. But she was smiling.

"Hey," Chuck yelled to the kids. "Can my sister have a ride?"

The girl stopped on the staircase and looked up. Her gaze traveled from Lucy across the group to Mary. The two looked at one another. It was her, the wannabe prep from English class. She didn't look too happy to see Mary, though why, Mary didn't know. The girl dropped her head and trudged up the steps, as though condemned to death.

Lucy squealed as Chuck dragged her by the wrist toward the head of the stairs. "Seriously," he said when the prep reached the top. "Can we try? Just once?"

The tassel on the hat, the flat chest, all that pink. The girl looked even younger than she normally did. Yet when she talked, she sounded like the crack of a billy club across a back: straight and hard.

"We're not supposed to," the girl said.

"What's the big deal? Give her a fucking ride," Tina said. "You afraid she's going to break it or something?"

The prep frowned. Her gaze shifted from Chuck to Tina, then to Mary. Eyes of deep blue, they looked plenty pissed. Yet underneath, Mary detected a request for help. She didn't move, though, because the girl wasn't in danger. Not yet, anyway. That, and Mary wanted to see what the girl would do. Fall down and cry? Or would she pull up the drawbridge again, as she had in class?

The girl's brother cupped a hand around his mouth and whispered into the prep's ear. She shook her head. Short, sharp. She looked at Chuck.

"My dad said we're not supposed to," the prep said.

Tina stepped to within punching distance. "You scared of us?" Tina's eyes dropped to the girl's fake black-and-white fur ankle boots, like the kind a granny might wear.

"What the hell are those, anyway?" Tina said, but the girl remained silent. "What, now you can't fucking talk?"

The girl lifted her chin, her mouth tight. "They're mukluks."

"What?" Tina said.

"Mukluks," the girl said louder. "Like Eskimos wear."

"What was that?" Tina said. "Muk-fucks?"

The prep's eyes jumped from one person to another. She

glanced over her shoulder toward the bathroom, but the fortress was locked. The prep leaned toward her brother and said something. Then they turned toward the road leading out of the preserve.

That was it, her big plan? To pretend Mary and her crowd didn't exist? Then what? Hike to the road and hitch a ride, a girl and a boy and their gigantic toboggan? Mary shook her head at the girl's naïveté in turning her back on enemies.

Sure enough, Tina jogged around and stopped in front of the prep, making her stop, too. Mary tensed but didn't move because sometimes that makes things worse. Instead, you watch closely and wait.

"Where you going, priss?" Tina said.

"Leave us alone," the prep said.

Tina took a step closer and looked at the boy. "What's your name, kid?"

The girl stepped in front of her brother, feet spread wide. "What's the matter with you? We didn't do anything to you. Is scaring younger kids all you can think of to do? You're just some big fat—"

"Catfight!" Chuck yelled, laughing.

Tina lunged at the girl, *lunged* at her like some goddamn bulldog with no self-control. Mary stepped forward, a hand out, but James jumped forward and got to Tina first and with a hand on each arm, dragged her backward. Though Tina was still within biting distance, the prep didn't shut up.

"—a big fat bully," the prep said. "It takes a lot of guts to pick on a kid smaller and younger than you. You must be so proud of yourself."

"Leave her alone," Mary said to Tina.

Tina straightened so suddenly James almost fell backward. Tina huffed, her face heated to a sweating red. She kept her unblinking eyes on the girl.

"Leave her alone," Mary said louder.

"Bitch," Tina said, spitting the word at the girl. Tina turned away while casting angry glances over her shoulder at the girl and complaining to Chuck, Lucy, and Bob. And god, how embarrassing that Tina's behavior confirmed the prep's suspicions, that Mary was a bitch who hung out with losers. Then again, why would she care what the prep thought? Look at her just standing there with clenched mittens, visibly shaking and glaring at Mary instead of thanking her. And instead of marching toward the road, the way now clear, the kid yanked the toboggan into position before the chute and sat down. To show the meanies they couldn't spoil her fun.

"Come on," she said to her brother.

The boy leaned over and whispered to her.

"Come *on*," the girl said, rope handle in her hands. Her brother sat behind her.

One tremendous body heave and one last Charles Manson glance at Mary, and the girl and her brother disappeared over the edge.

Yet the girl had stuck up for her brother, and in the process, managed not to blubber. And though incredibly ignorant to think you can wish away what you don't want to face, maybe there's something smart about walking away from trouble. An act that requires guts, courage, maybe both. So that even though a girl might be short and skinny and wear sweaters decorated with whales, maybe she'd be the kind of person who could pull you out of some serious shit. Which is cool.

And Mary smiled.

Chapter 3

Chuck stopped The Beast in front of Mary's house, braking so hard the momentum thrust everyone forward and rocked them back. His driving skills rivaled that of cartoony, almost-blind Mr. Magoo and Danny's longtime friend, Marco.

"Can't believe they gave you a license," Mary said from where she sat squeezed in the back between Bob and James.

"What?" Chuck said.

She didn't answer. James opened the door and got out.

"See you tonight," Bob whispered, as though only for her.

She didn't look at him. "Guess so."

She got out and slung her purse over her shoulder. James caught her in his arms and leaned back against the car, pulling her pelvis to his. Though she was five feet eight, James had a few inches on her, enough to look down into her eyes. He smiled a smile that jumped her mind to mukluks, then Eskimos. Where they had a million different words for snow, so James had a million different smiles, one for every occasion. He had a smile that could piss off his dad in one second flat, and another for his mom, to tell her he loved her, despite her nightly wine buzz. He had a smile that could charm teachers into giving him another chance. His best smile, though, is one that says even if he can't commit to you for longer than the present, or discuss anything deeper than the lunch menu, he'll never betray you. She laid her cheek against his chest. He kissed her head.

"Loosen up, babe," he said. "It'll be okay. You'll get it."

She nodded and turned away. Head down and arms lifted away from her for balance, she worked her way over the icy, lumpy sidewalk to the icy, lumpy front steps no one bothered to shovel.

"Tell Danny to hurry so we don't freeze to death," James said. "Chuck's too cheap to keep the car running."

Light blazed from the porch bulb, the living room window, and the second-floor bedrooms, nobody but her seeming to care about the light bill. Then again, among the three of them left here—her, Danny, and their dad—only she had a steady income with which to pay the electric, gas, and grocery bills. Danny usually paid the phone bill and helped with food, but he hopped jobs, ever searching for the perfect labor, one that would net him free art materials. But he'd lost his last job a month ago when his car died. Which left Frank. She only ever thought of him by his first name, but if she didn't call him *Dad*, he got pissy. Frank only ever managed to hold a job for a week, maybe two.

She didn't bother with a key. Nobody locked up. She pushed the front door, which stuck. She slammed her palm a foot above the lock to unjam the door.

"Who left all the lights on?" she yelled. The house remained quiet except for a rhythmic thud from Danny's room. She kept her coat on against the cool sixty-degree air, a temperature that hadn't changed since she'd driven a nail into the wall so people couldn't turn up the thermostat. As she walked down the hall past the living room, she glanced sideways to see Jerry passed out on the brown couch, beer in hand. He and Frank, both near fifty now, had gotten to know one another years ago on some job. A few favors in finding Frank work, and Jerry thought he lived here.

His eyes fluttered open, "Hi Mar," he said, his voice that of an old, shit-faced Yogi Bear.

She unbuttoned her coat and continued down the hall, across the bare wooden floor, and past the gouged walls. When she entered the kitchen, she stopped and stared at the table. At the small, bang-bottomed pot on the table. A pot empty save for a dirty fork and the light yellow sauce of the macaroni and cheese she had made last night. The food she'd saved, knowing she wouldn't be eating lunch again today because she didn't get paid until Friday.

"What the fuck! Who ate my mac and cheese?" She strode from the kitchen through a second doorway leading into the dining room. As she blew past the card table, she slapped a folding chair out of her way, the metal landing with a crack. She brushed past the Christmas tree she'd bought on sale, causing dry needles to shower to the floor. She stopped in front of Jerry. Him and his shaggy gray hair, saggy cheeks, and stupid, liquor-relaxed brown eyes.

"Did you eat my mac and cheese, Jerry?" she said.

"Well, I—"

"Did – you – eat – my – mac – and – cheese?"

"I was hungry," Jerry said, the s slushy.

"Because that was *my* mac and cheese, you asshole. *I* bought it!" She lifted her foot and kicked the cigarette-scarred coffee table, making him flinch. "Do you even live here? No, so don't eat the fucking food." She turned and flew up the stairs. And goddamn, when she interviewed for the bank job tomorrow, she'd do such a good job they'd have to hire her. And with the increase in pay, she'd buy a storage trunk with a lock so nobody could steal her food anymore. Then she'd save for her own place where Frank's bum friends couldn't hang out.

She threw open Danny's door and found him on his bed in stocking feet, a beer in one hand and a joint in the other. A crook-necked lamp on his side table cast light on his chest, leaving his face in shadow. Led Zeppelin played on the stereo. She flipped down the volume by half and paced the wood floor.

"That asshole Jerry ate my mac and cheese. The perv," she said. She plopped down on the saggy-mattressed double bed. She looked sideways at Danny. He stared at her with half-closed eyes. He smiled. No more than a lift to the right side of his mouth, but that was enough. Where James would never betray her, Danny would never leave her.

"I was just so hungry, you know?" she said. Like that explained everything. Tonight. Her life.

Danny nodded. "You going to be okay?"

That was what he'd asked the day they buried their mother. She'd only been five. All she had left was her mother's worn teal robe and a handful of wispy memories that came to Mary as little ghost sensations: the feel of a hand on her head, the smell of lilac powder, the cheap dime-store kind little kids buy their moms with saved pennies. Instead of a Technicolor funeral scene, she remembered laying under her bed in her favorite red velvet dress. A dress she didn't care at all about on this particular day, just as she didn't give a fuck about how her white tights sagged in her crotch or how her long hair clung to her face, which she hated, but didn't move to push away. Because she had to watch out now. Mom was gone, and Mary had to be careful. They'd be after her, and though she didn't know who *they* were, she knew they were real. So she wasn't coming out from under the bed. Not for anyone. Especially not into that creepy, dimming half-light of a sleeting December dusk.

Then Danny came in. He got down on all fours, his clip-on tie dragging on the floor. He looked at her, his eyes blue as their father's, but nicer. The high cheekbones, the black hair and long lashes. He had a lovely Irish face, Mom used to say. *You going to be okay?* Danny had asked. Despite her tears, she nodded. They looked at one another. Then Danny said, *I'll save you a piece of cake.*

And again tonight, he said, *You going to be okay?*

And again she nodded. She stared at the chest of drawers that used to belong to her oldest brother, Mike, who, after a number of incarcerations, had become a mechanic and moved to Gary, Indiana. They heard from him once a year, maybe twice.

"James and the rest are downstairs waiting to see if you'll buy beer for a party tonight," she said.

"A party where?"

"Harold Kawalski's."

"Are that kid's parents ever home?"

She smiled.

Danny smiled. "You want me to?"

She shrugged. "If you feel like it."

Danny licked his lips, the ones girls at school died to kiss, especially the cheerleader types hot for the whole bad-boy thing.

"Okay," he said. In slo-mo, he set down his beer and extinguished the joint with a few finger pinches. He swung his legs over the edge of the bed and sat next to her. "Tell you what. While I'm there, I'll get you some Sno Balls."

He smiled and stood. A little taller than James and just as lean, Danny swayed for a moment, the Sears Tower in a high wind. He laughed a little. "God," he said and walked to his black leather boots. Before he left, he said, "Johnny's crashed next door."

Mary looked at the wall that separated Danny's room from the one he and Johnny used to share. Johnny, the second-oldest brother, lived more in the city than not. A prodigal addict, he occasionally came home to sleep, as in crept in and out again, no hellos or goodbyes. Johnny would be forever Johnny, and ditto for Mike and Frank. Of them all, only she and Danny seemed to care about what happened to each other. Johnny, Mike, Frank, and Mary-Danny: four units that shared a last name, and for a time, a living space. Things had always been like that and always would be. So why would something like that bother you all of a sudden?

The image came, of the prep leaning in to kiss her mother. A careless gesture, as though they did that all the time. Mary pushed off of the bed and walked to her bedroom door. She used her key to unlock the padlock Danny installed two years ago at her request. She opened the door, unzipped her boots, and threw them in the corner next to the red beanbag chair. She stood in front of her white dresser with the blobby pink flowers down the side—the ones Mom let Mary paint—and took off her silver hoop earrings. She pulled the silver rings from each finger and tossed them into an overflowing music box with a ballerina that had stopped twirling when the Sugar Plum Fairy music died.

Mary hop-shimmied out of her jeans and stood in nothing but her graying bra, blue knee socks, and orange bikini panties with *Monday* written across the butt. Even to her, her belly seemed stretched too tight between her jutting hipbones. She heard a creak and turned to see fingers pushing her door open, fingers hairy, thick, and old. She slammed her body against the door. A howl rose from the other side and the fingers pulled back. She kept pushing, but Jerry must have gotten his foot in the door, which was probably why she hadn't crushed his hand.

"You stupid shit!" she yelled and pressed her shoulder against the wood. And what was wrong with her, that she'd forgotten to lock her door from the inside?

"You shouldn't yell at me like that, Mary," Jerry said. He leaned harder on the door, his two-hundred-plus pounds against her hundred and twenty. "Always ignoring me or yelling at me, acting like you're the queen, and I known you since you was little—" He pushed harder and the door opened wider, making her stocking feet slide on the wood floor. Her eyes raced around the room until spotting the weapon. She let go of the door, jumped onto her bed, and grabbed Danny's old baseball bat. The door flew open and Jerry skidded into the room. She hopped off her bed, assumed a batter's stance like her brothers had taught her, and made a line drive to Jerry's side. Not enough to crack his ribs because then she'd have to call an ambulance, which would make Jerry even more of a pain in the ass, but hard enough. Jerry exhaled with a grunt and stumbled sideways, farther into her room. Not cool. She turned and swung leftie to get him back in front of the door.

Mary lifted the bat for a third swing but Jerry grabbed the end. She yanked the wood out of his hand and drove the tip into Jerry's stomach. He stumbled into the hallway and fell onto his back. She stood over him with the bat high over her shoulder, legs crouched and ready.

"You stupid shit!" she said. "Get out or I'm going to crack you over the head, you fuck."

Jerry rolled over onto all fours and climbed to his feet. She followed him down the stairs, her skin gleaming with sweat despite the chilled air. He grabbed his heavy mechanic's coat from the wobbly coat rack and opened the front door. She shoved him out, slammed the door, and turned the lock, then ran and locked the back door.

Mary ran upstairs and threw the bat in the corner of her room. She grabbed her robe and strode to the bathroom where she locked the door behind her and took a shower. Her hands trembled while she sudsed her hair, raked her legs with a dull razor, and rubbed her body dry. She wrapped a towel around her head, and in her blue knee socks and her mother's worn robe, stumped down the stairs to the kitchen. Jerry coming in, eating her mac and cheese, sitting in her living room. Then he had the audacity to enter her room without permission? The piece of shit.

She threw open the pantry door that never closed right

and stood with hands on hips. Three big shelves and the only things on them were two cans of waxed beans, a half box of potato flakes, an almost-empty box of cornflakes, a bag of white bread with a few slices left, and a box of kitty treats for a stray she fed until the scabbed tabby stopped showing up. She pulled out the cereal and bread and threw them on the table. She opened the freezer to find a tray of almost-evaporated ice cubes and a box containing two frozen fish sticks. She closed the freezer and opened the fridge. No milk, when she'd only bought some two days ago. She took out a sticky jar of strawberry jam.

Mary lit a gas burner, lodged a piece of stale bread between the tines of a fork, and toasted the slice over the flames. When done, she sat at the table, her meal before her. Two pieces of toast on a plastic daisy plate, a bowl of old Corn Flakes, and a glass of water.

She stared at the meal. She thought of the prep and the look on her face when Mary and her friends had ruined her day. She'd been happy, and they'd scared her. And what does that mean, when just seeing someone happy makes you want to make that person miserable?

What was the prep having for dinner tonight? Who sat at her table? Because there was no way she had to eat alone.

Chapter 4

Thurs., Dec. 21

Mary made for her usual desk by the window. She sank into the seat and dropped her head onto folded arms. A bad rhythm banged in her head like monkeys going berserk with a drum set. Her stomach boiled from last night's five beers, four shots, and the joint, and Jesus, would someone just strangle her already? And worst of all, when the bell rang in fifty minutes, she couldn't go home to crash because she had to work. Runny Rose Milk skin care lotion on sale for eighty-seven cents, aisle four. Pukey Listerine mouthwash a buck ninety-seven, aisle six. And then there would be Big Lil, the queen of from-hell managers.

Though maybe the *worst* worst part was that Mary could have had Danny call her in sick, which she normally did on Hangover Mondays. But she had wanted to see what the prep would do. When the girl walked into class today, she'd most likely do something predictable, like ignore Mary or sit in a new desk as far from her as possible. But the prep had acted unpredictably at the toboggan chute by ignoring danger, so maybe the kid would amaze Mary again.

Mary turned her head toward the door and with her cheek on the desk, waited. Students flowed through the hall where locker doors slammed. Girls fake-laughed and sneakers squeaked on the wet tile floor. The fat kid with the protruding lower lip came in and dropped into his seat near the back followed by the Vietnamese girl and the kid with nasty head-gear for his braces.

Then the prep walked in, ponytail a-swinging. And of course she wore jeans that matched the sweater that matched the stupid wood-handled purse with her initials sewn on the cloth bag part. A disappointingly common pissed-off expression accessorized the whole outfit. The downturned eyes, the tight-ass walk, the sharp left turn at her aisle. She dropped her books on the desk she normally sat in—her desk, the one she wouldn't let Mary scare her away from—crossed her legs and opened a paperback. Her posture conveyed snooty as expertly as only naïve, self-righteous people could. The prep probably didn't even know how close she'd come to getting fucked-up by Tina. Rather than think about that possibility, the prep had probably lain in bed last night, planning this grand entrance and what she'd say if Mary made some smart remark. What a shame if all that effort went to waste.

So Mary said, "Hi."

The prep didn't blink, didn't flinch. Then again, she'd proven herself to be a kid who could ignore reality. In her head, she probably felt strong as Mighty Mouse. Then again, skating past the truth can make you weak, too. Can turn you into someone addicted to lying to yourself. *I'm happy, happy, all the time happy. Can't you see how fucking happy I am?* Like the smiling celebrities on the cover of *Good Housekeeping*— Cheryl Ladd, Jackie Kennedy Onassis, Elizabeth Taylor— when you know they're probably drunks and pill pushers, divorcées and *Exorcist* stand-ins like Mary's boss. But maybe the prep didn't see how desperately she protected her perfect world, which was interesting.

When Mary sat up, a tidal wave of nausea crashed over her

head. She closed her eyes and breathed through her mouth, because puking in public was not cool. When her stomach quieted, she opened her eyes and crawled them toward the prep's desk to where she'd written her name, first and last, on the front of her binder. Mary leaned forward for a closer look. Still pretending to read, the prep shoved her purse over the writing. But not fast enough.

The bell rang. Mr. O'Brien walked in wearing his brown corduroy blazer, which he did every Monday. He carried steaming coffee in his favorite mug that had a picture of Garfield waving a Chicago Bears pennant, the team a hopeful for this year's Super Bowl, something every guy in school seemed to feel the need to mention.

"Good afternoon, my budding Hemingways," Mr. O'Brien said. "Let's open to page one eighty nine."

The prep opened *Great Expectations*.

Mr. O'Brien's eyes swept the room and stopped on Mary. His expression became a picture of amazement. "Without a book again, are we Mary?" he said, one hand in his pocket and the other holding his book.

"Thanks for pointing that out," she said.

"Get a copy and join us," Mr. O'Brien said. "A discussion is always that much less when deprived of a great mind."

The fat boy with the protruding lip laughed. She stared at him over her shoulder without blinking. He dropped his eyes. She kept her eyes on him a moment longer, then reached sideways toward the shelf under the window to get a copy. She opened to the right page. She considered Mr. O'Brien with half-closed eyes, daring him to call on her for an insightful comment on a book she'd never read.

A pudgy girl walked in, handed Mr. O'Brien a green slip from the office, and left.

He read the note and looked at Mary. "It's your lucky day, Mary. Mr. Hoggarty wants to see you."

Which means you somehow have to get to your feet without swaying, fainting, or throwing up. She did and even managed to pluck the green slip from Mr. O'Brien's hand and stroll out, not a care in the world. But when clear of the classroom, her upper body tipped forward as waves of heat rolled over her. Her feet moved faster and faster but couldn't seem to catch up with her body. She ran toward an exit, slammed against the metal bar, and pushed open the door to the outside. She turned and leaned against the door, folded over, hands on her knees. She closed her eyes, expecting her guts to spill out through her mouth, but nothing came. Strong wind, somewhere in the teens, blew on her face and down her T-shirt while gusts of snow crystals swirled at her feet. When sure she wasn't going to heave, she lifted her head and opened her eyes. Life sometimes reduced to what you see before you, in this case: a thin layer of snow over brown grass with cars in the background and pavement gray as the sky. She could just leave school. Go hang out at Mr. Amar's before she had to work. Nobody would be surprised, much less care. And now that the prep had made her attitude clear, that Mary no longer existed, why stay?

Yet she stepped back inside. She stood a moment, waiting for a reason to appear, but none did. Maybe there was no reason and she would stay in school just because, and how weird. Or maybe there was an explanation, but one she couldn't see, which was even more disturbing, because normally she knew all the angles. That's how you survive, by knowing the facts, assessing the odds. If you don't, you could walk smack into something bad, and not movie bad, either, but rather something real and irreversible.

When she got to the office she said, "Hi, Mrs. D."

The receptionist, a grandma-old lady named Mrs. Donofsky, looked up and smiled. "Hello, Mary. Go ahead on in."

Mary walked past her counselor's office, with *Mrs. Barnao*

on the door, to the last office labeled *Mr. Stephen Hoggarty, Associate Principal.*

"Hi Mr. Hoggarty," she said.

Mr. Hoggarty rose from his seat and extended a hand, "Hello, Miss Donahue."

They shook. She dropped into a cushioned chair. Mr. Hoggarty sat behind his desk. A former Navy SEAL, he had short-cropped blond hair and light blue eyes. Where some teachers try to get chummy with you by sitting on the side of their desks and doing the *Hey, how are ya?* thing, Mr. Hoggarty kept you at arm's length. When the bell rang, he went home to his world and you went home to yours, everyone clear that life isn't fair.

"How's the new baby?" she said.

"Very well, thank you, although Jeffrey seems to have his days and nights mixed up. But he'll have it figured out before long." Mr. Hoggarty folded his hands on the desk, his thumbs in a pyramid. "I called you in because it's come to my attention you're ahead of schedule in using your allotted tardies and truancies for the year. At this rate you'll have hit the limit by February. Then I'll have to send a letter to your father requesting a parent conference, which we both know he won't attend. I'll also have to schedule you for Saturday School, which would interfere with your job and so pose a financial hardship. How do you plan to solve this problem?"

Mary shrugged and smiled. "Win the lottery and fly to Jamaica?"

Mr. Hoggarty didn't smile. "First of all, Miss Donahue, you're not old enough to play the lottery. For the sake of argument, however, let's say you were. If you won, you would need to understand the tax implications of your fortune—i.e., math—as well as the complexities of finance to an extent that would keep yourself from getting bamboozled by fraudulent financial managers. That and you would have to understand where Jamaica is—i.e., geography—and how to get there. Have you ever been on a plane, Miss Donahue?"

Mary said nothing.

"Then I'll ask you again: what do you plan to do to solve this problem?" Mr. Hoggarty said.

Mary pulled at a beige thread sticking out of her coat button. If he were anybody else, she'd tell him to go fuck himself. But she owed Mr. Hoggarty for the part he played in last year's Lecherous Counselor Incident involving her slime-ball, pot-bellied perv of an advisor who'd made some suggestions he shouldn't have. She complained to Mr. Hoggarty, who could have done what most adults did by siding with their fellow adults. Instead, he'd fired the bastard.

"Miss Donahue."

Mary looked up. Mr. Hoggarty stared at her, and not with reproach, either, but with something worse. Concern, maybe, which is something you shouldn't show unless you really do care.

"If a person," he said, "goes out to sea with nothing to protect him—no boat, no life preserver, nothing to prepare him for his ordeal—that person, no matter how smart he is, how witty, how streetwise or strong, will, without question, drown."

Mary remained silent. The heater kicked on, rattling the metal register.

"I propose we meet again after Christmas break," Mr. Hoggarty said. "That will give you time to plan a solution, which I have no doubt you will. You're a smart girl. In the meantime, you might consider this program," and he handed her a brochure. *You Can Be a Nurse's Aide, Too.* "It's a work-study program you could begin next year."

Mary opened the brochure and pretended to read because she owed the man that much. "Thanks," she said. She could feel him staring at her, studying her, those military eyes probably not missing the rings under her own eyes.

"It looks like you have your days and nights confused, too," he said.

She tried to smile. "Maybe."

Outside the office, she shoved the brochure to the bottom of her pocket. She stopped in the bathroom. She smoked. She read graffiti. She estimated when the bell would ring. Before it did, she walked back to the classroom. But rather than go in, she stopped near the door and leaned against a locker. Maybe if she didn't feel so sick, something would come to mind. A solution for Mr. Hoggarty. Maybe she'd also figure out how her life could be so goddamn Grand Canyon apart from his, or even that of the prep's. Why did they seem to have everything and she had shit? And how nice of Mr. Hoggarty to give her that mental image of the poor schmuck treading water in the middle of the ocean until she got too tired and went under. Why did he assume that would be Mary's fate? *Will, without question.* Yet even a person lost at sea has some chance of rescue, right?

The bell rang. A moment followed, one that rumbled until the doors blew open and students flooded the hallway. The prep came out, but she had her eyes down and didn't see Mary. The prep turned the opposite way and walked down the hall away from Mary. She followed.

The prep turned down the next corridor and opened her locker, the second from the left of Room 104. Standing about five feet behind the prep, Mary could see over the girl's shoulder and into her locker. A heart-shaped mirror hung on the inside of the door along with a booklet with musical notes drawn on the front. Above the mirror she'd taped two photos, one of a white-and-black cat with blue eyes and the other of the prep's overexposed face and those of three other girls, their smiles crowding an alight birthday cake.

Lockers slammed up and down the hall. Students yelled to one another. The hall would soon clear, leaving Mary standing there, looking stupid.

So she said, "Hey."

Rather than turn toward Mary, the prep remained facing her locker and looked up and off to the right, like somebody had called her over the intercom box hanging on the wall by the ceiling, but that couldn't be right. So the prep bent over and stuffed books into a big canvas bag with *Interlochen* stitched on the side in red letters.

"Hey," Mary said, louder this time.

This time the girl looked over her shoulder. The moment she saw Mary, the prep's face seemed to suck inward. Eyebrows, mouth, cheeks.

"Oh, it's you," she said. *Yee-oo.* She turned her back to Mary and yanked a coat off of a hook inside the locker. An evergreen wool dress coat instead of the pink ski jacket.

"What's your name?" Mary said.

"Oh, yeah, like I'd tell *you*," the girl said, her responsible-big-sister tone replaced by that of an enraged victim. She slipped off her leather shoes, jammed them into the canvas bag, and put on her snow boots. Not the mukluks, either, but something more respectable. When she should have worn her mukluks to show people she didn't give a shit what they thought. But she obviously did. She pulled a white wool hat over her head and shoved her hair underneath.

"I'm Mary."

"Big whoop," the prep said.

"Come on," Mary said. "Don't be such a tight-ass."

The prep spun around. "Oh, yeah? I'm the one who's uptight? Who's so scared of what her friends think she can't stand up to them when they're making fun of people who didn't do anything? So scared you just stood there watching while they harassed my little brother. Oh, yeah, yeah, now *that's* admirable."

The prep heaved the canvas bag over her shoulder. "In fact, you know what? I bet you wouldn't dare do something like tobogganing. That's for sissies, right? When really you wouldn't have the guts. What a coward." She turned and strode off.

"Shit," Mary said under her breath. She lifted her voice. "Kathleen."

The prep turned back. "Oh, great. Now you know my name. What's next? You going to prank call me? Or are you going to get all your friends together and corner me in the bathroom and make fun of me like you do the retarded kids?"

Mary never made fun of the *specials*. And who was Kathleen to call anybody a coward when she probably had no idea what it meant to fight for yourself on a daily basis? Mary had *fuck you* on her lips, but then noticed how Kathleen's shoulders shook and her eyes filled with tears. Rather than cry, though, Kathleen lifted her chin, nose in the air, to contain her tears.

The hall had emptied except for a few students.

"I just..." Mary said. "I wouldn't have let them hurt you."

Kathleen dropped her chin and looked at Mary from beneath dark brows. *"Wouldn't let them.* Gee, how nice of you." She turned away.

"Kat," Mary said.

Kathleen remained still, her back turned. "My name's Kathleen." She glanced over her shoulder, flying five-thousand knives at Mary, but she didn't move.

"Is it fun? Tobogganing?" Mary said. Asking a question when you should never ask questions because when you do, you have to wait for the answer, and waiting makes you look pathetic. But there was no choice now. She kept her lips closed and eyes on Kathleen, who stared back, so obviously furious and suspicious. Then something crawled into her expression. A notion, maybe, that she was looking at something she didn't understand, and how that can confuse you, feeling what you don't recognize, but suspect could bring trouble down on your head.

"Yeah," Kathleen said. Her lips parted again. Ready to say something. But then she closed her mouth and turned. She walked away, probably oblivious to the fact she knew everything Mary needed to learn about how to get to a better life. Information Mary would now have to wait to get.

Chapter 5

Mon., Dec. 25

Mary opened her eyes. She lay on her side, body toasty and pulled into itself within her nest made of a blue quilt, and over that, a dark green wool Army blanket. The feeling lovely and calm because today was Christmas. All businesses would be closed. She'd interviewed for the bank job two weeks ago and every day since had the terrible urge to call the bank manager to see what he'd decided. But today the bank was closed and the manager gone, so she might as well relax. Tonight she'd make sure to corner her cousin, Darby, who Mary had put down as a reference. The only one to have made good in their sorry extended family, Darby would most likely tell Mary to wait until after New Year's when things were less busy and all that shit.

Mind eased a bit, her eyes drifted to her dresser. To the red rose James had given her last night and that stemmed from a Gallo wine bottle she'd filled with water. And next to that, her Mickey Mouse clock reading eleven-fifteen. And beside the clock, a framed photo of Mom smiling down at a swaddled baby Mary. Though a black-and-white photo, Danny claimed Mary's hair was the same color as Mom's, that of the drink she made for each of her four kids on New Year's Eve, of apple juice with one maraschino cherry.

Mary pushed off the covers. She sat up and hung her bare feet off the edge of her bed, hair falling to her waist. She waited a moment, the warmth of sleep bleeding to a chill. Then she got down on hands and knees and pulled a long, flat cardboard box from beneath her bed. She took out a pair of sweatpants, a sweatshirt and a black-and-white wool hat she'd found when shopping in the lost-and-found box at school. She pulled on Mom's teal robe and slipped her feet into the broken-backed canvas shoes she used as slippers.

Rubbing her cold hands, she walked to the window. God forbid that the weather should vary from its normal dreariness of sleet and gray sky. The sidewalks had iced over into watered glass. Tree branches scratched the back of the house. Wind rattled the panes. Otherwise the house remained quiet. Hopefully that meant Frank's bum friends had cleared out, rather than passed out downstairs. She picked up a brown paper grocery bag from beside the dresser, unlocked her door, and tiptoed across the hall to Danny's room. She went in and rolled up the vinyl shade halfway. A pearl light washed over the bed where Danny slept on his side, a patch of curly black hair visible from beneath his quilt. She sat on the side of the bed. When Danny didn't stir, she bounced up and down. When he still didn't move, she bounced higher, her ass clearing the mattress. Danny rolled to his back and squinted at her. Then he closed his eyes and sighed.

Mary set the grocery bag on his belly. "Merry Christmas."

Danny rubbed his eyes and sat up, his chest bare. He opened the bag, pulled out a flat package, and tore the wrinkled snowman paper she'd saved from last year.

He looked at the book and smiled. *The Catcher in the Rye.*

"It's a used copy, but I figured you wouldn't care," she said. "Mr. O'Brien said you were supposed to read it last year, but didn't."

Danny laughed. "Sounds about right."

"He remembers you, you know." She didn't tell Danny what else Mr. O'Brien had said. *He could have done so much better, your brother.* Could have, like Danny, was dead or something.

"Keep going. I got you something else, too," she said.

Danny reached into the bag and pulled out a soft, football-sized bulk she'd wrapped in the Sunday comics because she'd run out of snowman paper. Danny ripped the paper, and a package of socks and one of underwear fell out.

"Oh, man, did I need these," Danny said, his tone reverential, as it should be. She hadn't known what to get him until she'd rummaged through his drawers and found nothing but a rag pile.

"I don't want you scaring off all those girls," she said.

Danny laughed. Then smiling innocently, he looked at she and arched his eyebrows, like what could she possibly be waiting for? She dropped her smile and let her head fall to the side.

"Come on, man," she said. "You play this stupid game every year."

He smiled, the innocence gone. "You were more fun when you were little." Back when he'd hide her gift in his room and make her hunt, a torture-the-little-sister kind of fun in which she'd trashed his room while looking.

Danny leaned over, and from beneath his bed pulled out a cardboard box about a half-foot tall and two-feet wide. She opened the flaps and for a moment, remained still, mouth open. Then she screamed; the sound drowned within her throat. She pulled out a jar of chunky peanut butter, and no on-sale off-brand shit, either. Skippy. The kind happy TV mothers spread on their darling children's white bread to make them happy, too. She shoved the glass cylinder into the crook of her arm. Then she drew out a box of Whitman chocolates, a can of Planters salted peanuts with the walking peanut guy wearing a top hat and cane, a box of Cap'n Crunch, and best of all, three packages of bright pink coconut-covered Sno Balls. She held the food in her arms as though encircling a worthy extended family while rocking from side to side on the bed, doing the Happy Food Dance.

Danny laughed. "You better hide it."

"No shit," she said.

"But there's *more*," Danny said with a *Wheel of Fortune* flourish to his tone.

To which she played her part. "*More?*"

Danny pulled a second package from beneath his bed. She dumped the food into the box and ripped the paper of the new gift. She stared for a moment at what she held, then stood and tore the plastic packaging, and shook out the pajamas. A flat of cardboard twirled to the ground along with a square of pajama bottoms. The pink flannel top featured a sleek, oval-eyed cat. She clutched the clothing in her arms and danced from foot to foot, doing the Happy Pajama Dance.

"I know it's pink and you don't like stuff like that," Danny said, "but I figured, you know, it might be nice to have something that isn't black. And it had the cat thing."

Mary Supermanned toward her brother and landed on his belly, making him grunt. She lay with her head against his beating heart, the pink pajamas in her arms, a favorite blankie she never had.

"Now you'll have to have a pajama party," Danny said.

"Ha," she said and sat up. Because what a joke, the idea of having a dweeby sleepover with frilly nightgowns and popcorn and shit. She first heard about sleepovers from some kid in her third-grade class. She ran home to invite Viola, the chunky, fuzzy-haired, early boob-growing kid down the block. *Wanna come, wanna come, huh, huh?* Only to be turned down by a Lithuanian fatty name Vi – O – la. And what did Vi – O - la do when Mary asked why not? Vi – O – la shrugged. Mary waited a week and asked again. The third time, she tackled

Viola, and sitting on her chest, threatened to dribble spit on her face unless she said why she wouldn't come. At which point Viola blabbed what her mother had said. *Over my dead body will my daughter stay in the same house as that drunk.*

"You want to go to church today?" Danny said.

She heard him, but her mind took a moment to shift from the feel of thick, frizzy hair clenched in her hands—somebody had eventually pulled her and Viola apart, though Mary couldn't remember who—to the image of St. John's decorated for Christmas. The gold-painted dome, the swooping angels, the smiling families who'd no doubt go home to eat a delicious dinner together. She lowered her eyes and shook her head.

"You sure?"

She nodded. She looked at Danny. "You hungry?"

"Always."

"Good," she said, because she'd gotten paid on Friday and had bought some goodies. "Is Johnny still around?"

"I think he took off last night."

"Is Char here?" she said, referring to Frank's girlfriend, a braless, creased cigarette-hacking hag who laughed whenever she shouldn't.

Danny rubbed his head with both hands. "I think she's spending the day with her daughter."

And what a surprise, that you could feel sorry for someone like Char.

"Danny?" she said.

He arched his brows.

"You believe in fate? Like—" She licked her lips. "Like that there wasn't anything Char could have done different? That even if she hadn't been a rotten mother, she was destined to have a slutty, drug-addicted daughter who looks like a zombie from *Night of the Living Dead?*"

Danny shrugged. "Mom used to say that once you made your bed you had to lay in it."

"But what does that mean? If you fuck up it's your own fault, as opposed to being destined to fuck up?"

"I guess."

Which means you have a choice in how things turn out. That rather than be dropped in the ocean against your will, you can decide not to go in the first place. But what if you just got in for a swim and accidentally stroked too far? A mistake you make because you don't know any better?

Mary gathered her gifts and camouflaged them in her closet. Then she went downstairs and stopped in the kitchen doorway. The mess truly impressive. But at least there weren't any drunken, unwashed bodies lying around. She opened the back door to a blast of gusting wind and flurrying snow and dragged in a metal garbage can. With one arm, she swept the beer and whiskey bottles into the bin along with peanut shells and paper cups of cigarette ash. After taking the can back outside and setting the shot glasses in the sink, she pulled a carton of eggs from their hiding place on the top shelf of the pantry. When Danny came down, she set before him a plate heaped with heavily-salted scrambled eggs and toast. She put a bottle of ketchup on the table, mixed him a cup of thick Swiss Miss hot chocolate, and sat in front of her own plate.

They ate. They talked. She licked strawberry jam off of her fingers while telling Danny about the party. Of how a tripping Chuck got mesmerized by the flame of his lighter and accidentally set the back of Bing's T-shirt on fire. And what was Colleen's bright idea? To douse the blaze with her beer. Fortunately before the alcohol hit Bing, little Julie V. kicked him out of the way. He fell on his back, suffocating the fire.

Then Danny told her he had a line on a job at the lumberyard across the train tracks. He'd get a steady supply of scrap wood.

"You going to carve it? The wood? Paul Bunyan, the ar*tiste*?" she said.

Danny smiled and pushed away his empty plate. "Maybe."

"You working on anything new?"

"Oh, you know. It's this one thing, really weird. I kind of started with a ball of twine I found in the supply closet at school."

His head clear, the high gone, his hands drew pictures in the air for her as excitement burned in his eyes like the blow-torches he used to shape metal into art. He crossed his arms over his chest and moved the conversation to his favorite subject, sculpture that messed with people's heads, like the stuff at the Chicago Museum of Contemporary Art. The type of work that made people scrunch their faces, wondering if the artist meant to make fools of them, or confuse them, or maybe just test how much they'd swallow before they caught on to the joke of trying to make sense of what made no sense. When Danny knew otherwise. The artist never thought of other people at all or what they'd think. The artwork just happens when you try to reach a state of *beyondness* where no rules exist and anything is possible. Something could be nothing, or everything. Look at Jackson Pollock who did all the squiggly painting that made people say things like, *Even I could do that.* But they hadn't done what he'd done, had they? They hadn't even thought about doing something outrageous, which was just as necessary as making something beautiful. And Georgia O'Keefe and her New York skyscrapers punching mile-high holes of light in the night sky; art not so much a thing as a way of thinking. *If you look hard enough,* Danny had once told her, *you can find art everywhere. Tattoos, auto detailing, lumber stocking—*

The stacking of tampon boxes in a dime store, she'd said, making Danny laugh.

Danny stopped talking. They sat a moment. The wind howled, but they were here, inside, together, and for a while, warm.

"You think she's going to get you in?" she said, referring to

Danny's art teacher, who'd recommended Danny for a spot at the art academy in the city.

"Doesn't work like that." Danny sat back. "You got to apply and submit a portfolio."

"What's that?"

"A collection of your best stuff."

"You have that?"

"I'm working on it."

"When's it due?"

Danny laughed. "Don't worry; I'll get it together." He sat with hands under his armpits, thumbs sticking up.

Mary speared toast crumbs with the tip of her fork. "It's just, you know. It's like she offered to help and it's not like you've got anything else lined up for after you graduate."

"I know."

"I mean, really."

"I know."

"Don't fuck it up."

Danny laughed. "Jesus, Mary."

"And Joseph," she said, according to their long-standing retort whenever he said, *Jesus, Mary*. But she didn't feel like joking. Not about this. "I'm just saying."

A thud sounded overhead. They both looked up toward the erratic-paced footsteps moving from Frank's bedroom to the bathroom. The door slammed shut.

"Santa's up," she said. She and Danny looked at one another. And laughed.

***

Mary stood at the base of the stairs, hands shoved to the bottom of her coat pockets. "Why don't you look in your dirty clothes pile?" she yelled. But instead of an answer, she heard only *slam, slam, slam*, the sound of a man looking for his other shoe.

Three o'clock and Jesus-fucking-Christ, could the man be any slower? They should have left an hour ago. If they were late to Aunt Eileen's, there went the chance to corner her Darling Daughter Darby, the Important Wife of an Attorney Husband running for state representative of his district. With that kind of title, you drop into your parents' sorry-ass family gathering of blue-collar drunks, but you only stay long enough to play the good daughter. Then you Cadillac your way to higher-class events that advance your career or that of your husband. Mary had purposely prepared for that category of uptight by dressing in a white blouse and black pants and toning down the makeup and jewelry. Now she looked boring as any woman who boarded the train for a white-collar job in the Loop.

Something thunked overhead. Mary shook her head, the man never going to find what he was looking for without help. She went into the living room and shoved the TV stand aside. She pulled the couch away from the wall, and there, amid the cigarette butts, dust clumps, and pretzel crumbs was one black dress shoe far beyond dress-shoe days, the shine gone and heel rubbed low on the outside corner.

She jogged upstairs with the shoe. "Danny, let's go," she yelled while crossing the hall to Frank's bedroom. She found him on his knees, head inside the closet. So thin his gray trousers hung low, showing the small of his white-skinned back.

"Your shoe," she said.

Frank reared up. Eyes wide. Mouth agog. Like she held a butcher knife instead of a shoe. Then his mouth slackened and he grabbed the shoe.

"Where'd you find it?" he said.

"Behind the couch."

He lifted a foot to put on the shoe, but fell to the side. She grabbed his elbow. He yanked his arm away.

"I got it," he said. Rather than move, he stared at her feet as he always did, with his face tight, intent. Like he looked straight at her when really he was just looking at her goddamn feet because he couldn't bring himself to look at her face.

"You think Aunt Eileen's going to make Christmas cake this year?" he said.

"Jesus, Dad," she said. "She makes it every year. *Every year*. So yeah, I think she's going make it this year, too. Let's go."

"I'm just asking," Frank said. He tied his shoes, hands shaking. He pushed himself up, taking a good ten seconds to unbend and straighten, the stiffness a result of too much heavy labor. He once mentioned he'd wanted to be a mason like his dad. But then Frank met his Theresa, his *colleen*, Gaelic for *Irish girl*. A good Irish Catholic girl, which meant no sex before marriage, baby. So Frisky Frank skipped trade school for the fast buck of construction work and away he went into an early manhood of hammering, nailing, hauling. Then his Theresa died at age thirty-three, and forever after, Frank drank more than he hammered.

"Christmas cake," Frank said. "My mother used to make Irish Christmas cake."

Mary rolled her eyes. But telling the tale made him happy when little else did. So that although she tapped her toe and chewed on her lower lip, she kept her mouth shut.

"Sometimes I can still smell the brandy. She'd start to cut me a slice, and my pop would say, 'Give him more. He's a growing boy.'" Frank laughed. "She would cut a colossal piece," and he spread his hands two feet apart. "She'd hand the plate down to me and laugh herself a good one. My eyes must have been big as saucers."

And she saw in his face what she'd never seen before, that his profile resembled a hilly landscape, maybe that of Ireland. The high, barren cheekbones. The upswinging hill of a nose. The lips like mountains ground to low mounds over the long, hard ages.

"We'd better go," she said.

***

They loaded into her father's 1966 green Buick and drove the fifteen miles to the South Side neighborhood where her dad grew up. According to him, this part of the city, though modest, was where the good Irishmen lived, the ones who'd dug the Erie Canal. When really the community was just a flat of bare trees and industry along the south branch of the Chicago River. The sidewalks cracked. The telephone lines sagged like laundry from a clothesline.

Aunt Eileen's house was a yellow brick submarine squeezed between other submarines separated by skinny sidewalks leading to narrow backyards. The door opened, and oh joy, the spectacle of the occasion. The too-warm air and matted brown shag carpeting smelling of pug dog. The painting of flowers above the orange couch, the lacy curtains adorning the bay window, the narrow stairs leading to a cramped second floor with a single slant-roofed bedroom. Everything here: known, known, and known, change apparently forbidden.

Enough people had arrived to make the house noisy and the air thick with cigarette smoke. A Christmas carol played in the background. Petite Aunt Eileen darted out from the kitchen dressed in brown slacks, a cream blouse, and a red apron with white snowflakes. She accepted the bottle of Jameson Frank handed her, followed by a brief hug.

"Frank, Mary, Danny," Aunt Eileen said. "How about that, you're all here!" Her hair, as always, was the same deep red of her youth, except for the purple tinge of hair dye. "Colleen's in the basement, Mary; and Harry's manning the bar, Frank, so just tell him what you want; and Danny, how good looking you are!" And she tugged on his wrist while he laughed. "We're eating soon. Everything will be laid out and—"

Aunt Eileen looked over her shoulder and yelled, "Harry, get the rolls out of the oven," then went to do the job herself.

"Come on, Dad," Danny said and pulled Frank toward the bar. Over his shoulder, Danny whispered to her, "You driving home?"

Code for *Is it your turn to stay sober?* It wasn't, but she wanted Danny to enjoy himself, so she said, "Yeah."

She couldn't get her license for another six months. But Danny had taught her to drive for these rare occasions when the three of them were out where alcohol was being served. That and if her friends got too wasted and insisted on going home instead of staying put for the night, she could drive them because that was exactly what she didn't need, her or one of her friends croaking in some fiery crash.

Mary threw her coat over the banister to the second floor, then nodded and smiled her way through the living room, her eyes skating from face to face. People hovered around the dining room table, laden with relish trays of black olives, pickles, carrot sticks, celery, and dip. Uncle Harry, wearing a Santa hat over his graying black curls, stood at a small garlanded tiki bar in the corner, pouring drinks.

Twenty-five, maybe thirty people had arrived, not counting who might be in the basement. The Donahues. A load of Boyles from Uncle Harry's side. Second cousins from the O'Connell clan, including Judy O'Connell's eight-year-old twins, a boy and girl, who raced after one another through the forest of adults.

Mary made her way to Uncle Harry. Not much taller than his wife, he had a gut almost twice her width.

"Uncle Harry, is Darby here yet?" she said.

"Not yet, but she promised to be by soon. She said she and Tom are *making the rounds*. Want a Fresca or something?"

A glass of pop. What you're supposed to drink until the adults get smashed, at which point you can help yourself to the booze.

"No thanks." She passed through the small kitchen and walked down the stairs to the basement.

No matter the time of year, the basement always smelled like the damp of a not-so-fresh grave. Three overhead lights hung from the center of the ceiling like upside down bowling pins. A smog of gray dust covered the bumpy blue-painted cement walls. Her thirteen-year-old cousin, Sean, played darts with some littler kid while three really young kids sat under the Ping-Pong table, giggling.

Sean pulled the darts from the board and turned. "Hi, Mar."

She nodded. "Sean."

"Hi, Mar," Colleen said from where she sat on a sagging brown corduroy couch, head resting on the back, and bare feet tucked up under her. The same age as Mary, Colleen was Darby's younger sister. Face round as a plate, Colleen had the same auburn hair as her mom and the wide-spaced gray eyes of her dad.

Mary sat beside Colleen, their hips touching.

"You look pale," Mary said, her voice low. "You high?"

"Naw."

Mary thought a moment. "You had it done?"

Colleen nodded without lifting her head. "Saturday."

"Didn't go so well?" Mary said.

"Not like last time."

"You bleeding a lot?"

Colleen nodded again.

"You call the doctor?"

"Yeah. He says I just got to wait."

Mary watched the three kids prance around on their hands and knees beneath the table, rearing up, reversing direction, shoes long gone.

"My mom found out," Colleen said.

"Shit."

"Yeah."

"She tell your dad?"

"You think I'd be here right now if she did?"

Which was true. If Uncle Harry had found out, he would have beat up Colleen and thrown her onto the street. Good old jolly Uncle Harry, the first to dispense punishment when he had his own shame to hide. What a hypocrite, like everybody here. If you follow any of them home and listen to the things they say to one another in private—shit they don't want you to hear—and see how they behave, handing out a smack here and there, you have to doubt the sincerity of their smiles. Were Kathleen's relatives like this? Cloaked in shine for the public, but with rusted underbellies? Mary looped her arm through Colleen's and sat listening to faint sleigh bells in the music drifting from upstairs.

The doorbell rang every minute now. Kids ran up and down the stairs. Aunt Eileen gave the call of "Food's on!" Mary told Colleen she'd get her something to eat and went upstairs. People jammed the kitchen and dining room, waiting to fill their paper plates at the buffet table. Beef in Guinness, rolls, green bean casserole, Irish soda bread, store-bought lasagna, a green-and-red gelatin mold shaped like a turkey, two whiskey cakes, salad, more rolls.

Mary rose to her tiptoes and perused the faces. She caught a glimpse of red hair pulled into a twist on the back of a woman's head. Mary squeezed between two uncles and approached Darby. Nylons, black pumps and a gray suit that fit her petite body precisely, she exuded style with an understated sexiness, rather than any overt sluttishness. She smiled and chatted with relatives while standing next to her tall, thin husband, his haircut neither too conservative nor too liberal. Mr. State Senator Hopeful Tom Menechino not too much of anything. He shook hands with some old guy and flashed a white, orthodontically-correct smile. And so he and Darby worked the room, two celebrities making the most of a bowling-alley gig.

Though Mary had to give Darby credit. After high school,

she got a secretarial degree and worked her way to the U.S. Senator's Chicago office where she met Prince Tom. That made Darby, at only twenty-four, too good for this house and these people. A bitch to admit, but true. She'd climbed out, no drunken, penniless future for her.

When Darby gave Great Aunt Kathy a hug and the old woman moved off, Mary moved in. At the same moment, Tom concluded his conversation and told his wife, "I'll get our coats."

Darby nodded at Tom, then smiled at Mary while offering an efficient hug. "How are you, Mary?"

"Fine," she said. "Going already?"

"Unfortunately Tom and I have to make the rounds tonight, which includes stopping by the Senator's home for an open house."

"I was just wondering if anybody from the bank had called you."

Darby's eyebrows lifted. "Bank?"

"Remember? I called and asked if you could be a reference for me? For the bank teller job."

Darby smiled and managed a shade of embarrassment. "I'm sorry to say I've been so busy I can barely remember what I had for my last meal, much less who I talked to." She glanced over Mary's shoulder, toward the front door and the more important next opportunity.

"It's just, I interviewed a while ago," Mary said, "so they should have called by now. A guy named Mr. Luskey?"

Darby looked at the ceiling for a moment. "Oh, that's right. Now I remember." She checked her gold watch.

"When did he call?"

"I think—" Darby bit her lip. "Almost two weeks ago, I think."

Jesus. Right after Mary had interviewed, and she still hadn't heard from him?

Tom approached wearing an expensive gray wool coat and a black muffler. He carried Darby's coat over his arm.

"Tom, you remember my cousin, Mary," Darby said.

Tom smiled, his eyes shining a spotlight on her. He shook Mary's hand as though she could vote already. "How do you do, Mary?"

"Great," she said. Ten days. "Can I finish talking to my cousin a minute?"

From the corner of her eye, she saw Darby shoot her husband a frown. But hubby was focused on Mary.

"Sure!" he said. "A little cousin-to-cousin talk. I'll warm up the car. Nice to meet you, Mary." He gave a last smile and cruised away.

Darby tilted her head, gave the polite smile back. "How can I help you?"

Mary now a nut job who had to be soothed.

"What did you tell Mr. Luskey?" she said.

"What?" Darby said. Like she suddenly couldn't hear over the noise. She walked toward the door, forcing Mary to follow. She repeated the question.

Darby smiled with apparent surprise. "What you asked me to say, that you're my cousin."

"Did you mention how I helped you deliver those pamphlets for your candidate last year?"

Darby stopped by the front door. "He wouldn't have been interested in that. It's not like you applied for a position at the State Department. It's only a bank teller job. "

Mary stood taller.

"I have to go. It was nice seeing you, Mary." Darby turned and opened the door.

"Hey," she said and followed Darby onto the small front stoop, the night cold an aching cloak around her. Darby held the metal railing, and in her high heels, took two careful steps down the stairs.

Mary took a step down and gripped Darby's free wrist.

Darby twisted around. "Cut it out! You're going to make me fall."

Mary dropped Darby's wrist. "What did you tell him?"

"Good grief! That you were my cousin."

"And what else? What did you say about me? Did you make me sound good or not? That's what this whole reference thing is about, right? Making somebody sound good so they get the job?"

"I have to go."

From where she stood a step above Darby, Mary leaned over her cousin. "And—what—else?"

Darby stared at her. "You ditch school. You get high every chance you get—"

"Oh, shit—"

"—like everyone else in this—"

"You fucked this up for me—"

"—family. If I were—"

"You told him I sucked."

"I told him you might not be dependable," Darby said, her tone tight, controlled. "I'm not going to lie for you."

"It would have been more money for me!" she said. "Don't you fucking understand? This was *my* chance to get out."

"If I were to recommend you and you didn't deliver—"

"I've got bills to pay! You have no idea—"

"—because you were too lazy to get up or started cursing out a customer like you're cursing me—"

"You know who helped pay for your sister's second abortion because nobody else would? Did you even know?"

Darby nostrils flared. "If I'd recommended you and you didn't deliver, my reputation would have been on the line, and that's not something I take lightly."

Mary's eyes narrowed. "She came to you, didn't she? Colleen. Your own sister. And you turned her down. Didn't want anybody tracing that shit back to you. Sullying your reputation—"

"I've worked hard for what I've got—"

"A suck-up unwilling to help anybody else get ahead. Well you haven't changed. You're just better dressed."

Darby took a step toward Mary. "You think I'm a suck-up? Why did you deliver those pamphlets for me? Because you're so interested in politics? To earn the pittance the job paid? Or because you thought you'd be able to collect on a favor someday? You probably don't even remember the candidate's name or her platform. You probably don't even know what a platform is, or for that matter, what the Electoral College is or the difference between a Democrat or a Republican. Because you don't care. You don't go to class. You don't have any plans beyond the next drink. Just like the rest of this family."

"Fuck you."

Darby closed her mouth. She stared at Mary a moment then went down the stairs. She got into her elegant car next to her elegant husband and Cadillaced her way into the night. Mary hugged her shaking body. She wiped her tears before they turned to ice. She went inside, the air super-heated and smelling of dog. To people who didn't know what had happened. How she wasn't going to get the job and what that meant.

"Let's get Mary to decide," Uncle Jimmy said and weaved toward her while people laughed. "Who's going to win the Super Bowl this year?" and he draped his arm around her shoulders.

She threw his arm off of her. More laughter. She pushed her way through the living room, the dining room, the kitchen. Unable to think anything but *the bitch, the bitch!* Darby, who'd crawled her way out from under—who knew the weight of impending failure—and yet knowingly gutted Mary.

She bit a corner of her fingernail, tore off the nail, and spit out the sliver while pushing her way to the back of the house. She turned at Aunt Eileen's bedroom and slammed the door. Light and cheap, the door barely made a noise other than a *whoosh*. A sound nobody would hear above the laughter and buzz of their boozed brains. So she opened the door and slammed it again, though harder, then opened the door and threw with her whole body. The effort made her sweat and ache to run, but where would she go? She paced the narrow space between the dresser and a bed piled high with coats. Three steps, turn; three steps, turn. She wiped her forehead with the back of her hand, her chest tight, her brain and body expanding as she felt what it would be like to be out there, floating in the ocean. You slip under once, then again and again until you finally drown.

But then she saw a blue phone on a white nightstand. A phone, with wires leading outside of this house and maybe this life. She pulled open the drawer beneath the phone and rummaged through a stack of *Playboy* magazines until finding a thick phone book of Chicago and the surrounding vicinity. She found the name, the number. She dialed. She stood. The phone rang on the other end. She ripped another nail with her teeth, feeling the sting of nail pulling away from skin. That you're forced to do something this desperate, because if you don't, goddamn. If you don't, you'll be young one minute and dead the next.

And still the phone rang.

She began to whisper, "Fu—" when a woman answered. The mother.

"Is Kathleen there?" Mary said.

The woman told her to wait. Laughter suddenly erupted amidst murmur in the background. Laughter made of lightness and freedom and piercing exclusion.

"Hello?" Kathleen said.

"Kathleen?"

"Yeah?"

"It's Mary."

"Who?"

"Mary. From English class."

Silence.

"I'm not calling to give you shit," Mary said. "I just—"

"I'm kind of busy right now."

"I know." She stared at the wooden crucifix on the wall above the bed. "I just wanted to—It's just, tonight I'm—" *Fucked up.* But you can't say that to an uptight Catholic girl. You have to say something normal and polite. Something that won't scare her.

"You want to go tobogganing sometime?" Mary said.

"What?"

Mary paused, shocked by what she'd just said. Now she had to act like she meant to say that.

"I've never been, and I was thinking maybe I should try it," she said. "I mean, you said it was fun, right? We could, I don't know, maybe meet? Maybe tomorrow or something, just for like a half hour—"

"I'm busy."

She used the back of her hand to wipe the tears off of her cheek while pacing up, pacing down. "Okay, not tomorrow then, but maybe sometime this week. And I wouldn't bring my friends or anything—"

"I don't think so."

She stopped and squeezed her eyes shut. How you never think you will, but then you do. You beg.

"Please," she said. "Please."

The moment seems made of Silly Putty that stretches long and longer, until no more than the width of a thread, ready to break. The only thing that sustains you is the sound of breathing. Not your own because you can't breathe. You're under water. But that of someone else, and nearby. The only person for miles, yet she doesn't want to show herself. Because you scared her. That and everyone knows if you reach out to someone who's drowning, the person can drag you down, and there goes your perfect life.

"I'll have to ask my mom," Kathleen said.

"Okay," Mary said and nodded, meaning she'd understood. That Kathleen had no intention of asking anybody anything. But that's the advantage of having people look down on you. They think you're too ignorant to see what's going on, which gives you the right to play dumb.

"Let me give you my number," Mary said. "You got something to write with?"

"Yeah," Kathleen said, though too fast to have actually picked up a pen or found a notepad.

"A pencil or something?" Mary said.

Kathleen sighed, the sound short, sharp. There came a rustle of paper, and in a resigned tone, "Go ahead."

Mary gave her home number. "Call me later tonight."

Kathleen said nothing.

"Or I'll call you," Mary said.

"No. I'll call."

"Merry Christmas."

"Right."

She listened to the click followed by the dial tone. She hung up and stared at the phone. At what she'd done.

Chapter 6

Tues, Dec. 26

Mary paced her porch in the morning cold, hands shoved to the bottom of her pockets. She craved a smoke. But you shouldn't reek of cigarettes the first time you meet the mother of Uptight Girl. Mom might refuse to let you in the car, or worse, give you a ride but treat you like a bad influence. Mary had gotten used to how disapproving parents looked at her, with narrowed eyes and mouths pinched tight. She shook her hair out of her face, still unable to believe she'd set herself up for this kind of failure. Jesus.

And Kathleen who'd called back last night and said, *Well, do you want to go?* in a tone high and tight, like a hostage being forced at gunpoint to read a confession. She didn't want to go, so why would she invite Mary? Because of her veiled promise to keep calling until Kathleen gave in? Had she even told her mom about the incident with Mary and her friends? No way. Good parents couldn't know something like that and still encourage their kids to take pity. Not unless they were the competitive religious types trying to rack up the get-to-heaven points by doing good deeds.

The street was not just empty, but a morning-after-Christmas desolate. Not even the bent old man with the bearded gray schnauzer had gone out yet. Why are you outside when you could be toasty inside, lazy with gifts, and your stomach full of eggnog and Christmas turkey? At least none of her friends would come by and ask who she was freezing her ass off waiting for. If they did, she'd say, *None of your business.* Which was true. As true as not wanting to take shit for hanging out with a prep-wannabe. She glanced at the rusted Harley parked in the driveway along with Danny's 1969 Dodge Dart with the killer sapphire exterior and dead engine. Just beyond her view, a brown station wagon turned the corner onto her street. She didn't move until the car had pulled alongside the curb in front of her house and come to a complete stop. Even then she sauntered down the porch stairs. *Saunter*, another one of Mr. O'Brien's words, this one meaning to convey a way of walking that shows you don't care, when really your skin feels ready to shiver off like a shedding snake.

The front passenger's-side door of the car opened. Kathleen got out, limbs dragging and mukluks nowhere to be seen. She stood with an arm on top of the car door, eyes half closed.

"Hi," Mary said.

"Yeah," Kathleen said.

Mary's mother leaned across the front seat and peered up at through the open door.

"Hi, Mary. I'm Mrs. McCarthy," she said. Then she smiled, this mom with the baseball-round face, dark blue eyes, and puff of short, brown hair. A mom who looked at Mary's feet and asked, "Do you have any snow boots?"

"Nope."

Mrs. McCarthy smiled. "That's okay. Come on."

"You have to sit in the middle," Kathleen said, tossing a limp wrist toward the back seat, which had been laid down to make room for the toboggan.

When she slid into the middle, she tried not to touch Mrs.

McCarthy. But the extra twenty pounds or so Mrs. M. carried made her thighs spread enough that when Kathleen pushed in, they all squeezed together. That didn't stop Kathleen from pressing herself against the door to get as far from Mary as possible. Kathleen stared out the window. The heater blew hot on Mary's knees.

Mrs. McCarthy pulled the car away from the curb. "Kathleen says you have the same English class."

"Yeah."

"She likes Mr. O'Brien. What about you?"

"He's okay."

Mrs. McCarthy asked what other classes Mary had and then about after-school activities, and Christ, but did this woman know how to give the third degree.

"I work," Mary said, "so I don't really have time for that kind of stuff."

"You work? Where?" Mrs. McCarthy said.

"Ben Franklin."

"The one on Plainfield Avenue?"

"Yeah."

"I shop there! It's one of my favorite stores," Mrs. McCarthy said. And how did she do that: sound truly delighted instead of faking it like the ladies on cleaning product commercials? "How long have you been working there?"

If she said two years, since she was thirteen, Mrs. McCarthy would know Mary had lied on her application. Was that the point of the smiles and questions, to uncover the dirt?

So Mary said, "A while."

"I think that's just great," Mrs. McCarthy said. She glanced sideways at Mary. "You must be a very independent young woman. Like me. I started cleaning houses when I was thirteen and paid for my own car when I was sixteen."

Mary nodded. "That's cool. What kind did you get?"

"A little blue Chevy convertible."

Which was something to picture, a younger, slimmer Mrs. McCarthy tooling around town in her convertible. *Audacious*, as Mr. O'Brien might say.

After a minute, Mrs. McCarthy said, "So. Did Kathleen tell you she babysits?"

"Nope."

"And she ice skates really well, too," Mrs. McCarthy said.

"Mom," Kathleen said, shooting a glare past Mary to Mom before returning to look out the window again.

Mrs. McCarthy drove the winding road to the empty parking lot by the toboggan chute. She parked and kept the engine running.

"Kathleen," Mrs. McCarthy said, "see if there's a hat on the floor of the backseat. I'm worried your ears are going to freeze off, Mary."

"I'm okay."

"I know, but I'd feel better."

Mary got out of the car. After the heat of the car, the cold air sheathed her in ice. When Kathleen walked to the back to get the toboggan, Mary leaned down to talk to Mrs. McCarthy through the open door.

"I have to work today at one," she said. "What time are you going to be back to pick us up?"

"I'm not going anywhere," Mrs. McCarthy said. "I'm going to sit and enjoy my book," and she lifted a paperback from her lap. "I never get a chance to read, and by the time I get home I'd have to turn around and come back, anyway." She smiled, one of joy and mischief so sincere that Mary understood. While Mrs. McCarthy might look like a chubby sucker of a suburban mom, she was sharp. A contender. A protector. An unsuspecting thug. She'd be cheerful, even hopeful, that all turned out for the best today, but if not, she'd be here this time to ward off those who meant Kathleen harm. That was what a mother was supposed to do, protect her kid, just like Mary's mother had.

"Have a good time," Mrs. McCarthy said.

Mary smiled. "Thanks."

And again with the mischief in her eyes. "My pleasure."

My pleasure. And this time Mary believed Mrs. McCarthy's
sincerity. She closed the car door. She turned and got hit in
the face by something soft that then fell to the ground.

Mary spit out the snow and started to say, "What the fu—"

"Your hat," Kathleen said and pointed down at Mary's feet
where the blue-and-orange Chicago Bears hat had fallen.

"You'd really make my mom's day if you wore that," Kathleen said from where she stood beside the chute, the toboggan
lined up and ready for the run. Mary shook the hat against
her leg, the pom-pom wobbling. She glanced right and left,
and Jesus, no one was even around, and even if they were,
why would she give a shit if they saw her wearing something
that for once kept her ears warm? She pulled on the hat and
walked to the chute.

Before getting on, she leaned forward for a better look at the
slide, a slender hook that plunged almost straight down for
fifty feet before curving to level ground. Mary's arms flew out
to the side, the feeling immediate, of dizziness and nausea.

She staggered back a step. "Shit!"

"It's not that bad," Kathleen said.

"The hell it isn't."

"Could you not do that?"

"Do what?"

"Swear."

"What?"

"Could you not curse all the time?"

Mary looked from the chute to Kathleen, then said, "It's
just, I once saw this picture, a photo in a magazine, and it
took up like two pages and it was of Niagara Falls, and just
looking at it, it was like you were hovering over the water
where it dumped over the edge. The water's all dark green

and then it just goes over and there's nothing there, and you think, oh my God, if I was in a little boat or something right at this spot, I'd have no chance. The current would be so strong you couldn't swim or get rescued or anything. You'd just go over and *bam!* That'd be it. Shit."

"Just sit down."

"I'm not going in front."

"Yeah, you are."

Mary leaned toward Kathleen. "No. I'm. Not."

"Or I'll tell my mom you smoke."

"So, who gives a shit?"

Eyes half-closed, Kathleen bent her mouth in a little garter-snake curve of lip. A smile that said she knew that for some reason, Mary would care what Mrs. M. thought. That even though Mrs. M. probably knew plenty of adults who smoked, she'd want better for Mary. Mrs. M. who'd started to work when she was thirteen and who'd saved her money to buy a car and who worried about Mary's ears and called her *an independent young woman.*

"Yeah, well, just hold onto this thing so it doesn't slip," Mary said.

"I am."

"No, you're not."

"Yeah, I *am.*"

Mary stepped onto the toboggan and inched forward. A moan slipped out her mouth. She clamped her lips shut. She lowered herself, heart beating hard enough she had to open her mouth to pant. She gripped the front of the toboggan and stared at the nothingness in front of her. A gust of wind *ahhhed* through the trees, blowing tufts of snow from waving limbs.

Kathleen shoved up behind Mary and lodged a leg under each thigh.

"What are you doing?" Mary said.

"Stop being a baby. I've got to anchor my legs under you. Now hold the reins." Mary did, and Kathleen put her arms around Mary's waist.

"You ready?" Kathleen said, her tone like the Grinch before he got all soft-hearted. Because she'd asked, but she had no intention of waiting for an answer, but instead heaved her hips forward once, twice. The toboggan inched toward the edge and tilted forward. Then came a moment of suspension, of the world teetering on its edge. The toboggan plunged down and the world shrank to a narrow strip of straight-down, head-long white. Cold air rushed into her screaming mouth as rushing air sucked tears from her eyes and tore her hair from its root. The toboggan hit the bottom curve, leveled out, and sailed across the snow for twenty yards before slowing to a stop.

She sat, mouth open. Kathleen jumped up and ran around to face Mary.

"You okay?" Kathleen said and put out a hand to help Mary up. But she could do nothing but sit for a moment. Then she grasped the hand and allowed herself to be pulled up. She stood a moment, dizzy. Her eyes wandered to the treetops and she felt the wind on her lips. A pressure rose fast in her throat and erupted.

"Woo-hoo!" she shrieked, arms shooting into the air. "Oh my god! I can't believe I did that! Lucy would have puked. And James! He would have loved it." Her boot heel caught on a chunk of snow and she fell over sideways. She rolled onto her back, her face to the blue sky and diamond sun. Kathleen's face appeared above. She smiled down at Mary.

"That," she said, "was fucking cool."

Kathleen winced around the eyes.

"I mean, very cool."

"Want to go again?"

Mary smacked the snow with an arm. "Hell, yes." She

jumped up and stumbled through the snow while helping Kathleen drag the toboggan up the wooden staircase. They went down fifteen more times, until her feet were frozen and her T-shirt and scalp soaked with sweat. Until she had to plod along, too winded to talk.

"You should stop smoking," Kathleen said.

"Yeah, yeah."

Mrs. McCarthy told them, "One more time," and then, "Okay, girls, this is it," and "I mean it."

***

When Kathleen and Mary shoved into the front seat, they sat with their thighs touching because who cared? Touching, not touching. What was a little pressure compared to death defied. And goddamn, how good it felt to laugh, the three of them together. They laughed mostly at Mary, who copped to the extent of her initial terror. They talked so fast she paid no attention to where they were going. She still felt the swooping in her belly. From the wonder of plunging into something new. From having everything turn out okay for once. No humiliation, no hangover, no crash. Not one bad thing waited for her at the bottom.

"Do you want to come over for hot chocolate?" Mrs. McCarthy said to Mary.

"My mom makes delectable hot chocolate," Kathleen said.

"Oh shit—" Mary covered her mouth, then uncovered it. "I mean, shoot. What time is it?"

"About noon," Mrs. McCarthy said. "You should have time, and then if you want, I can drive you to work. If it's okay with your parents."

Mary kept her eyes on the road. "No, I—"

"You should come," Kathleen said and jabbed Mary in the ribs with an elbow. "There's leftover Christmas cookies."

Mrs. McCarthy started to say something, then stopped.

"I better just go home," Mary said.

"You could meet my cat," Kathleen said. "She's black and white, but we call her Ginger." She laughed and said she'd named the cat after the movie star character on *Gilligan's Island*, and everybody knew that TV show. How a boat of tourists gets stranded on an island and try to escape in a hundred different ways, though they never did.

"You should come," Kathleen said.

Mary licked her lips.

"What, are you scared or something?" Kathleen said and poked Mary in the ribs again, when Kathleen should just keep her goddamn elbow to herself.

"Now Kathleen, it's okay if she can't come today," Mrs. McCarthy said. "She can do it another time. We'll take you home so you can change out of those wet clothes. Otherwise, you'll be miserable at work."

"It's just—"

"It's okay. Another time," said Mrs. McCarthy.

Mary looked at the woman's profile. Chin lifted. No longer laughing. A woman who knew that for a girl to call someone she didn't know, begging to do something as random as tobogganing, was an act of desperation. Nobody could understand something like that, unless at some point, she'd been desperate herself. Which made Mrs. McCarthy and Mary two desperadoes who knew a part of life Kathleen didn't and might never know. Mrs. McCarthy, who wanted to see Mary change out of her wet clothes so she wouldn't be miserable, when nobody worried about her like that. So she should be gracious for once and accept their hospitality.

But Jesus. What if.

What if what? What could be worse than going home to the cold and unpeopled emptiness of your own house? Yet she still didn't say anything. She rubbed her thighs, the heater having made her skin itch beneath her wet jeans. She clutched the hat in her hand, the T-shirt a chill against her heart.

"Actually," she said, "The hot chocolate sounds pretty good."

"I'll show you my sewing machine," Kathleen said. "Mom and Dad bought me a new one last Christmas and it can do button-holes really good."

"Well," Mrs. McCarthy said.

"Well," Kathleen said. "I made my dress for our Christmas Eve party this year. Full-length. I know that probably sounds stupid, but it's kind of like putting together a puzzle. And it really turned out nice."

Mrs. McCarthy turned down a street about five blocks from where Mary lived. Mrs. McCarthy pulled into the drive alongside a tall white two-story with black shutters. The house was surrounded by evergreens trimmed into popcorn balls of various sizes. A huge red bow hung from a black light pole by the steps leading to a front door decorated with a wreath of shiny red-and-white balls. Mrs. McCarthy drove into the garage. Kathleen led Mary through the clutter of bikes, coiled hoses, a picnic table, and stacked plastic chairs. All the while, Kathleen talked about who lived down the street and how her home economics teacher assigned projects that were too easy. The defensive priss had fled, replaced by this new Chatty Cathy, so open and friendly. Normally Mary would have made a smart-ass remark about that. Nothing harsh, but instead a friendly dig. Because Jesus, that was all it took to gain her trust, a few toboggan runs and a few laughs?

But Mary couldn't talk for the growing threat she felt, though about what, she didn't know.

All three took off their boots in the mudroom and hung their coats on wooden pegs. Kathleen opened the door and warm air rushed in, swaddling Mary. She squinted, the kitchen bright from a central hanging light shaped like a lantern. The walls were covered in blue-and-white-checked wallpaper. A long wooden table ran down the middle of the room. On the counter sat a cookie jar shaped liked a fat woman wearing a chef's hat and a white apron that read, in black letters, *A balanced diet is a cookie in each hand.*

Mrs. McCarthy put her arm around Kathleen and squeezed. "Go show her the rest of the house while I get the hot chocolate ready."

Kathleen rested her head on her mom's shoulder and smiled. "My mom makes really good hot chocolate." She stood within her mother's embrace, yet pushed away. "I'll show you our glamorous basement first," and Kathleen headed through a doorway by the stove.

Mrs. McCarthy opened a pantry door. When passing, Mary glanced inside to see four rows of shelves stocked from top to bottom. Three boxes of cereal that had been opened. And entire shelf of canned goods. Flats of pop stacked on the floor.

"Come on," Kathleen said.

Mary heard the laughter of boys and guessed one had to be Kathleen's brother. When she reached the bottom of the stairs, there he was, jumping around in his stocking feet, throwing a Nerf ball through a hoop stuck to the wall while a friend waited for the rebound.

"I keep all my stuff in here," Kathleen said and put a hand on an old dresser beside her sewing machine. "Like scissors, patterns, extra material, and stuff."

The Nerf ball bounced off the wall and landed near Mary. Kathleen's brother spun around. When he saw Mary, he stopped. He was sweaty around the bangs and mad as hell around the mouth and eyes. He remembered her from the forest preserve then, though this time he wasn't scared shitless. Not when he stood in his own house with his mother upstairs.

"Come on, Kevin," the other boy said and threw the ball at the hoop.

Kathleen glanced from Kevin to Mary with a nervous smile. "This is my brother, Kevin."

"Hi," Mary said.

Kevin turned away and waited for his friend to throw him the ball. Kathleen glared at Kevin's back. "Don't mind him. He's just being a doorknob." Then she headed up the stairs, turning long enough to whisper over her shoulder. "He's still kind of mad about the other day."

Kathleen led the way through the kitchen to the dining room, living room, and stairs leading to the bedrooms. While the same size as Mary's house, this home was the opposite in every way. Instead of bare windows, curtains closed out the night. Instead of blank walls, paintings hung at intervals. The dark wood banisters gleamed and carpeting covered the floor. The limbs of the full Christmas tree sagged under pounds of silver tinsel and ornaments. Crystals hung from candle-shaped lights in the bathroom on either side of a gold-framed mirror. There were photos in the hallway of Kathleen and her brother at various stages of geekdom. Books lined the book-shelves. A dictionary, the Hardy Boys, *National Geographic*. There were stacks of clean towels in the upstairs hall closet and a medicine chest filled with aspirin, cold medicine, and Band-Aids that a mother buys to make you feel better when you're sick, and if you're too sick, she makes you stay in bed instead of letting you crawl to work so your next paycheck won't be short.

When they reached Kathleen's bedroom, Kathleen walked in while Mary remained in the doorway, staring at all that lavender: from the swirl of ruffled curtains to the bedspread and carpet. A bookshelf displayed souvenirs from past vaca-tions. A penguin, Pink Panther, and other stuffed animals crowded the made bed, this a girlie girl's bedroom like those on TV. Except this was worse because this was real and the people who lived here were real and their happiness was real, and that, Mary realized—but too late, too goddamn late—was what you should be afraid of.

"And this is my cat," Kathleen said. She scooped the animal off of her bed and scratched its head. "You want to hold her?"

"I've got to go," Mary said. Her lips moved, but she didn't feel them. She turned and sailed across the upstairs hall, down the stairs, and past the shining dining room table. She curved around the refrigerator with the heart-shaped magnets. Past the wooden wall plaques with the too-cute sayings of *Welcome, Willkommen, Bienvenu!* Past Mrs. McCarthy.

"Mary," Mrs. McCarthy said, the delivery almost a shout that made Mary stop and turn. Though she saw Mrs. McCarthy's lips moving, Mary could hear almost nothing because of the clanging in her ears. "Wait," Mrs. McCarthy said. She dug fast through a drawer of containers and pulled out a thermos.

"It's okay—" she said, hearing herself as an echo in her head.

"You wait," Mrs. McCarthy said. She ladled hot chocolate into the thermos, her movements careful but urgent. "It's made with milk. Are you allergic to milk?"

"No."

Mrs. McCarthy stuffed two marshmallows down the opening and screwed on the top. She handed the thermos to Mary.

"No—"

"Take it. And some cookies," Mrs. McCarthy said, holding up a plate. "I insist."

Mary looked down. At a plate of frosted gingerbread men with silver candy buttons and cinnamon-dot eyes. She held her mouth firm because she would not allow herself to cry. No fucking way. She grabbed two cookies and stuffed them in her pocket.

"I can drive you," Mrs. McCarthy said. Because she knew, didn't she? The humiliation of such ignorance. Here you think you know how some people live and make yourself feel better by believing they aren't as happy as they look and you aren't as miserable as you feel. So you think, *Hell, what have I got to lose.* But then you trip into their world, tra-la-la, and oops, realize you've been wrong all along. They're not pretending and you are.

She opened her mouth, but couldn't speak for the enormity of what she now understood. How much closer to hell she lived than did Kathleen. Which meant Mary had to climb even higher than she thought to get out. And if she had any thoughts at least part of the way would be easy, she didn't now. Every step would be a muscle-straining, cliff-hanging crawl. So why even try?

She turned and threw open the door to the mudroom, jammed her feet into her boots, and pulled on her coat. The screen door banged closed behind her. She strode around the house, down the driveway, and onto the sidewalk, the thermos tucked under her arm and hands stuffed into her pockets along with the cookies. She wanted to Frisbee those shitty little brown men with their silver buttons so she could watch their heads explode against a frozen tree. But they were Christmas cookies and she was starving. When in the same situation, Kathleen, if upset about how much better others lived, wouldn't think twice. She'd fly those red-eyed bastards far as she could because she'd know there'd be something just as sweet, maybe sweeter, waiting for her at home, along with more towels, more lights, more fucking kisses on the head. A girl who could waste because she wasn't starving for anything.

And Mary's jaw locked. With rage, with shame. That she'd been so naïve about how they lived, those who weren't infected. Well, fuck them and their happy oblivion.

Chapter 7

Mon., Jan. 1, 1979

Mary sat on the sagging couch in Chuck and Lucy's basement, knee bouncing. This was supposed to be a New Year's Eve party, but there was nothing new about any of it. Now after 3 a.m., the snow had been falling since midnight, burying them here, yet no one but her seemed to care. People packed the house: upstairs, downstairs, some friends, most acquaintances, a few strangers. People who obviously didn't have any plans for tomorrow, or the next day either, or the next. But she did. When the world reopened for business, she'd be out the door. Filling out job applications. Looking for references. And this time she wouldn't let anybody screw with her chances of getting what she wanted. She'd list only friendlies on the application, people who'd promise to say good things about her when prospective employers called. And she'd ask for a specific date by which she could expect a response. A minute after that deadline passed, she'd call said employer, and every day, too, until she got an answer, instead of waiting like a fool. And instead of getting bitchy—*What the hell, man? Why are you making me wait?*—she'd be Mrs. McCarthy polite.

Though she had a plan, the heebie-jeebies had nested in her gut, something to do with this blizzard being a possible *metaphor*, as Mr. O'Brien might say. That despite her best effort, the obstacles in her way might suffocate her chances. Bob's presence only made the feeling of claustrophobia worse. Every time she turned around he was there, leaning against the wall, hands in his pockets, staring at her. Lying in wait, but for what? Did he think his creepy persistence would eventually win her heart?

She took a drag on her cigarette and let her eyes wander, first to Tina, who was making out with a kid twenty pounds lighter and most likely a freshman, to the lit neon Pabst beer sign on the wall and the popcorn and plastic cups littering the shag rug. Aerosmith vibrated the walls. The air reeked of weed, cigarettes, and laundry detergent, like somebody spilled a box of Tide and hadn't cleaned up, which was probably what happened. And to think she could have given up all of this excitement to attend Kathleen's girls-only sleepover.

Kathleen had called twice, probably to find out why Mary had freaked and run out of their house like a fucking coward. Danny had taken the messages, the second of which had included an invitation to Kathleen's party. How fucking naïve. To think Mary would fit in with a bunch of giggling good girls, or that those girls would welcome her.

Two boys stood facing one another in front of her. They dropped into a boxing stance. They gripped each other's right hand and thumb-wrestled while a few guys and girls looked on, laughing. One of the contenders was Steve, a blubbery kid with light red hair. The other was a freshman named Ken, a geek with white blond hair to his shoulders and the same petite body as his older sister, Julie V. She said her brother had won a science fair competition for two or three years in a row, yet here he stood, out for a swim with the sharks. Why would you follow in your older sister's delinquent footsteps if you have brains? Maybe Ken wasn't so smart after all.

Steve dropped Ken's hand. "You're too wasted," Steve said.

"You're all like…" and he let his tongue loll while punching the air with limp wrists.

Ken slapped Steve's fists away. "No more wasted than you."

The couch jerked. James jumped over the back of the couch and landed snugly against her, his body thrumming, probably from speed.

"What's up?" he said.

"Absolutely nothing."

Lucy sat down next to James, eyes bleary and smile tranquil, nobody able to conjure oblivion like Lucy on ludes, sedatives probably the only way to deal with an oldest brother like John. A truck driver, he reigned over his younger brother and sister like an inbred czar who considered Lucy his personal whore. Chuck had become Lucy's sole defender, something people didn't know, those who whispered about how Chuck and Lucy seemed a little too close for a brother and sister. Those who didn't know shit about how much energy the two had to expend to remain vigilant against an attack that could come at any time. Thank God Evil John often rode off in his truck to pull long-distance loads, or take off for Milwaukee with his buddies during a weekend of drinking and going to topless bars. Then Chuck and Lucy could relax and actually hang out at home as opposed to anywhere but.

"God, this is so lame," said a girl who stood against the wall, watching Steve and Ken. "You guys should just go at it and slap the shit out of each other."

"You want us to fight? Give us something to fight about," Steve said. Suggestions poured in. *World hunger. Pretend he's a homo. Pretend he's your dad.*

Then Ken laughed and said, "Let's fight to see who gets to make it with Lucy. I'll pretend to be Chuck."

All movement stilled. Someone whistled, a low tone that slid lower still, an incoming missile. Ken straightened and looked around. People glanced at Lucy, who'd apparently missed the comment and swayed where she sat on the couch, her eyes closed, arms raised and hips rocking in a private dance. Mary saw somebody slip up the stairs, no doubt to tell Chuck.

"Hey, dumbshit," Mary told Ken. "You've got about ten seconds to get out of here before Chuck shows up."

But Ken was inexperienced, and therefore stupid and slow. And the way his eyes ricocheted around the room said he still didn't know what he'd done wrong.

"Get him out of here," she told James. "Use the basement door."

Footsteps pounded the wooden stairs. At the sight of Chuck, those around Ken blew outward.

James got between Ken and Chuck. James put a hand on Chuck's chest. "Come on, man—"

Chuck whacked James's arm to the side and glared at Ken. "What did you say, asshole?"

Lucy's eyes fluttered open. "What's going on?"

Chuck tried to get around James, who remained the only barrier protecting Ken's ninety-eight pounds, maybe, and Chuck's two hundred.

"What did you say about me and my sister, asshole?" Chuck said. Then he lunged around James and caught Ken by the T-shirt. He lifted the boy with both hands. The T-shirt ripped and Ken fell.

"What did he do?" Lucy said and stood. "Chuck—"

Julie V. came clumping down the stairs in her platform boots, voice a screech. "Don't hurt him, Chuck! If you fucking lay a hand on him—"

Chuck hauled Ken up and swung. The blow drove Ken backward. He fell on the floor in front of her. Chuck took a giant step and pulled Ken to his feet. Julie jumped onto Chuck's back.

"You'll kill him!" she said.

Chuck swung again. Ken's head snapped back and he fell

again, the right side of his mouth ripped open and his white hair streaked with dark blood.

"Chuck! Stop!" Lucy said, crying.

Mary jumped over the back of the couch and ran to the Pabst sign on the wall. She pulled the two-by-two square of metal from the wall, turned, and brought the sign down on Chuck's head. He fell and pulled into a fetal position, hands clasped on the back of his head. He cursed between gritted teeth, his eyes shut tight.

She stood over Ken, who groaned. The white of his right eye had filled with blood and a flap of lip hung loose.

"Get him out of here," she said to James. "And take Lucy with you."

James and Kevin grabbed Ken and hauled him up the stairs. Julie followed, alternately crying for her brother and cursing Chuck while Lucy followed, crying, too.

"Who fucking did that?" Chuck said, his voice strained with pain. He rolled onto his back, legs stretched out, a hand behind his head.

She squatted and brought her face close to Chuck's. "I did."

"What the fuck, Mary?"

"You could have killed him, you doorknob," she said. "Think what that would mean. You're eighteen now. Legal. You'd be tried as an adult. No six months in juvie like last time. You want to leave Lucy with John for however long it takes you to get out of jail?"

Chuck rolled over onto his side, then his belly. He pushed onto all fours and let his head hang. His shoulders shook for a moment, tears falling into the rug. She sat back on her heels. Chuck's breathing slowed and his shoulders calmed.

"Thanks," Chuck said and drew a hand across his nose.

"Go stick your head in a bucket of ice," she said, her voice steady but body shaking. She helped Chuck to a stand where he swayed for a moment, his eyes closed.

"It just blows, you know?" he said.

"Yeah."

He rubbed his cheek against his shoulder and slogged upstairs. She followed. With every step, the music from the upstairs stereo grew louder until the beat pounded her heart in a knock-against-knock rhythm. Drums and an electric guitar, if blasted loud enough, gave the impression that everything was all right. That the party had kicked into overdrive in a universe bursting with fun. And yet the fluorescent light in the kitchen turned everyone's skin to plastic. Every chair seemed filled with sex, couples either making out or fingering one another, and why couldn't they fucking get a room? She worked her way through the crowd, annoyed there never seemed to be enough room to maneuver. Never enough space to spread out and think. She pushed through the kitchen and into the dinky dining room and the living room with granny lamps on garage-sale tables. And where the hell had James gone, anyway? She continued down the hall and leaned against the wall behind a long line of people waiting to get into the house's only bathroom. She tried not to think about the piece of lip hanging from Ken's mouth or Kathleen's lavender room and what would that be like, waking from sleep and knowing nothing bad would happen? Like when you go downstairs and pancakes are waiting for you, your Mom on the other end of the spatula.

When her turn came, she closed and locked the door. She peed while staring at the wall, some white tiles missing, like teeth from a smile. When done, she washed her hands. She looked into the mirror. A shadow covered her jaw and spread upward across her face. She leaned closer and scratched with a wet finger. The dots dissolved in the water on her fingers and ran down her hand. Blood.

"Fuck," she said and ripped off her coat. She twisted both valves to full force and filled her hands with water. She splashed her face, then scrubbed.

"Mary," James called from outside the door, his voice a forever away.

She kept scrubbing, water everywhere, in her mouth, in her hair, her body a Jiffy-Pop explosion and mind fixed on Kathleen. How if she was here right now, she'd probably be crying in a closet somewhere, traumatized by the violence. By the horror of one person wearing another's blood, or maybe even swallowing it. Mary gagged, but nothing came out. She held a trembling hand to her lips, because Jesus, in her *mouth*. In this, her world, where fights were expected and constant. Like the time Bing broke his ankle trying to kick in the window of Jay McIntyre's black Corvette, or when Julie V. ripped out Stacy Comiskey's earring. Incidents Mary never thought about, but now did because of Kathleen. She seemed to hover over Mary's life, a preppy angel, clucking her tongue at everything she saw and heard, no part of Mary's life worth saving.

Somebody banged on the door.

"Mar, you in there?" James said.

The bathroom didn't have a towel, so she pulled a flap of her T-shirt from where she'd tucked it into her jeans. She wiped her face and opened the door.

James leaned an arm on the doorframe. "I've been looking all over for you." The worry in his blue eyes matched his smile of concern. For all of Kathleen's luck, she didn't have a James, a vice guaranteed to distract you from thoughts of blood, horror, and judgment. She moved into James and rode her hands up under his shirt to his shoulder blades. She raised her mouth, his taste that of a last sip of beer. Bitter, warm, delicious. She pressed her hips against his and pressed him backward, out of the bathroom door. Whistles sounded up and down the hall until James pushed away from her, his lips unlocking with a pop. He looked at her, his eyes surprised and hungry bright. He ducked beneath her arm and hoisted her over his shoulder. He gave a Tarzan yowl and people in the kitchen looked and laughed. Chuck saluted with a beer in one hand while holding a bag of frozen peas to the back of his head. Beside him stood Bummer Bob, who inhaled, causing his cigarette tip to flare a searing orange. James trotted her down the hall, his shoulder thumping her belly.

"God, I'm going to puke," she yelled, laughing.

James threw open the door to John's room and tossed her on the bed where she bounced on the mashed mattress. He locked the door. She turned on the bedside lamp, unclasped her bra, and laid back. James jumped on the bed and danced around her, both of them laughing. Then he jumped to the floor and stood at the foot of the bed, breathing hard like a runner who just won. He smiled, the prize at hand.

"You got a raincoat for Jimmy?" she whispered.

James tossed the condom. She caught the packet in one hand. She unzipped her jeans. Slowly. Knowing how waiting made impatient James crazy. When the last tooth of the zipper had been unlocked, James gripped the ragged bottom of her jeans. She gripped the bedpost. One yank and off came the pants. James threw them aside with the flair of a matador, as Mrs. Dariano from social studies might say. James stared at her, discovering her New Year's Eve surprise, of not wearing underwear. James whistled. He stepped up onto the bed and stood over her, then fell to his knees, his crotch above hers. He peeled off her T-shirt and threw that, too, and then the bra, until Mary lay naked beneath him. He looked down and there she was, a goddess reflected in his light blue eyes. The power of her hips and concave belly and of her breasts with the wine nipples, ready to drink. And if Kathleen were looking down, she'd say, *Oh my goodness!* Mary laughed, the sound sharp-edged. She pulled James down to her, and goddamn.

***

She opened her eyes to blackness. She closed her eyes. The next time she opened them, a slice of light from beneath the dingy curtains made the room gray. The house was quiet. The music gone. She picked up the alarm clock on the bedside table and squinted at the hands. She cursed, dragged herself out of bed, and collected her clothes from the various places James had tossed them. She dressed and put on her coat, then sat on the bed to put on her boots.

"James," she said, twisting around to shake him by the shoulder. "Come on, man. I got to be at work in a half hour."

He didn't move, and probably wouldn't; James a dead-to-the-world sleeper, even without the drugs. Fortunately, the night after a party guaranteed bodies would be strewn about. She'd rouse somebody and beg for a ride. She kissed James on the cheek and shoved off the bed.

When she reached the kitchen, she stopped, the instinct immediate to move back out of sight. But she didn't move fast enough. Bob looked up from where he sat at the table, hunched over a cereal bowl. He finished chewing and used a tongue to dig a piece of food from his molar while watching her in that blinkless gaze.

"Have a good time last night?" he said, his tone emotionless, yet fluid. And what did he mean, *Have a good time?* At the party, or with James?

"You know where Chuck is?" she said.

"Went to breakfast. Around five. Him, Havermeyer. Some others." Bob shrugged. "Need a ride?"

"No, thanks."

"Going to be kind of hard to walk."

He thumbed over his shoulder to the window above the sink. To a world trapped in a chokehold of white. Snow bent the limbs of an evergreen into so many frowns.

"You sure you don't need a ride?" Bob said.

She scratched her shoulder to cover the shiver of willies. "A girl who was here last night lives near me," she said without looking at him. "I'll see if she's still here." She walked past Bob like he was nothing to her, which was true. Yet what did it mean when you have to remind yourself of that? When someone's look makes you feel like you're the next victim in a horror movie?

Once in the dining room, she quickened her pace and moved to the living room where she leaned over a boy face down on the couch. She didn't know him and so moved on to a girl curled up on the floor beneath a coat. A Brenda something or other: a freshman who wouldn't have a license, much less a car.

A chair leg scraped the kitchen floor. Bob was getting up, filling her with a strong urge to get out, get away. As though if she didn't, unseen hands would grip her throat and squeeze and in the moment before she blacked out, she'd see everything she'd never done. The messages she'd never returned. The dark rooms she'd never left.

She bounded on tiptoe across the room and opened the front door and slipped out. She jumped down the stairs into a foot of snow and kicked her way toward the street while glancing over her shoulder, and how, right now, Bob might be walking around to see where she'd gone. She jogged past his lime green Charger in the driveway and continued for two blocks before turning left and then right again onto the rural four-lane highway leading from this bass-ackward unincorporated area toward town, toward people and police. Though the road had been cleared, it was flanked by ten-foot snow mounds made from previous plowings. If Bob came, she'd have nowhere to hide. She turned and walked backward, her thumb out and heart hoping for a friendly passerby. The road stretched empty. By now, Bob might be opening the front door, his eyes following her footsteps this way.

A light blue car rose over the hill, driving toward her.

"Come on," she whispered, because if Bob saw her, he'd know she'd rather slog through snow and risk a ride with a possible ax murderer than drive with him. Then he wouldn't invite her to his birthday party for sure. Yet the thought wasn't funny, just like it wasn't funny to think about the girl who'd been strangled in the woods across from school. And how awful, that your last moments would be spent in terror, loneliness, and a bitter wind. An outcome a mom like Mrs. McCarthy would never let happen to her daughter. Just like she wouldn't let Kathleen attend Mary-type parties where boys like Bob lurked. A good mother knew where her daughter was at all times. And who she was with and what she was doing, and if called in an emergency, that mom would drop everything to rescue her kid, no matter the weather or time of day or night, no questions asked.

"Come on, come on!" she said through gritted teeth even as she smiled for whoever drove the car, which seemed to crawl toward her, tires grinding snow. Then behind the car, she saw Bob's car turn onto the road in her direction.

The blue car slowed. She jogged toward the vehicle and reached for the handle. She looked down and saw a tiny, elderly woman peering up from the passenger side while a tiny, elderly man sat in the driver's seat. Mary scooted to the back passenger side, yanked the car handle, and hopped in. Door closed, she slumped.

The elderly man, wearing a black overcoat and matching fedora, craned his head to look at her. "Are you all right, young lady?"

"Yeah, but let's go."

Chapter 8

Mon., Jan. 8

For the remainder of Christmas break, Mary stayed up late, got up early, worked long hours, and filled out job applications. When her alarm went off Monday morning, the first day back to school, she felt good. Overly good to the point of expectant, and even anxious, that something good could actually result from her honest effort at finding a better job. Rather than wait for a ride from James or one of her brother's friends, she ate a spoonful of peanut butter, a handful of Cap'n Crunch, and took off on foot.

And Christ, look at the sky: made of ash. Another snowstorm had raged last night, leaving six inches of snow. Darkness reigned like midnight with only the yellow streetlights to show the way. She kicked through the accumulation on the sidewalk, her heart pumping hard enough to keep her warm. When she got to school, she pulled open the door and heated air washed over her iced face and numb thighs. She stamped her feet. Clots of snow fell off her shoulders. She crossed the entryway, jogged up four steps, and took a right down B wing.

Though an empty hallway, she heard laughter from the other end. She looked up and three girls came around the corner. One of them was Kathleen. She had her eyes on the ground and so didn't see Mary. Kathleen and her stupid wood-handled purse and giggling friends with their pony-tails and braces, and what were they laughing about? The thought came of slipping into a classroom and letting them pass. But avoiding people made a person pathetic. And she wanted to see if Kathleen would ignore the big bad burnout. Mary guessed the prep would because Kathleen had proven herself to be a champion ignorer. That and she had a right to snub Mary.

She walked toward the trio. Kathleen never once looked up, and how did she survive in such oblivion? She and her friends were three strides away now, then two, then one. Only in the moment before they passed did Kathleen glance up. A moment in which a person has no idea you're there, but then she sees you. An unguarded moment where the person can't hide her reaction to you. And in this moment, Kathleen's eyes reflected relief. A person honest-to-God happy to see Mary and know she was okay.

Then Kathleen looked away and passed by.

Mary stopped.

Passed by. As Kathleen should have because Mary had acted badly. Had stormed out of Kathleen's house without explana-tion and ignored her attempts to say hello and her invitation to come in and get warm and be happy. Good for Kathleen. And you're happy you made her stronger, and maybe harder, too. But your heart burns with the wish you'd acted better. But you don't know how.

Maybe Mary had done Kathleen a favor by not pretending to be friends because they couldn't, could they? Mary jogged her shoulders and tilted her head from side to side, trying to stay loose, careless, yet feeling hot and tight and unhappy.

More students filtered into the hall while locker doors slammed and people called to one other. Vibrations rebounded off of metal, tile, concrete, and glass. Everything hard and unforgiving. To just ignore Mary, when nobody ignored her. Yet she'd deserved it.

Someone called her name. She turned to see Christine, this year's Winter Ball queen. Despite the Barbie look—blonde hair, blue eyes, petite build—Christine blew every stereotype. She aced school like a brain, smoked with Mary and her crowd like a burnout, partied with the jocks, and hung with the theater groupies. She dropped by, asked questions, kept an eye out: the world a party she hosted with a cool far beyond most around her.

Christine smiled. "I hear you clocked Chuck."

She rolled her eyes. "Jesus, who hasn't heard?"

Christine laughed, then leaned closer. Five feet looking up at five-eight like the two were on the same level. "I heard Duncan McCormick might have another party."

She shrugged, having heard the same.

"If it comes off, do you think it'll be as entertaining as I heard the last one was?" Christine said.

As entertaining the key phrase. While Duncan had a garage full of pinball machines guys loved and an impressive repertoire of drinking games, neither would interest a chick like Christine. Which only left drugs.

"He dabbles in the experimental," Mary said.

Christine lowered her chin and looked up from under a rim of thick, mascara-blackened lashes, her smile smacking a Playboy Bunny twist, the kind that must get such cleavage queens a fat tip.

"As in unusually-altered mental states?" she said.

"His cousin's a chemist. They mix and match."

"Interesting?"

How could a person explain last summer's party? That after swallowing something tiny, you drop down a rabbit hole and wake to a world soft and bendy. Images funnel through you intravenously, pouring out of your senses. The best part being how you emerge in not just goddess mood, but feeling like Aphrodite herself; and oh man, the memory. Like porn gone pure.

Mary smiled. "Mind-blowing."

A corner of Christine's mouth lifted, a bingo in her eyes. She thanked Mary and peeled away, a leaf from a stem, leaving no chance for Mary to mention the one kid who'd gone to Duncan's party and wound up in the hospital. Rumors continued to float. Of an overdose that left the kid comatose and brain dead. Though maybe he'd just moved away.

Night like that, who knew what could happen?

***

The snow stopped falling before first period, then started again at noon. Mary sat near the window in social studies and watched, an elbow on the desk and a fist on her cheek. She listened, sort of, to Mrs. Dariano, who went on and on about governmental policies of exclusion while pacing back and forth across the room, each step of her thick-soled shoes doing a *tock, tock.* She stopped when the intercom crackled.

"Oh, please," a skinny boy in the back whispered loud enough to make people laugh.

Mr. Hoggarty's voice came over the sound system. "Due to the continued snowfall, we're dismissing school early—"

A cheering erupted, one that could be heard in, across, and down the hall while accompanied by the drumming of hands on desks and feet on the floor. Students were already out of their seats, heading for the door, while Mrs. Dariano yelled out the homework for tomorrow. Mary buttoned her coat and strode past her teacher.

"Nice to see you, Mary," Mrs. Dariano said. "Any chance you'll get me that essay on Zimbabwe any time soon?"

She smiled and kept moving. "As Mr. O'Brien says, *Hope is a free commodity.*"

"Mary," Mrs. Dariano called.

But she was out the door. She left school via the gym exit. Though the sidewalk had been plowed, the path had already filled again with the falling snow. Nobody would be in the alcove today, so she'd just go to work early. At least she'd be warm and could get something to eat from the vending machine. Yet she'd gotten up this morning feeling like something significant might happen, but nothing had, and how that can make you pissy and antsy at the same time. Then she looked up to see someone crossing her path. Someone dressed in a dark green coat and white mittens. Mary narrowed her eyes, seeing for the first time what Danny meant when he said you've got to watch and wait and think. That opportunities don't necessarily drop at your feet, but instead require pursuit.

Mary followed Kathleen north across the four-lane road filled with cars rolling through the snow mush. Kathleen had a block's lead and walked fast enough Mary had to pick up her pace.

"Kat," she yelled.

But Kathleen kept on. Mary walked faster, slipped on a piece of ice and almost fell, her purse swinging out in an arc before slamming her in the side. "Shit! Goddamn snow—Kat!"

Kathleen looked up into the trees. Why did she do that. look off in some bizarre direction? Couldn't she hear that Mary's voice came from behind? Now only ten yards away, Mary yelled again. Kathleen turned. This time, though, she didn't seem either surprised or happy to see Mary.

She neared and stopped. "So," she said, trying to catch her breath and sound uninterested at the same time, a tough gig. Now she suddenly didn't know what to say, maybe because she had no experience pursuing anyone. "Why'd you ignore me this morning?"

"I didn't ignore you," Kathleen said.

"The hell you didn't. You walked right by me without saying anything."

"Well, it wasn't like you said hi to me, either. And you didn't answer my calls, which is really impolite."

"I know."

"You know? So why'd you do it?"

Mary shrugged.

"That's all?" Kathleen said and gave an exaggerated shrug to mimic Mary. "Don't you ever have any homework?"

"What?"

"I never see you carrying books."

Mary kept her eyes on Kathleen. On the point. "You afraid to be seen with me?"

"No," Kathleen said. Yet she dropped her eyes.

"No as in yes. How come?"

Kathleen looked up. "I'm not—"

"Don't bullshit me, Kat."

"Stop calling me that."

Mary leaned forward. "So—*Kat*—are you afraid to be seen talking to me?"

Kathleen threw out a mittened hand. "Oh, so now all of a sudden we're being honest."

"Yeah."

"Oh, well, so as long as we're being honest."

"So are you?"

"Yeah," Kathleen said, her cheeks a blotched red and white.

"Why?"

"Because you're a burnout."

She stared at Kathleen. The snow between them like white noise made of silence. They both knew the hierarchy. Preps. Jocks. Geeks. Burnouts. A social strata similar to the geological one Mr. Van Dyke talked about last year in earth science. How one layer presses down on the previous one, with new layers added all the time with neither pause nor mercy. Eventually the weight grew unbearable and squashed varying sediments together into inescapable rivers of grit. Mary and her crowd comprised the very bottom layer. The shittiest place to be stuck, the weight so heavy you can't escape.

"So by associating with a burnout you are one?" Mary said.

"Oh, right, and like you haven't gone out of your way to keep from introducing me to your friends because I'm too uncool."

"You met them already."

"Uh-uh, I did *not* meet them. You did *not* introduce me. You just let them give me trouble." The jaw and cheek muscles of Kathleen's face jumped. "You wouldn't really introduce me, like as a friend because you'd be afraid of what they'd say about you hanging out with someone you think is such a Girl Scout—"

"Were you?"

"That's not the point!" She huffed, creating white clouds of breath. "You'd be embarrassed because *I* don't smoke and *I* don't do drugs and *I* don't date hot guys and flunk my classes."

Mary smiled a little. "And why is it you don't?"

"And why is it you do?" Kathleen shouted before casting her blazing eyes to the ground. A boy walked their way. Books under his arm, he had his head down in a way that said he'd heard the yelling and would pretend he hadn't so long as they just let him pass without hassling him. Yet he was nobody Mary knew, so she didn't move. He started to climb onto the hill of snow piled beside the sidewalk, his boots slipping and hand out for balance. Then Kathleen, ever so fucking polite, stepped out of his way so he could get back on the sidewalk. He glanced at her and smiled. She smiled. Like everything was okay when it wasn't. What a fake. And sure enough, when Kathleen turned to Mary, the smile disappeared.

"It's like you want to fail," Kathleen said, "and live a deplorable life of misery when all you'd have to do is homework sometimes and stuff."

She leaned closer to Kathleen. "You have no goddamned idea what you're talking about."

"Well maybe I don't, but at least I try. None of you try."

"Oh, so now I represent all the burnouts."

"Well, you do. You're like the queen of them or something."

"How the hell would you know?"

"At least I call people back."

Tough girl Kathleen with the thousand emotions fighting for space on that tiny oval stage. A kid in white mittens who said things like *a deplorable life of misery* with a straight face. Something about her that could piss you off and at the same time make you face yourself. She smiled.

"It's not funny!" Kathleen said.

"It's not."

"Then what are you laughing at?"

Mary didn't want to laugh, but did anyway. "I'm not laughing at you."

"You are!"

"It's just that you're right."

Kathleen pressed her lips tight, having apparently expected Mary's reasoning to go left, only to have it go right.

"I'm sorry," Mary said, still smiling but feeling more sincere than she had in a long time. "I should have called. I was just—"

Just what? What could she tell Kathleen that she'd understand or wouldn't scare her? About Darby's treachery and not getting the job? About Mary's envy at all Kathleen had? About the horror of wearing someone else's blood?

Mary knocked her head sideways. "—Just messed up. It was really nice of you to check in on me. And to invite me to your party. I bet yours was more fun than the one I went to."

Kathleen's eyes held the heat of a battle she'd won but wished she hadn't had to fight. She must not know what to think. Mary didn't, either.

So Mary stamped her feet to shake off the snow that had accumulated. "So you think James is hot, huh?"

Kathleen frowned, as though aggravated she couldn't control the blush that increased the redness of her cold cheeks. Mary laughed again. "I'm just teasing." She wiped off as much of her smile as she could. "How come you got stuck walking home?"

"My mom isn't home yet," Kathleen said, her tone still grumpy.

"She works?"

"Half-time."

"As what?"

"An ambulance dispatcher."

"Bet she's busy today."

Kathleen glanced over her shoulder, toward home.

"Come on, don't be mad."

But Kathleen didn't answer.

"Why'd you call, anyway?"

"To see if you wanted to go ice-skating."

"I've never been."

Now Kathleen stared at Mary, this time with eyes wide and mouth open. "You don't know how to ice-skate, either?"

Mary yet again the just-hatched idiot, when Kathleen probably didn't know how to roll a joint. "Yeah, well, is the offer still open?"

Kathleen shrugged.

"I'll think about it," Mary said. "Call me."

"Yeah, but will you actually call me back?" Kathleen said. "And at school, even if you're in front of all your friends, will you say hi to me and tell them to knock it off if they say mean stuff?"

Mary smiled and held out her bare hand. Kathleen stared, face solemn, eyes wearing the unforgiving expression of *Don't screw up again*. She lifted her mittened paw and they shook. A simple gesture, yet one that immediately and surprisingly eased the tightness in Mary's chest.

"See you," she said.

"Wait." Kathleen opened her shoulder bag and pulled out a see-through baggie with half of a sandwich inside.

"Sorry. It got smooshed a little," Kathleen said, handing over the bag. "My friend brought birthday cake and we had that for lunch and—" She shrugged. "My mom thinks you're too skinny."

"Gee, thanks."

Kathleen's eyes widened. "No, I mean, it's not bad. She didn't mean it in a bad way—"

"I know," Mary said. She smiled a little. "Thanks."

Kathleen smiled a little, too. "Bye."

Mary knocked her head back. The burnout signal for *See ya*.

Kathleen turned and continued in the same direction she'd been walking when Mary called out. The same direction she had to go. But instead of suggesting they walk together, she watched until Kathleen made a right and disappeared behind a house. And how amazing that the feeling remained of a lightness not yet gone, not yet overshadowed by the reality that just as every high had its crash, for every good moment where you correct something stupid you did, you pay a price. And what a bumper-sticker truth: the better you feel, the farther you fall. She wandered her eyes over to the darkening sky. And because she still felt clean and clear, despite knowing a cosmic debt would be collected, she flipped heaven the bird, put her head down, and trudged on.

Chapter 9

Wed. to Fri., Jan. 10 – 12

Mary lay on her bed, staring up at the metal sculpture that turned slowly on a chain attached to a hook in the ceiling. If the watermelon-sized ball fell right now on this black winter night in the piss-yellow of her overhead light, the weight would crush her ribs. Break her heart. But the sculpture wouldn't fall, would never fall, the hook and chain too strong. She watched the object turn, the welded metal shiny with light and reflection, the lines of the piece neither harsh nor sharp, but curved outward like ribbons in a wind. And not a cold wind, either—not a winter wind—but a warm breeze made of spring, the first of the season. Air that melted snow and made you leave your coat at home even though the temperature hovered in the low sixties, the promise there of warmth, and soon.

She found the sculpture hanging in her room when she got home from work last night. You open the door. You switch on the light. You stop. And how your heart thrills because you know your brother has finally given you this belated Christmas gift. She should have known by how Danny barred her from his basement workshop for the past two weeks. She would have thanked Danny by now—pummeled him with gratitude—but he hadn't come home yet. She'd have to wait, then, to ask what he'd meant to convey, if anything. Then again, he'd probably say, *Use a few brain cells. Figure out what it means to you.*

She yawned and closed her math book. She collected the papers spread across her bed. She'd done her homework, something she never would have done if not for Kathleen. Her you-never-do-homework accusation had worked its spiky way under Mary's skin with incredible speed until she found herself thinking, *Why not play by Kathleen's rules for a while?* Though doing homework probably wouldn't make a significant difference in Mary's life—not by itself, anyway—trying couldn't hurt. Maybe there's even be a payoff someday, like that she'd make more money or have an edge in the stock market. At the very least, she'd be able to say she tried, and if things didn't work out, she could torture Kathleen with an *I told you so.* That the world didn't operate by a neat set of rules that if followed guaranteed success.

She checked her alarm clock, the time near midnight. She yawned, but got up anyway and went down to the kitchen. She took the calendar off the wall, scrounged a stub of pencil from a drawer, and opened to the current month. Then she considered the ninety-plus days left of school and how to survive them under Mr. Hoggarty and Kathleen's system, which encourages you to be less honest about who you are in favor of appearing more law-abiding, pleasant, and trustworthy. That when you appear more law-abiding, pleasant, and trustworthy, people cut you more slack. Give you the benefit of the doubt. That left the question of how you cut school—a necessity for breaking up the monotony and taking a breath from authority—without looking delinquent? So she'd plan which days she cut and have Danny call her in sick. Never mind that planning which days to cut is an *oxymoron*, as Mr. O'Brien would say—and you love that, a word with *moron* folded in—since the whole point of cutting is to exercise the freedom to take off whenever the hell you want.

She could only afford three days. She drew a star on April 13, her sixteenth birthday, then on May 7, James's birthday. She marked Danny's birthday, too, of Feb. 22, though he'd be busy with his friends until finally coming home to eat the yellow cake with chocolate frosting she always made for him. So she erased that star, amazed at her willpower. Two days instead of three, then.

She hung up the calendar, walked upstairs, and stopped at the threshold of her room. She studied the sculpture. The metal, the bend, the revolution of shine. Something in the center looked familiar. Something so common as to go unnoticed, like a seatbelt buckle? And, Jesus, yeah. He'd melted a seatbelt into the middle, and why hadn't she seen that before? Identifying one car part, she saw the rest. The waves of fender, the warped gas cap, a cigarette lighter morphed into a bell clapper. The sculpture a Frankenstein compilation of pieces from Danny's crapped-out 1969 Dodge Dart buried under its shroud in the driveway. She imagined Danny out in the cold, scavenging parts for freedom's sake, the humor released, the riddle made of shrapnel from a blown-apart auto.

The feeling sudden, intense. That if Kathleen stood here right now, Mary could let loose. Could say, *Is that fucking cool, or what?* And Kathleen would forgive the curse because she'd understand what Mary meant. Would understand art in a way Mary's other friends couldn't.

But even if Mary asked, which she wouldn't, Kathleen would never come.

***

The bell rang, and social studies ended. She put her pen in her purse and pulled the stapled sheaf of papers from the back of her notebook. She joined the flow of students heading for the door where Mrs. Dariano stood with arms crossed, saying, "*Kwaherini*," Swahili for *Goodbye*.

She handed her report to Mrs. Dariano, who peered at Mary over the rim of her bifocals. She looked ready to say something stupid, like how shocked she was Mary actually turned in her homework. But instead, Mrs. Dariano smiled and let Mary pass, proving that not all adults were idiots who didn't know when to shut up. She continued down the hall, skimming a sheet of vocabulary words for a quiz in the next class. Someone called her name. She looked up to see Mr. Hoggarty across the crowded hall.

"Got to get to class," she said above the noise and walked past him.

"Make an appointment to see me," Mr. Hoggarty said.

She turned and walked backward. "No need. It's all taken care of."

"You've devised a plan?"

"Yup." She turned and walked on. Mr. Hoggarty probably continued to watch her. He wouldn't be frowning, though, because if she said she'd made a plan, he'd believe her until proven otherwise. But he'd be curious. She smiled.

***

A customer hoisted her basket to the counter in front of Mary's register. She glanced at the big clock on the store's back wall, the time two minutes to six. Kathleen would be here soon. And how idiotic that Mary had, for a second time, agreed to humiliate herself, this time by ice-skating. Jesus. What would be next? A quilting bee? And how all this good family fun shit could kill you. Fortunately, there was zero chance any of her friends would see her, not that she gave a rat's ass.

Toilet paper. *Ring*. White thread. *Ring*. On-sale Christmas cards. *Ring*. The door opened. Cold air rushed in along with Kathleen. She wore her pink coat and hat, and on her feet, there they were: the mukluks. Finally.

"Be with you in a minute," she said to Kathleen. Then Mary handed the customer her bag just as Mary's manager, Lillette, approached, doing her pug-dog waddle and wearing a foam-rubber smile just for Kathleen.

"Can I help you, young lady?" Lillette said. Implying Mary hadn't done her job of properly greeting a customer, never mind that she had been a model employee for the past two years. Always on time, always willing to work, her drawer balancing to the penny at the end of every shift.

"Oh, no thanks. I'm just waiting for Mary," Kathleen said.

"Really?" Lillette said. Then she lifted her penciled eyebrows as though silently asking why a wholesome-looking girl like Kathleen would have anything to do with a delinquent like Mary.

"Ms. Gordon, this is my—" and she cleared her throat, "—friend, Kathleen."

"And what are you girls up to tonight?" Lillette said.

"We're going ice-skating," Kathleen said.

Lillette's eyebrows jumped higher. She looked at Mary and smiled. Not little and tight, but big and teddy-bear fuzzy. "I used to love ice-skating. I'd pretend I was Sonja Henie. Well, you'd better get going, Mary. I hope you girls have a wonderful time."

"Thanks," Mary said, wanting to know who the hell Sonja Henie was, and even more importantly, where the hell had the aliens taken the real Lillette? Or does hanging out with clean-living people like Kathleen make you look more Spic and Span yourself?

When she approached the McCarthy-mobile, she slowed. Who was the guy in the front seat next to Mrs. McCarthy? Mr.

McCarthy, no doubt, when Mary had assumed this would be a chick trio like on the toboggan day, just her, Mrs. McCarthy, and Kathleen. But apparently not. Kevin glared from the back seat. Then she returned her gaze to Papa Bear, a smile on his long, thin face. A family outing was bad enough, but when you throw in a man, shit. Because a man was never *just* a dad or *just* an uncle or *just* anything other than a body where the balls beat the brains nine times out of ten.

Kathleen got into the backseat next to her brother and left the door open.

"Geez, Mary. Get in. You're letting all the hot air out," Kathleen said.

But still Mary hesitated, knowing that sometimes you should punt.

"Mary, honey, what's wrong?" Mrs. McCarthy said.

She refocused on Mrs. McCarthy. At those deep, lake-blue eyes that looked not only at Mary, but all the way around her and inside her too. Mrs. McCarthy, Master Arm-Twister, Mom-of-Might Protector. Yet when Mary got in and closed the door and the car pulled away from the curb, she knew this was a mistake, one Mrs. McCarthy didn't understand. Now instead of just worrying about making an idiot of herself, she'd have to watch out for Mr. Clean. To make sure his fingers didn't do the walking.

At least when men look lecherous, you have fair warning and can stay the hell away. Whereas a man's harmless appearance—a *Father Knows Best* image—can camouflage the most perverted of hearts. Look at Uncle Harry with his jolly smile and beer gut. Who'd suspect he'd be the kind to rape a girl into pregnancy so she'd have to marry him? No one. And then there was Mary's counselor, who'd suggested she taste what made him sweet. Not to mention countless friends of Frank and friends of her oldest brothers and fathers of her friends and stock boys who'd come and gone at work and on and on. Christ.

Mr. McCarthy reached a hand over the back seat toward Mary, to shake. She stared at the hand, then the face. The long oval, the slightly misshapen ears, the innocent blue eyes. This, the guy Mrs. McCarthy had linked up with. She shook his hand, but she didn't smile.

"We're so glad you came, Mary," Mrs. McCarthy said. "We may have to leave early, though. They said there's going to be a big snowstorm tonight. I guess it's on its way."

Kathleen plopped a grocery bag into Mary's lap.

"There's a hat in there, and mittens and a scarf and stuff," Kathleen said. "What else, Mom?"

"Extra socks, long johns," Mrs. McCarthy said.

Mary would have said it, *There's no way I'm wearing long johns*. But she was too busy watching Mr. McCarthy for that first disappointing sign that though he played Decent Dad, he was male and therefore a douchebag. What would he do first? Cast a glance back, eyes aimed at her crotch? And when they got there, what reason would he find for resting a hand on her lower back for longer than he should?

"And we brought hot chocolate," Kathleen said. "And pretzels. The braided kind."

Her stomach growled.

"How was your Christmas, Mary?" Mr. McCarthy said.

Mary once again under interrogation. She told them about her holiday break—except for the partying, fighting, drugs, and sex—deletions that made her sound impressively boring. She did tell them about the sculpture Danny made for her, though. Mr. McCarthy asked where Danny planned to go to college, and she said the art institute. How Danny was putting together a portfolio. Mr. McCarthy seemed impressed.

"What do you think you might want to be?" he said.

Christ. Like she'd ever thought about it, whereas the preps and brains at school seemed to have discussions with their parents shortly after emerging from the womb.

What's it going to be, son? Doctor or lawyer?

Waa!

"Maybe a lawyer," she said.

Mr. McCarthy nodded, as though taking her seriously, and Jesus, she should have said brain surgeon.

"You should think about the University of Chicago then," Mr. McCarthy said. "It has a great law school. My brother graduated from there. If you want, I'll give you his phone number. You could give him a call and ask him about the program."

They pulled into the forest preserve drive and wound through the night woods. They passed the toboggan chute and came to a parking lot by the ice-skating rink. A bonfire raged in the open-air pavilion. Orange flames leapt against a black sky while bodies walked, twirled, and ran through the dark, and how weird. Mary had been to plenty of parties where people had milled around a fire, but they moved slower, their shoulders rounded, the feel of a dimmed hanging out, low and dark. Whereas tonight seemed to pop with speed. People threw snowballs. Others walked to the rink in their skates, took a few fast strides, and glided out onto the ice. Kids, teens, adults: all of them together on a Friday night. Like that was normal.

"Come on, Mary," Kathleen said, carrying the grocery bag. She followed her parents and brother up the hill to the pavilion. Mary started up the hill, but the snow was packed down and slick from foot traffic. She slid backward on her smooth-soled boots. She could yell for Kathleen to give a hand, but how stupid. Mary couldn't get up a hill? She kicked steps with the toes of her boots. When she started to slide backward again, she fell forward onto her knees, cursing, her bare hands clawing the icy slope. She heard laughter and looked up. Kathleen was bent over, laughing so hard the tassel atop her hat bounced.

"Goddamn," Mary said beneath her breath. "Will you help me out here? My hands are freezing off."

Kathleen loped down the slope and extended her hand. Mary grabbed and held. Kathleen leaned back and pulled Mary to a stand. They approached the pavilion, where Mrs. McCarthy was laughing, too.

"Have a little trouble?" Mrs. McCarthy said.

A real pack of hyenas, these McCarthys. Ready to laugh at you at every turn. When nobody laughed at her. She kept her mouth shut and stuck her iced hands in her pockets. Mrs. McCarthy sent Kathleen to get the bag of clothes.

"Let me see your hands," Mrs. McCarthy said.

Mary pulled a hand from her pocket.

"Both," Mrs. McCarthy said.

She drew out her other hand, the fingers long and dead white.

Mrs. McCarthy took off her gloves and stuck them in her pockets. Then she took Mary's hands and put them together, like when a person prayed. Mrs. McCarthy rubbed Mary's hands fast until the heat rose in her skin. Real touchy-feely, too, these McCarthys, with their hugs, kisses, handshakes, and hand-warmings. But she didn't withdraw her hands; the warmth nice and the gesture somehow easy. That with Mrs. McCarthy, you don't have to worry.

"Now," Mrs. McCarthy said, keeping her eyes on their hands. "I know hats and scarves and long johns are not gorgeous. But it's really cold out and you'll be miserable if you don't dress warmer, so if you could see your way clear to putting on the things we brought, including the long johns..." She stopped rubbing but continued to hold Mary's hands while smiling. "I won't tell anyone."

And how you don't speak sometimes because you can't. That if you do, your voice might shake and kill a moment like this when your faces are close, so close you can see the freckles across her nose, and the crack on her lower lip, and the bonfire in her eyes that traveled through her arms to warm you.

"You're kind of a tough lady, aren't you?" Mary said.

Mrs. McCarthy smiled.

Mary wedged her way into a tiny stall in the bathroom, shimmied off her jeans, put on the extra socks and long johns, then spent the next ten minutes trying to get her jeans back on. To the point where she took off her coat. To the point where she was sweating across her forehead, under her arms, and down her back. To the point where she got tired of swearing, Kathleen nothing but a pain in the ass who kept popping in to say, *You okay?* When Mary finally got her jeans on, the zipper ready to split, she put on the sweater and her coat followed by the hat, scarf, and gloves. She could barely bend her knees, let alone put on her boots. She walked into the wood-floored pavilion in her socks.

Kathleen already had her skates on. She told Mary to sit down, like that would be easy. She managed to drop to a bench but had to lean back because her legs wouldn't bend. The heat from the fire behind her made her back blaze.

"Here's your skates," Kathleen said and handed Mary a pair. "Put them on and I'll come back for you. I've got to get out of here and cool off. I'm broiling."

"Wait—"

"Don't worry, I'll come back." Kathleen clunked away in her skates.

She sweated and cursed, but finally pulled on her skates and tied them. Now she was supposed to walk on these things?

"Go ahead and stand," a man said. "Let's see what kind of job you've done."

And there was Mr. McCarthy, smiling down at her. A dad watching out for his daughter's friend, and what a good guy he seemed to be. Mary skimmed her eyes over the crowd on the skating rink, but didn't see Kathleen or Mrs. McCarthy or even Raging Little Brother. She ignored Mr. McCarthy's outstretched hand and stood. Her ankles caved and she fell toward Mr. McCarthy who grabbed her wrist.

"Whoa, there," he said.

She pulled her wrist from his grasp. "I'm all right"

"Go ahead and have a seat and I'll tighten up the laces."

She remained standing and kept her eyes on the distance between his knees and hers and how that distance had better not shrink.

"Come on," Mr. McCarthy said. "You can't go out like that. You won't have a chance of remaining upright."

Mr. McCarthy hadn't done anything inappropriate yet, which meant she had to play this adult game of social pretending. That she was a grateful, unsuspecting kid and he was a decent man. She sat down.

Mr. McCarthy kneeled before her and fitted the blade of her right skate between his thighs. His leg muscles contracted and loosened as he plucked the laces of her boot with his thin fingers, his wedding ring glinting in the firelight. And here you're trying to do everything right, everything you're supposed to, by filling out applications, turning in homework, playing by the rules. Then along comes a man who has the power to screw up everything by whispering an inappropriate suggestion or squeezing where he shouldn't. Then what do you do? Let him get away with that shit because you somehow can't stand the thought of not having a friend like Kathleen? Because Mary could no longer imagine a life without someone like Mrs. McCarthy to warm her hands when they burned with freeze? Then again, there was no way she would put up with someone else's shit. If Mr. McCarthy tried anything, she'd clock the asshole and the rest would be history, one she could imagine in Technicolor. Of Mr. McCarthy holding his bloody nose while Mrs. McCarthy and Kathleen asked what happened. And if Mary told them? They'd be crushed. Or maybe they wouldn't believe her. Either way, her connection to the McCarthys would be blown because nobody liked being forced to see the truth about someone they loved.

Mr. McCarthy finished tying the laces of the second boot and lowered her foot to the ground. He lifted his eyes from her feet to her face. A direct jump instead of a snaky slide up her body. And the way he looked at her, not with sexual desire but a kindergarten happy.

"Okay. Hop up," he said and stood.

She got up, the boots so tight her ankles had become steel posts.

Mr. McCarthy stood and put his fists on his hips. "Good?"

She nodded.

"Let me give you a hand down to the rink," he said, and instead of taking her upper arm where his fingers could brush her boob, he squeezed her funny bone hard enough to make her wince. But she kept her mouth shut. He led her out into the open. Where she could breathe, her legs shaking badly.

He led her through the falling snow to the rink, a field the park service flooded every winter. Kathleen and Mrs. McCarthy skated toward Mary and stopped, Kathleen by turning to the side, her skate blades sending up a spray of shaved ice while Mrs. McCarthy dragged a foot behind her.

"You look pretty good," Kathleen said, smiling at Mary. Mrs. McCarthy smiled, too, first at Mary, then at Mr. McCarthy, who smiled back at his wife, then at Mary. Everybody so goddamned happy.

"We'll take it from here, Dan," Mrs. McCarthy said. She leaned toward him and he toward her and the way they laughed, they looked young instead of old. They kissed. A pluck on the lips.

"Good luck, ladies," Mr. McCarthy said and skated off.

Kathleen and Mrs. McCarthy surrounded Mary on either side, hooked their arms under hers, and pulled her onto the ice.

"God, would you slow down?" she said.

"You're doing great," Mrs. McCarthy said. "So great you don't need me anymore." She let go of Mary and glided forward, then turned and skated backward a few feet in front. "Don't worry. I'm here if you need me."

"You're such a chicken," Kathleen said, laughing.

The temptation jumped from Mary's throat with such force, she had to clamp her lips tight against the urge to tell Kathleen to shut up. Then she and her mom began firing suggestions from all sides.

"Okay now, pick up your feet."

"Don't lean forward so much."

"Now release your grip on Kathleen a bit."

Until without warning, Kathleen dropped Mary's arm and skated out of reach, leaving her to flap her arms like an idiot. Mrs. McCarthy took Mary's hands and skated backward, pulling her. "Now push off with one foot."

Mary licked her lips and pushed into a glide.

"You're doing marvelous, honey," Mrs. McCarthy said.

She released one of Mary's hands, then the other. She sailed at a baby pace, arms out and legs shaking, but the glide feeling surprisingly cool. She was doing this. Wearing long johns among people who had no idea who she was and didn't care. People who were here to just have a good time in a world of stone cold sober, and she among them, one of them.

Kathleen showed up so fast, Mary almost fell over. "God, Kat."

"We're going to play Crack the Whip! Come on." She grabbed Mary's hand and towed her to parents and brother.

"You're doing great," Mr. McCarthy said. "We've been watching you for a while. Very impressive."

"She wants to play Crack the Whip," Kathleen said.

"All right!" Kevin said, a demon glint in his eyes. "Put her at the end!"

Mrs. McCarthy frowned at her son. "Be nice, Kevin." Then she said to her husband, "I don't know, Dan. She's just learning."

"All she has to do is be able to glide," Kathleen said.

"Would somebody mind telling me what Crack the Whip is?" Mary said.

"We hold hands," Kathleen said, "to make one long line and the person in the lead pulls everybody. Like a snake."

Mr. McCarthy set the order. Him first, then Mary, Mrs. McCarthy, Kathleen, and at the end, Kevin. Hands linked, Mr. McCarthy bent over and pushed off, dragging the rest of them, at first slowly, then faster and faster. Past couples. Past kids splayed on the ice. Then Mr. McCarthy stopped and pulled hard. The momentum swung Mary around, followed by Mrs. McCarthy, Kathleen, and at the end, Kevin, who whipped around. He let go of his sister's wrist and raised his arms, bullet-bound across the rink.

"Christ," she said. No wonder the little twerp wanted her at the end.

Kathleen took a turn at the end, after which she said to Mary, "Your turn."

"There's no god—there's no way I'm going on the end"

"Don't make her go if she doesn't want to," Mrs. McCarthy said. But she was smiling and had used a wimpy-assed tone that obligated Mary to take her turn. The line formed fast. Mr. McCarthy to Kathleen to Mrs. McCarthy to Ken, who grabbed Mary's wrist. Though she tried to pull her arm free so she could take his hand, he held tight and laughed, the little shit. Mr. McCarthy pulled.

"Oh my god!" Mary yelled, her one arm flailing in space. Faster and faster they went, the snow flying in her face. Then Mr. McCarthy stopped and pulled hard, whipping the chain of bodies. Mary swung out, and like Kathleen and Kevin had, raced across the ice. Though unlike them, she screamed nonstop. Then Kevin let go of her. She raced across the ice—arms out, hat flying off, feet bumping over the uneven surface—toward a four-foot wall of shoveled snow that rimmed the rink, and goddamn. Wouldn't that have been nice if somebody had taught her how to stop? She plowed into the wall. Her body curled over and her face planted in the snow. Too stunned to move, she realized she wasn't dead. When she lifted her head, snow fell off of her chin and nose. She rolled onto her back and sat up.

"Oh my gosh, Mary, are you all right?" Mrs. McCarthy said. "What were we thinking? Oh Lord above."

She blinked. Water dripped from her lashes. Snow had gotten down her shirt, her bra, and now melted over her heart. Mrs. McCarthy stood with her hands out toward Mary, ready to help. But she just sat. Kathleen pulled up, followed by her dad and Kevin. The four of them stood there in front of her and stared, each expression different. Kathleen trying not to laugh. Kevin worried he'd broken the guest, but only some-what. Mr. McCarthy surprised, but pleased. Mrs. McCarthy more amused now than worried, though guilty for being so. All of them funny as she must look. And she laughed.

Chapter 10

Wed., Jan. 17

Mary sat on a step stool in the dime store, pricing L'eggs pantyhose. She wanted to thank Kathleen. For the toboganning, the ice-skating, the smooshed sandwiches. And for no longer worrying about knowing a burnout. Mary felt sure if she passed Kathleen and her friends and said, *Hi*, Kathleen would smile and say, *Hi*, too. One person stepping out for another, which took courage. If people step out for you, you step out for them, the reason she had been trying to think of how to express her gratitude, though the word seemed too heavy and corny for what she felt.

When the idea fell on her head, a laugh popped out of her mouth, the concept perfect. Personal without being dorky. Including just enough risk to tweak Kathleen's rule-oriented heart, though not in a mean way. Yet Mary had never done anything like this before, which made the notion at first seem hilarious in a never-in-a-million-years way. But the more she studied the prospect, the more she understood how to make this work. The more real the possibility, the more anxious she got, because something like this could leave you hanging. And even if you planned well, a ton of things outside of your control can still go wrong. Kathleen might be out sick or the weather might be crappy or a teacher might interfere, and what a hassle, this caring enough to try such a stunt in the first place.

That night she had a nightmare in which an old lady pelted her with toilet paper rolls for handing back the wrong change. She woke early, feeling tired, edgy. In the gray light, the plan seemed like a sitcom plot, or worse, that of a sappy after-school special. But she had a debt to pay, so she'd do this and no longer owe Kathleen, or at least not as much. Mary got to school early. She kept her face blank while striding through the crowded halls. She spotted Kathleen behind her open locker door and tiptoed up until standing behind the flimsy metal panel.

When Kathleen closed the door, her shoulder's jumped. "Geez, Mary, it's like you love giving me a heart attack."

The moment so *Three Stooges,* she smiled. The change within her sudden and unexpected, rushing her veins with something good that washed away her doubt. Kathleen was a decent person and Mary felt like a decent person doing this, planning something cool, something special for someone who deserved the thanks.

"Meet me by the gym soon when lunch starts," Mary said.

"Why?"

She walked backward, away from Kathleen. "Don't be late. And wear your coat. And your mukluks, if you've got them."

"I don't—"

"Be there." She turned and walked away, still smiling.

In home economics, she learned the properties of yeast. In math, she asked the Vietnamese girl how *congruent* differed from *reflective.* In biology, her lab partner—a geek named Jim—dissected a frog while explaining everything in an amazed manner, maybe because she'd not only shown up but seemed interested. Then she dressed out for gym and faded this way and that on the volleyball court, allowing the jocks to dive for the ball so she wouldn't have to.

When the bell rang at the end of class, she made for the locker room and dressed as fast as she could without looking hurried because that makes you look eager, and therefore desperate. When she got to the gym exit, she breezed past Kathleen and pushed through the door to the parking lot. She held the door open with her foot. But instead of following, Kathleen stood with her coat over her arm, looking her normal worried and suspicious self.

"Come on," Mary said.

"Where we going?" Kathleen said.

"It's a surprise."

Kathleen didn't move.

So Mary said, "Trust me," and kept her unblinking eyes on Kathleen because that's how you get a good Catholic girl to do what you want, by making her feel guilty. If Kathleen didn't go, she'd prove that although she liked to think of herself as a good Christian who showed mercy on the downtrodden, she didn't really trust anyone below her socioeconomic status. On the other hand, if she went with Mary, Kathleen risked ruining her record of exemplary citizenry. Either way would force her to face imperfection, something Kathleen couldn't seem to tolerate.

Kathleen pried open her lips just wide enough to say, "It won't take that long?"

Mary smiled. "Naw."

She led the way across the parking lot under a sky white as skin on its way to frostbite. She headed toward an eight-foot-high snow bank the plows made when clearing the area after the weekend blizzard that had closed school on Monday.

"Where are you taking me?" Kathleen said.

She turned.

Kathleen had stopped about five feet back.

"I told you, it's a surprise," Mary said.

"Off campus?"

"Not telling."

"We're not supposed to leave campus."

"And?"

"What if we get caught?"

"We won't. Now come on."

But Kathleen didn't move.

The world stilled and in that stillness, Mary saw her mistake. How, in the planning of this little adventure, she'd forgotten herself and fallen into the trap of thinking she could control someone else, when you can't. Of wanting something so badly you sink into make-believe, that clown house where two-dimensional fools of your own make and model do and say what you want. Whereas Kathleen was real. If Mary had considered that, she would have known that while leaving school grounds was nothing to her, Kathleen would feel like a criminal. Maybe that was why she flourished, because she was that afraid of what might happen if she broke the rules that kept her imprisoned within the illusion she was free and comfortable and right.

"So don't fucking come." She turned and walked toward the snow bank.

"Mary," Kathleen yelled.

But she didn't stop. She kicked steps up the snowdrift and plunge-stepped down the other side. Hidden from view now, she waded across a fifty-yard field of snow between the school and the strip mall. When she got to the covered walkway, she stamped her feet and took off, the brick walls echoing her strides. That she'd exposed herself to that kind of shit, and for someone so rigid she couldn't bend the least little bit, not even when somebody was trying to do something nice for her. *Trust me*, Mary had said. Yet Kathleen had probably only heard a burnout tempting her from the straight and narrow. Mary dropped her head against the wind. She passed the ice-cream store, the art supply store, and a dry cleaners before turning the corner and pushing through the front door of a dim, narrow shop with newspapers and magazines stacked in wooden racks down either wall. In the back, a refrigerated case for soda sat next to a doorway to a storage room.

The door to the shop closed behind her and she stood a moment in the empty store, her breath the rasping pant of a heart scraping sandpaper.

But then the door opened again. She turned. Kathleen entered, a gust of wind following. She glared at Mary.

"You didn't have to walk so fast," Kathleen said.

"And you didn't have to be such a b—"

"Mary," Mr. A. said from the back of the store.

But she didn't turn. She stared at Kathleen, who had the audacity to look furious, like she'd been forced to follow. A girl who thought she had the maturity to make a decision, yet seemed unwilling to accept the responsibility.

Mary turned her back on Kathleen to face Mr. Amar. Short, heavy, his caterpillar eyebrows matched the mustache that drooped over his upper lip. He walked toward her from the back of the store, chewing something. He must have been eating lunch in the storage room.

He swallowed and smiled. "And how are you today?" he said, his voice deep with age and shaped by an accent from a youth spent in Istanbul. He had a wife and five kids and had been in America for thirty-four years, all things Mary had learned since she first came to this store with James on her last birthday.

"Hi Mr. A.," she said, her tone lame, even to her own ears. Mr. A.'s smile faded as his eyes drifted over her shoulder to Kathleen.

"And who's this?" he said.

Mary stepped back. Mr. A. walked forward and extended his hand to Kathleen.

"Mr. Amar, this is Kat," she said. "Kat, this is Mr. Amar."

"Kathleen," Kathleen said. She offered Mr. A. her hand and a Betty Crocker smile.

"How do you do, Kathleen?" Mr. A. said.

"Fine, thank you," Kathleen said.

Fine, thank you.

Mr. A. patted his round belly and looked from Kathleen to Mary. "What can I get you ladies today?"

"The usual." She walked to the refrigerated case against the back wall and pulled out two oblong, shrink-wrapped sandwiches and handed them to Mr. Amar. He disappeared into the back room.

She turned to Kathleen and with droll eyes and a droll tone said, "What do you want to drink?"

Kathleen walked closer. "What?"

"I'm treating you to lunch. What do you want to drink?"

Kathleen's eyes widened. "I... You're treating me to lunch?"

"Yup," she said. "For taking me toboganning and shit. Now are you going to make up your mind or what?"

Kathleen gazed through the glass doors of the case. "Grape."

She took out a grape pop and a Dr. Pepper and closed the door. She handed Kathleen the purple can. Kathleen frowned at the drink, then lifted her eyes to Mary.

"But, I mean, it's kind of..." Kathleen said. "I'll... I'll be happy to pay."

She stared at Kathleen; there no apparent end to her ability to insult a person. First she doesn't trust you, then she blames you, then she implies you're too poor to afford the expense.

"I wouldn't have used the word *treat* if I hadn't meant it," Mary said. "And I know I don't have expensive shit like you, but I do have a job, which means I can pay for a few goddamn sandwiches and drinks, unless, that is, you want me to beg you for the privilege."

Kathleen licked her lips, her eyes blinking. "I didn't—I mean—I think I messed this up."

"You think?"

"It's just—"

Mr. A. walked out holding two sandwiches with a paper towel under each. The bread and meat steamed from three minutes in a toaster oven. He handed a sandwich to Kathleen, then Mary.

"I'll be right back," he said. He returned with a milk crate in each hand. "Have a seat, ladies." He put down the crates next to the refrigerated case, pulled a stack of napkins from his trouser pocket, and handed them to Kathleen with a smile.

"Now if you ladies will excuse me, I'd like to finish my own lunch." Mr. Amar gave her a look, one that said she should behave herself. "Will you let me know if a customer comes?"

She nodded, and Mr. A. left. She sat on her crate, feeling more like throwing up than eating. But she'd come for this goddamn roast beef and cheese sandwich, her favorite of all treats. One she'd wanted to share with Kathleen, but forget that. Mary would eat and when done, take off, her debt paid. She took a bite, her lips burning from the cheese.

"This is really nice of you," Kathleen said.

She didn't look up. From the corner of her eye, she saw Kathleen sit, and after a moment, take a bite. Then Kathleen groaned like you do when your mouth loves what you just put inside. The Happy Mouth Dance.

"Oh my gosh," Kathleen said. "It's so... Oh my gosh."

Mary shook her head; Kathleen the only person Mary knew who required a gun to the head to convince her that something most people knew would be fantastic might actually be so. Mary ate fast until finally popping the last piece of sandwich into her mouth and chewed then swallowed the last of her pop. She could go now, just get up and walk out, leaving the money on Mr. A.'s counter. But the food had taken the edge off of her anger, leaving her too tired and deflated to move.

"That was so good," Kathleen said.

She glanced sideways to see Kathleen lick her fingers and wipe her mouth with the paper towel. Then she sat up straight. "Oh my gosh, what time is it?"

"Relax. We've got fifteen minutes."

"How do you know? You're not wearing a watch."

She shrugged. "I just know."

They sat, the shop quiet.

"How do you know about this place?" Kathleen said.

Mary used her tongue to dislodge a wad of bread from her top-right molar. "You have to have someplace to go when you cut."

"You mean, cut school?"

"Yeah."

"How come you cut?"

Mary shrugged.

"Aren't you worried it'll look bad on your transcript?"

"What's a transcript?"

Kathleen gaped; Mary, apparently, once again a dunce.

"It's..." Kathleen said. "I don't know, a transcript. A list of courses you take in high school and what grades you get. If you want to go to college, you have to send a transcript with the college application. Especially if you plan to go to law school. That's really competitive."

Law school again. Christ.

She rubbed her forehead. "You mean you've never cut school?"

Kathleen shook her head.

"Have you ever done anything you weren't supposed to?" she said.

The door opened. A swirl of wind lifted the ends of Kathleen's hair. An old lady in black rubber boots came in. When she saw Mary and Kathleen, she smiled, then selected a newspaper, which she put on the counter with a box of mints.

"Hey Mr. A.," Mary called. "Customer."

The woman smiled and nodded at Mary and wandered to a nearby stand of greeting cards.

Kathleen stood. "Shouldn't we get going?"

The door opened, and a man in a suit and black overcoat came in. He strode past Mary and Kathleen without looking at them and grabbed a sandwich and a Coke from the refrigerated case. He got to the counter just as Mr. Amar walked out of the back room. The man pushed the woman's newspaper aside and set down his items. Mr. Amar prepared to ring them up.

Mary stood and buttoned her coat. "Hey Mr. A., the lady was here first."

Mr. Amar looked at the man.

"I'm kind of in a hurry," the man said.

Mr. Amar looked at the old woman. "Are these your things?" and he pointed to the newspaper.

"Yes," the woman said, "but if he's in a hurry—"

"I am sure he'll be happy to wait," Mr. Amar said.

He rang up her items.

The businessman glared at her. She walked to the counter. She slipped an arm between the woman and the businessman and dropped a five-dollar bill on the counter. Though her chest was only inches from the man's, she didn't bother to look at him.

"See you Mr. A.," she said.

"Your change," Mr. Amar said.

"Start a line of credit for me. It'll be a first." She pushed backward out of the door, cold wrapping around her and wind blowing hair out of her face. She and Kathleen walked in silence past the shops, through the field of snow, back over the snowdrift and across the parking lot. When they neared the gym doors, Mary felt a hand on her arm. She stopped and looked from Kathleen's mittened hand, then into her face. Her eyes were for once clear of pity.

"Thanks," Kathleen said.

Thanks bestowed, a goodbye implied, an end at hand. Yet Kathleen didn't move. The corner of her mouth turned up into a half-smile. Of something strange. Awe, maybe, though the kind that was unsure. Like when you find yourself admiring someone you never thought you would.

"With that man back there," Kathleen said. "How could you do that? How could you talk to an adult like that?"

"How come you couldn't?" she said, though not in a mean way. She just really didn't know. She turned and walked into school.

***

Danny held a lid over the pot and poured the boiling water into the kitchen sink. He glanced at Mary. His eyes red-rimmed. He'd offered her some weed, but she hadn't felt like getting high, not when she had to get up in six hours. She sat in a chair, her upper body splayed across the table, the time near midnight.

"You hungry?" Danny said.

"Naw."

Danny slid the noodles onto a plate, salted them, and sat down, an open beer before him. He speared some noodles and ate with elbows on the table and back bowed. The refrigerator clicked three times, rattled then hummed.

"Chuck wanted me to ask if you'd make a run for a party this weekend," she said.

"What party?"

"Duncan McCormick's."

Danny looked at her for a moment. She held his gaze. She hadn't told him she'd gone to Duncan's last party in June. She liked the secret of having attended a party her older brother had thought might get too nuts and so had avoided. That and he would have freaked if he knew what had gone on. He wouldn't have yelled at her for going, but he would have been concerned, and in such a sad way, such a disappointed way, that she would have been sorry for going.

"I don't know," Danny said. "Maybe. If I'm around." He stirred his noodles.

She lifted her upper body off of the table and sat, hunched. "Danny?"

He looked at her again. And what a beautiful face, the eyes gentle, like he couldn't be mean if he tried. Maybe that was why girls liked him so much. The real reason, the one beyond his looks. Because they knew he wouldn't hurt them.

"Do you know what a transcript is?" she said.

Danny took another bite. "Yeah, it's like, a sheet with your grades on it. You got to send it to colleges when you apply."

She straightened. "How did you know that?"

Danny shrugged.

"You got to tell me stuff like that," she said.

"How am I supposed to know what you want to know?"

"I don't know. Just. Talk to me more or something."

He took a swallow of beer.

"With this art school, what if you don't get a scholarship?" she said.

"I don't know. I guess I won't go."

"But you're working. You could pay."

"Yeah, but it costs more than I make."

"Couldn't you borrow it or something? Like from a bank?"

"Maybe."

"You've got to go."

"We'll see."

But she wanted to say, no, that wasn't the right answer. *We'll see* too breezy, too unappreciative of what could happen if he didn't go, *what could happen* the part that scared her most. Because without the school, without a plan, Danny's future seemed gone, wiped out, a blank that swallowed him, and her, too. And how the thought made you want to scream, of watching a shimmer, a brilliance fade, fade into the dull of yet another uneducated, underpaid, alcoholic Donahue.

Danny pushed away his plate.

She stared at him.

"What?" he said.

"You think I could go?"

Danny scratched his eyebrow. "To college? I don't know. Maybe if you went to a place that didn't cost too much."

"Really?"

"Why are you so surprised? It's not like you're dumb or anything. It's just the money."

Her eyes wandered over the green counters and white sink stained brown. *It's not like you're dumb or anything.* She was as smart as Darby, maybe even smarter, because Mary now knew the difference between congruent and reflective, congruent meaning two things are the same. Whereas reflective meant one thing mirrored another. If congruent, you can be the same as someone else—have the same genes, the same name, the same history—but still be ignorant of those facts or prone to deny them, which increases your chance of falling into the same trap. But with reflective, you have no choice but to look at yourself. *Mirror, mirror on the wall, who's fairest of them all?* Look at Darby. Maybe she pretended she wasn't a Donahue. Whereas Mary knew where she came from, which pointed to where she was headed. She could feel the next exit—the next escape route—coming up fast. Next, and maybe last.

"Danny?" she said. "Do you think we live a deplorable life of misery?"

Danny laughed. "Where'd that come from?" But when she kept her eyes on him, his smile fell away. He shook his head. "No. Some people got it a lot worse. Look at that Jim Jones guy." The wacko cult leader who'd, last November, handed out cyanide Kool-Aid to his followers, husbands to wives, parents to children, until they all lay dead and rotting in the heat of a weird, little South American country.

She tossed her head. "But what does that mean? That your life sucks so bad you've got to look at nut jobs like that to make yourself feel better?"

Danny ran his hands through his hair. "Come on, Mar. We've got a place to stay. And you know, you and I, we look out for each other. I mean, shit, some people—" He blew air through his lips and shook his head. "Some people don't have anybody." If he'd been thinking of their older brother, Johnny, he didn't say so, and neither did she. Danny pushed his chair back and stood. He walked to the doorway and stopped. "You going to McCormick's party?"

She shrugged.

"Be careful," he said. "Watch the shit he gives you. See what it does to somebody else before you take it."

"Yeah, yeah, I know—"

"Better yet, stick with something you know. If you need anything, I can get whatever you want."

Like she couldn't. "I *know*."

"I'm serious."

"I know," she said.

Danny kept his eyes on her a moment longer, then disappeared; her brother here one minute and gone the next, the difference between the two sudden. Too sudden. So sudden as to suck out her insides and fill her—overwhelm her—with loneliness. She shivered and rolled out her lower lip. A pout of uncertainty, though she didn't know about what. Maybe about time and how minutes can vanish; there no snatching back what you've already lost. She reached out and with one finger, pulled Danny's plate of unfinished noodles in front of her. She picked up his fork and ate the remains.

Chapter 11

Sat., Jan. 20

Duncan McCormick held his last party in June after his lawyer dad had flown off to Thailand on business. At the time, Duncan's parents had been playing nasty in a divorce that had skyrocketed the mom to her sister in California, leaving poor, only-child Duncan all alone. Or at least that was the story Mary heard. Duncan was a senior now and had been accepted to Harvard. Shorter than her, he had wavy brown hair to his shoulders and despite the glasses, a cute face that conveyed the feeling he'd help anyone, no matter what his or her social strata. Duncan had been voted Most Likely to Succeed, an honor almost certainly bestowed by his fellow seniors in thanks for his party the previous summer. Nobody had walked away inexperienced from that gig, and all had seemed to enjoy themselves, probably because no one had to sweat the social divide. Duncan invited whomever he wanted and when people crossed the threshold into his house, they understood all labels and their corresponding burdens, including past grievances, would be dropped. Burnouts, jocks, and geeks mixed without friction.

Duncan's parties differed from standard music-and-drug gatherings in three ways. First, if invited to a McCormick bash, you understand the invitation is exclusive, so you don't bring anyone else, such restraint a rarity on the party scene. Secondly, the guest of honor was Duncan's chemist cousin, Dave, who supplied the drugs, some of which he'd created. A fat guy in his thirties, Dave wore bowling shirts with his name on the left breast and worked for Argonne National Labs. Lastly, Duncan's parties rocked because of their ideal location.

Duncan lived in what looked like a mini White House, what with the four white columns around a semicircular porch leading to the front door. The three-story home had five bedrooms, a third-floor ballroom, and a tiny elevator big enough to haul Julie V. up and down between the first and third floors, a contraption Mary learned was called a dumb-waiter, as in *dumb waiter*, and what a hoot. The house was the only home on a short, dead-end road. A row of tall, tight evergreens separated the back yard from a busy street while woods surrounded the home on the remaining three sides of the acre lot. Without neighbors around to complain, the cops had no reason to cruise such a short street. When she had first seen the house last summer, she'd been impressed. The place looked like something out of *Good Housekeeping*, especially with all the roses in bloom. But the house didn't look like that tonight.

James parked across the street. She got out and slammed the door. She stood in the lung-freezing cold as the wind blew and clouds misted across a translucent moon. The trees, so full in the summer, extended their now-bony reach toward the sky. A thick, leafless vine crawled the front of the house like a boa constrictor that appeared stationary, yet gained an inch, then another and another without you noticing.

The two front windows had no curtains. The window to the left of the front door was lit by a black light that reduced the people inside to skeletons wearing patches of glowing white. A shirt here, a jacket stripe there, a smile of teeth that appeared out of nowhere and hung suspended in the air until disappearing. The dining room window to the right featured a strobe that added to the nightmare, making the ghosties inside move in jerky slow-mo, their limbs jangling.

James got out of the driver's side and walked around to her. She wore her best T-shirt from the Pink Floyd *Animals* concert of 1977, her favorite silver hoop earrings, and even mascara. She'd been expecting another *Sleeping Beauty* ball. Whereas freak show seemed the theme of this party.

"Fucking creepy," she said. "It's like *Alice in Wonderland* meets *The Texas Chainsaw Massacre.*"

"Man, so long as I get what I had last time, they can hack off anything they want," James said. He smiled at the house, his curly brown hair blowing back off of his shoulders. He stood, taut and ready, like a prince itching for the fast chase that would race him into oblivion without one look back at his princess. At least that was his tendency at parties, to get distracted and disappear, leaving her alone. Normally she didn't mind and would do what she wanted until he wandered back. But tonight felt different. Anxious. Strange.

"Stay with me tonight," she said.

"What?" James looked at her.

"You always run off and disappear. Don't do that tonight, all right?"

"Why?"

"I don't know, just—God, do I have to have a reason for everything?"

James slipped his arm around her waist and pulled her into his side. "You okay?"

Mary stared at the house. "Yeah," she said, because if she told him she didn't feel like getting high tonight, he'd be on her with *Why not? What's wrong?* Like not wanting to get high was abnormal.

"You've been acting kind of weird lately," James said. "Is it that time of the month?"

Mary pulled away. "Jesus, what is it with you guys, thinking you can say something like that to a chick?"

James lifted both hands in surrender. "God, babe. All I'm saying is you've been quiet lately and, you know, to tell you the truth, kind of a pain in the ass."

"Well maybe I've got a reason for being a pain in the ass. You ever consider that?" she said, her voice climbing higher, squeezing tighter. "I mean, people don't just stay the same forever. Things happen, you know?"

James took her face in his hands.

She softened. "I don't know, it's just kind of weird. Like sometimes you can just wake up and—Shit, I don't know."

James leaned his forehead on hers, their noses touching. His breath warmed her lips. "Most things in life, man, it's just bullshit, you know?" he said. "Total, Grade-A bullshit. So whatever's bugging you, punt it, babe. It's going to be okay, you know?"

It's going to be okay, when her heart raced and she didn't know why. Yet she nodded. James tilted her face up and kissed her, a winter kiss on a frozen road. He put his arm around her waist and they walked toward the house.

James didn't bother knocking, but instead pushed into the warm darkness. The air thrummed with the beat of music she'd never heard before, a synthesized ground rhythm that sounded like the German electronic shit Duncan preferred. Just in front of her was the central staircase leading to the second floor.

"Mary Berry! Jimbo!" Bing yelled. His huge shadow loomed from lesser shadows, and his arms wrapped around her and squeezed. He pulled away and pushed a cold plastic cup into her hand, then gave one to James, who drank the beer almost to the bottom while Bing laughed. Then Bing leaned down to her ear, his lips brushing her lobe, making her shiver.

"The pharmacist is in the den," Bing said. He pulled away before she could ask who else was here. James pressed his hand to her lower back, pushing her forward. He guided her into the strobing dining room where her white skin lit to a neon death. She held her beer in one hand while working her way into the crowd, unable to see anyone in the flashing darkness. The furniture wasn't just pushed to the wall like last time, but gone. Paintings taken off the walls. Rugs rolled up. Like whoever lived here had one foot in another life, this house nothing but a husk of what had been. Maybe if she came back tomorrow the place would be vacant, the door chained, making her wonder whether tonight ever happened.

Mary no longer felt James's fingers on her back. She turned around. He was gone.

"Shit," she said. Now she had to wait until he showed up again. She moved through the crowd toward the kitchen and pushed aside the sheet covering the doorway. She squinted in the bright light, everything white. Walls, cabinets, floor. Julie V. hung over the shoulder of some guy who spun her around, making her hair fly outward.

"Mar!" Chuck yelled from where he stood by a keg, filling a cup.

Mary opened her mouth to ask the whereabouts of Lucy, but Chuck looked over her shoulder and smiled at whoever stood behind her.

"Dave, my man. Want a beer?" Chuck said.

Mary turned and looked into the eyes of Duncan's cousin, Dave, aka The Pharmacist. He smiled with his lips closed, his face round and skin freckled. He had light red hair and eyes on the muddy side of brown. He didn't seem to blink much, especially when looking at the ladies, which he did often, as she noted last summer. She had yet to find a man who wasn't something of a lech, except maybe for Mr. McCarthy. Maybe. But where most leches were crude and obvious, Dave seemed different. Weirder in a way that makes you uneasy, but not enough that you stay away from him or what he has to offer.

"I remember you from last year," Dave said, his voice so soft she leaned toward him. "Come." He took her free hand and led her away. She set her beer on the counter and as she passed Chuck, looked at him over her shoulder. Chuck shrugged and smiled, like some people had all the luck.

Dave led her through a hallway that ran along the back of the house to a dimly-lit, wood-paneled den. The moment Dave entered, a cheer rose from those waiting in a line of some twenty people, most of whom she knew, at least in passing. The line began at a piece of white tape on the wood floor about eight feet from a broad, dark wood desk. Old, expensive, lawyerly. Behind the desk, a wan yellow light emanated from wall sconces on either side of a fireplace mantel. Though the music wasn't so loud in here, people kept their talk to a murmur and their eyes on Dave. He led her past the line to the desk.

"Hey, how come she gets to cut?" said a short, skinny kid fifth in line, a guy she recognized as an asshole wrestler.

Dave turned to the boy. "Go to the back of the line," Dave said, his voice calm in a teacherly way.

The wrestler threw his head back, hands exploding toward the ceiling. "What the fuck?"

"This is kindergarten," Dave said. "You're acting badly. Go to the back of the line or you won't get your juice and cookies." The wrestler shook his head and walked to the back of the line, his lips buttoned.

Dave walked around the desk and sat in a leather swivel chair. He unlocked a drawer and pulled out a rectangular plastic box a foot long. He opened the lid. People fell into a hush. She could almost feel them craning their necks to see. The box was segmented into square-inch compartments, most filled with pills; ovals, circles, cylinders, green, white, silver, pink, glossy, a flat matte. Three compartments, however, contained one pill each. Dave used tweezers to pluck a lone blue-green pill from its compartment. He held up the dot like in the commercials where the jeweler holds a diamond to the light so you can appreciate the gem's brilliance. Dave spoke. She leaned forward.

"I believe," Dave said, "that some people deserve drugs as individually tailored as perfume. Something worthy of who they are and the magic they contain. Something that will help them achieve their full potential." He took her hand and turned her palm toward the ceiling. He dropped the pill into her hand.

"What is it?" she said.

Dave smiled, tight, secret, and almost girlish. "Last time, only more so."

Last time, only more so, and Jesus, what an Eden. Yet she'd gone home from that party, slept off the high, and the summer had passed into fall and then into this winter and she still hadn't gone anywhere or done anything. Nothing had changed and nothing would, unless she stopped this shit.

Mary moved to drop the pill in her pocket. But Dave reached out and put a hand on her forearm, making her stop.

"Ah-ah-ah," Dave said. A parent talking to a child who thought she could leave the table without eating her peas. "I must insist you either return the gift or swallow it. I can't have party-poopers going home to show their parents—their policeman uncle, perhaps—what they got in their goodie bags."

Mary looked at the pill, knowing that sometimes life comes down to this, a point of color in the palm of your hand, the decision either yes or no, to resist or not. Though only two choices, the decision isn't always simple, not when people watch you. People who think you're fearless and who, if they discover you do get scared, will cut you down with machine gun fire.

What did Kathleen know about such moments? About the real reason you never consider going to a girlie party of pink and pizza, because rather than have no cares, you have so many you're not able to laugh and giggle with abandon. So many, in fact, that when the chance comes to escape for a while, you think, *Swallow it down, so you can sink into that little blue-green ocean and float, and how nice.* She lifted her hand and with the tip of her tongue pulled the pill into her mouth. She closed her eyes and swallowed. When she opened her eyes, Dave smiled.

"Enjoy," he said.

Mary walked away. Someone called her name, but she didn't turn. She went into the living room, needing to find James before the world folded over. She moved sideways into the crowd of dancing corpses, the relentless rhythm driving into her brain. She grew warm and allowed her coat to slip off, though slip off of what, she didn't know, because her body had disappeared. Her mind somehow directed her limbs from afar, arms and legs that kept her from falling down even though she couldn't feel them. She turned her face up and closed her eyes, the music pulsing her heart. James. Not here, but somewhere else. Her existence stretched out, touch and taste heightening so that a drip of sweat behind her ear felt like a caress. Or maybe someone really had stroked her neck. She turned her head and saw nothing but a dancing stripe of violet white. Her mind drifted further away. Into the distance where she glimpsed Kathleen. Here? Never. Heat descended, rolling over her body, a tidal wave of suffocation she couldn't remember.

Her eyes opened, closed. Her appendages took her away in search of air, of cool, but failed. The temperature rose. Her heart beat faster until she heard herself gasping. *More so*, Dave had said. And where the hell had James gone? Had she just said his name aloud? She couldn't tell, the blood through her veins blaring. Time flushed. Fingers of sweat pressed her neck and the sides of her face. Her foot lifted, up one stair, then another. She needed to get away. From the heat, the pace, the severity of this heart pump. She found a doorknob in her hand, turned, and pushed. Shadows yelled at her to get out. She tried more knobs, more doors, but there was no room, no admittance, no James. So she climbed again, toward the third floor, the bare wood under her boot heels causing a ring upon echo.

She stood in a vacant hall at the threshold of a huge room, naked and hollow. A creamy moonlight beam streamed through a floor-to-ceiling window. Feet moved her to the window where she looked at the ground far below, her fall certain unless she leaned back, so she did, her skin slick and hair clinging to her neck. James. She felt her lips move, but couldn't hear any sound. The heat grew heavier, pushing down on her eyes, on her body until she dropped to her knees. And still the heat increased until her thoughts roiled, the movement so fast she couldn't hang on to anything but the question of what separated them, two white girls who lived in the same town. Bodies? Clothes? Money? Why did one have everything and the other nothing? Or did the reason have to do with instinct? With genes? Because if so, there was no changing either, which meant, what? The end? That she should give up? And when had she ever given up? Then again, instinct, genes.

James. Please.

And then he was behind her. He lifted her to a stand and remained with his chest pressed against her back. His hands moved down, over her breasts and hips. He unbuttoned her jeans and slipped his hand around her hipbone, across her pelvis, and down into her underwear. His fingers curled upward, into her. She breathed harder. She turned her head sideways until her mouth met his. Her body followed, turning to him. She slid her hands through his short hair, his big belly against her.

Short hair, big belly, face fleshy and oh, shit. She pulled her face away, meaning to be fast, but the motion poured like glue, her head a thousand pounds of drag. She dropped through his arms to her knees and crawled toward the door, and what would Kathleen think if she saw this? Mary slithering like a half-crushed bug trying not to get squashed. But he fell atop her anyway, smashing her to the floor. A sharp pain cast a crack down the left side of her chest. He flipped her over, his tongue lapping at her neck. *Only for you*, Dave had said, and she'd swallowed, despite what Danny had warned and what Kathleen would think. So that now Mary had to listen to what a wacko murmured in her ear, how she shouldn't struggle, and fuck that. But then you black out.

Until you feel your elbow in an eye. Maybe a chin. She rolled over, her rib knifing her enough she held an arm to her chest to keep from passing out. She got to her knees, her feet. She knocked her head into the slanted ceiling of the hall and fell. He grabbed her hair. She punched him with her fist. He grunted. She crawled to the stairs and started down, one hand at a time. He grabbed her hair again and she yelled and didn't stop. Not when she pulled herself up by a railing. Not when she laid herself over the banister and slid down on the right side of her chest, her left side screaming. Though his hands no longer grabbed for her, everything felt too late. She wailed without end, her body sweating and mouth locked to *on*. She listened to her voice, then to the sound of running and yelling, of fists and thuds. Of screams. Faces swirled past. She thrashed her mind onward, forcing her limbs to move to the bottom and through the cutting strobe. She pushed the sheet aside and staggered into the bright of the kitchen because this was where she'd seen one, a phone, by the refrigerator. She reached out. Someone behind her dropped a hand on her shoulder. *Leave me alone*, and she swung an arm. The back of her fist smacked skin. The hand disappeared from her shoulder. She pressed her left arm to her ribcage and breathing shallowly, took the phone off the hook. The numbers were so blurry she had to move her eyes within inches and will the numerals to stop dancing. She dialed for a year, maybe more, while the ocean around her roared. When a voice on the other end answered, she yelled. To be heard.

"Mrs. McCarthy. It's—It's—Oh fuck—" Mary pulled the phone away from her ear, leaned forward and threw up. Her body shook. Her teeth clicked. Spit hung from her lip. She lifted the phone to her ear and heard a small voice asking if she needed help. But she couldn't answer. The voice, teenie-tiny, told her to hang up and call the police. She wished the voice would just listen, would just—

"Is—" and she swallowed. "Is Kathleen there? I have to talk, just ask her—" But now the trembling controlled her. Shook her until the phone fell from her hand. Her shoulder hit the wall. "Just ask..." she murmured while sliding down the wall until she sat on the floor, vomit soaking through her jeans. She stared at where the phone lay, thousands of miles away on the floor beside her, everything too late, anyway. She tried to keep her eyes open. "Just ask, what the hell, you know?" But her eyes closed. "What the hell?"

Chapter 12

Sun., Jan. 21

Mary opened her eyes, the light through the window of her room a hazy white tinged with orange. Her eyelids, man. Just too goddamn heavy to keep open. They fell shut. There were voices downstairs, muted and persistent, yet unhurried. Though hot, she didn't have the energy to push off what buried her. Blankets, and a lot of them, judging by their weight. She had that strange, distorted fun-house feel of having slept too long and missed something important. She was either sick or late for work or both. She opened her eyes again. A little wider this time. Forcing them to focus, she could make out ice crystals covering the outside of her window, fragmenting the sun into a bloody mess. She licked her lips, and shit, what a sting. She used her tongue to feel her swollen lower lip, which had somehow been split from top to bottom. Something limp and heavy pressed down on her forehead, making her crazy. Unable to stand the pressure, the heat, she lifted a hand to remove the washcloth and a bullet of pain shot through her left side. She hissed, and panting, waited for the nausea to subside. Then, more slowly, she lifted her hand and pushed away the damp cloth.

The floor creaked. She almost turned her head, but stopped.

The trick, apparently, to move slowly, first the head, then the eyes so the world wouldn't jackhammer. There in the doorway stood Danny, holding a glass of water. And the way he looked at her—Jesus, who'd died?

He walked to her bed and pushed hair off of her forehead, his fingers cool. "How you doing?"

Mary opened her mouth. She tried to speak, but her voice shattered into glass shards that coated her throat, every swallow a massacre.

"Can you take a drink?" Danny said.

Mary nodded. He worked his arm beneath her back and lifted. The pain squeezed her eyes shut. When her panting quieted, she opened her eyes and with shaking fingers, directed the glass to her lips. She swallowed, the water—the relief—outrageous. So outrageous her eyes fell shut. She sank back to her pillow.

But the light: that particular shade of sunset instead of a sunrise. She wasn't just late for work, she was a no-show, and she wouldn't get paid and maybe would get fired. She started to rise again. "Shit, I've—"

"I called you in sick today," he said. He put two fingers on her shoulder to keep down. Two fingers, when normally she could wrestle him to the ground. "Can you eat?" he said.

Mary shook her head.

"Just so you know, people have been calling all day. To find out how you're doing," he said. "Chuck, Tina. Everybody else. And a Kathleen somebody. But that can wait."

Mary had been sick lots of other times and nobody had called. She opened her mouth to ask, *How come?*, but he turned his head to the side and called for James.

Feet ran across the hall in maybe five strides. James skidded to a stop in the doorway. "Oh my god, babe." He rushed in, dropped to his knees beside her bed, his hands reaching for her. But then he stopped. He sat back on his heels and his arms dropped. Was she contagious or something? He rubbed his hands on his thighs, up, down, up, down, while scanning her entire body, and Christ, he was making her nervous. He rocketed to his feet.

"We got him, Mar. We got him," he said.

"Damn, man, would you stop moving around?" she said, his up and down making her want to puke. "Got who?"

Danny and James stared at her. Or rather gaped, like Kathleen did.

Mary's dad appeared in the doorway. He walked to her side. "What happened last night?" he said.

"I told—" James said.

"Goddamnit," Frank said and whipped his head toward James. "I know what you told me. Now I want to hear what Mary says, so keep your goddamned trap shut." Frank turned his face back to her. But she couldn't see his eyes for the glare of light on his glasses, a glint that made the silence stretch to butcher knife long and sharp, because the question implied there was a right answer and a wrong one and she knew neither.

"I think it's because of a... of a leftover hotdog I brought her from our fridge," James said in a rush. "I didn't want to tell you, because—I didn't mean to. I mean, I didn't know. It must have been spoiled. I thought she'd be hungry—"

"Is that what happened, Mary?" Frank said. "This is all because of a spoiled hotdog?"

Mary nodded. If James felt the need to lie, the truth must be worse.

"What the hell's the matter with you?" Frank said to James. "You give her your spoiled scraps like she's a dog? Then you disappear? Look at her, for Christ's sake." Frank stepped close to James until only inches separated them. "Puking so hard she fell down and cracked a rib. And look at her busted lip! How long was she laying there before you figured out she might be in trouble?"

Danny gripped the man's upper arm and pulled back, knuckles going white from the effort. "She's okay, Dad."

Danny. Frank. James. Which reminded her of that statue, the one where soldiers struggled to hoist the American flag, but somehow opposite, because the three men needed pulling apart to keep one from the other, a Danny from a Frank and a Frank from a James. Because if Frank lifted a fist to James, he didn't look like he'd defend himself, the beating somehow deserved. And how Danny had lied, not to mention the cracked rib, the split lip, and oh, Jesus, what had happened?

But sometimes thinking harder didn't help. Not when your thoughts come rushing at you in frozen fragments that strobe, like at McCormick's party. Flash. Flash. Flash. No one moving. Just still shots. Photographs that go beyond the visual to include the taste of unbrushed breath. The stale, spicy smell of a man's deodorant. The feel of short fingers. Of someone besides James, and what that someone could have put inside of you?

Frank looked down at her. "You all right?" he said.

"Yeah," she said, even as a tear slid from the corner of her eye, feeling cold and unconnected to her. A marble someone had placed on her face and then released. The glass bead rolled over her cheekbone and dissolved into a pool within her ear. "Just, you know, tired."

You say these things and tell yourself to hang on for just a few more seconds, months, years. Whatever length of time necessary for your father to leave, because you know that though he stares at you with the only expression he possesses that can pass for caring—a y*eah, well, you'll get over it*—his generosity only extends as far as your innocence. Staring at you, battering to get in and you don't think you can keep the door barred for much longer.

Then Frank walked out. The moment he did, she fell to slaughter. Her eyes locked shut. Her body shook. Her teeth clicked. She heard Danny and James whisper until she wanted to tear them apart for what they knew and she didn't.

She opened her eyes to slits and looked from one to the other. To force them. To threaten them. To make them throw off their urge to protect a female when they couldn't and hadn't. But her jaw wouldn't open.

Danny looked at James. "Don't fuck with her, man. Just tell her."

James nodded. Danny walked out and closed the door behind him. James sat on the edge of her bed. He didn't drop onto the mattress and bounce like he normally did, but instead lowered himself. She put her hand on his forearm and pulled herself to a sitting position, her teeth clenched. She planted her eyes within his, because that's how you get James to tell you the truth. You let him know you see through his bullshit and if he doesn't spit out the facts, you'll show him ten shades of hell.

"Did he—" She swallowed. "Did he fuck me?"

James statued into stone, unmoving and mouth tight. Yet his jaw muscles jumped and wouldn't stop. Then his body jerked a little, then bigger and jerkier. He cried, the sound a gaping hack that echoed off her bare floor.

And as he cried, he talked—*I don't know. I don't* know. *I'm so sorry, and God, babe*—and yet he didn't seem to say anything. Or maybe you just can't hear, even though your insides have stilled to an odd calm that allows your mind to lift. And from above, you look down on a girl in trouble, just some idiot named Mary. And as you consider her from on high, the idiot's boyfriend closes his arms around the girl and with his lips near her ear, whispers what the idiot now remembers. How she screamed and wouldn't stop. How her attacker had tried to drag her back upstairs. How Chuck came to the rescue along with twenty other guys, so that when James got there, the stairway was covered with bodies, all punching and kicking.

First the football players helped beat the shit out of the asshole. Then they threw him in a car and drove off. Then Chuck found her in the kitchen, where she'd collapsed. Then James wanted to take her to the hospital, but that meant explaining, and besides, she was breathing okay, so they brought her home.

"But Russell. Man." James shook his head, tears dripping off his chin. He wiped his nose on the sleeve of his sweatshirt. "You gave him a black eye before we even laid hands on him. You—"

"Russell?" she said. "What are you talking about?"

James stared at her. When she didn't say anything, he said, "Russell. The guy who attacked you."

"It wasn't Dave?"

James frowned. "What are you talking about? What's with Dave?"

"I—It was dark. He's the one who..." But the words died, and her eyes drifted to the crystal-fractured window. Not Dave, but Russell, a stupid, blubbery, red-haired second-string football player. A kid who, on any other day, she could pound into the ground. Yet now he could claim he'd fucked the Queen of the Burnouts.

Mary gripped James's sweatshirt and twisted. "And you didn't call the goddamn cops?"

"We couldn't, Mar," James said, trying to push her hand down, but she wouldn't let go.

"Why not?" she said.

"Because—" James palmed the tears from each eye, the move distracted, desperate. "God, Mar, there were like twelve guys on him. They had to carry him out, you know? *Carry* him out. The guy was unconscious, and God, babe, I've never seen that much blood."

Mary's hand dropped. "Did they kill him?" she whispered.

James stood and gripped his head with both hands. He

blew a rush of air out of his mouth and said, "I don't know. We've got to wait. To hear something. Shit. I don't know." He paced. "We didn't know what he did to you, you know? You were screaming, then you were gone. And it was like, did he stab you and you'd crawled off to die? So we looked, and when Chuck found you, you punched him. You didn't know it was him or anything, but man, right in the throat. You almost crushed his windpipe. He thought you were trying to call the police. That you'd get arrested. That everybody would."

Twenty guys jumping to her aid, which was good, but Jesus. Twenty full-grown muscled guys beating one flabby boy to a pulp. And where had James been the whole night, when he said he'd stay with her? So that Chuck had to take charge, as always, ever watching out for her, or for that matter, for any girl threatened by guys like his predator older brother who thought they could force themselves on a girl.

Chuck and the others had all been trying to do right by her, which the police wouldn't understand. Instead, the cops would arrest those trying to defend her while taking the opportunity to bust underage drinkers. If she'd seen the fight, she wouldn't have called the police, either.

That left only one question. If she'd been found with a phone in her hand, who'd she been trying to call? It had to be someone she thought would rescue her. Someone like—

Mary caught a breath. She held on. She grabbed another and clutched that one, too, followed by a third, her lungs a party balloon ready to pop.

James lunged at her, hands on her shoulders. "Mary! What's wrong?"

Mary shook her head, her face burning.

"Breathe!" James said.

Mary fluttered her hands. "I got to—Get me to the—I think I'm going to—" She pushed the blankets aside. James put an arm around her waist, and when she stood, pulled down her

T-shirt to cover her underwear. He helped her to the bathroom. She closed the door and twisted the lock. She lodged a hand on either side of the sink basin to keep from falling down. She hung her head. That Chuck had found her in the kitchen with the phone in hand. Had she called? Had she really called? But why else would Kathleen be among those who'd called to find out how Mary was doing?

If Mary had called, she couldn't remember what she'd said, not that the words mattered now. Whatever she'd said must have come out in an incoherent, drug-induced slur, and how that would freak out Kathleen and send her running to her mother. No more hot chocolate with milk for Mary. No more hand-warmings. No more Kathleen gawking at what Mary did or said. And goddamn, what does it mean when you might have been raped and the thought of losing a friend feels worse?

"No," she said in a high, thin whine. James banged on the door. Yelled for her to open up. That if anything happened, he'd find the money and take care of the problem. Everything would be okay. She sank to her knees, to the floor, the bathroom echoing the jeer.

***

At some point, though, you have to unlock the door and leave, which Mary did. She limped past James. She climbed into bed and pulled the covers to her chin. So he couldn't touch her. So nobody could. She closed her eyes. When James sat beside her, she hissed. The mattress sprang up again, James's weight gone. She could feel him standing over her, just as she could feel his need to relieve his guilt. For abandoning her when she'd asked him not to leave her. He pleaded with her to talk to him, to tell him what was going on. *Come on, babe*. And how you want to give in. To roll sideways and make room for someone to curl behind you, his arm around your waist and face against your cheek while you cry forever and he whispers, *Mary, my poor Mar*, and tells you everything will be okay. But if you do, if you sink into the soft folds of make-believe, you might never crawl out again.

So she kept her mouth shut. James had been James and she'd done what she'd done and shit had happened. Now she owned the stench, because who'd feel sorry for her? *If she hadn't been so shit-faced...* Whereas Russell had gotten kicked around, but would recover to tell the tale to his smiling, admiring, lecherous friends. *Come on man, how was she?* Though she had no memory of what he'd done, she'd have to live with never knowing. She'd forever carry the image of Russell touching her, and worse, of how she'd initially responded, all of which made her want to throw up.

After a while, James stopped talking. Even so, she could feel him there, and for a long time. Then he left. When the door closed, she opened her eyes and watched the white-orange twilight demur into a deeper orange before closing down to a dark gray, the kind that makes you feel like you're floating in an ocean as night falls, no one for thousands of miles.

A light knock sounded on the door. She closed her eyes. The door opened. Someone came in and stopped by her bed. When he didn't speak, she opened her eyes to see Danny looking down. He had a glass of water in his hand.

"You got to drink," Danny said. "Flush that shit out of your system. You think you can eat? I could bring you something."

Mary cleared her throat. "I'll come down," she said, her voice sandpapered from screaming.

"You should stay in bed."

Mary shook her head.

"Want me to help you?"

She shook her head again but didn't move.

Neither did Danny. "You don't always have to do everything yourself," he said. "You could let people help."

Mary didn't say anything.

"I'll get something ready for you," Danny said.

He left the door open. The hall light cast triangles of yellow into her room. She pushed off the covers. She slid her arms into the robe and her bare feet into the canvas shoes. She walked downstairs at a granny pace, one arm lodged beneath her broken rib and the other on the wall. Frank looked up from where he sat on the couch before the TV, holding a beer can on his knee.

"Feel better?" he said.

Mary nodded, even though she sweated and felt light-headed from her fast, shallow breathing. She continued to the kitchen where she found a bowl of chicken noodle soup and a glass of water on the table. She could hear Danny downstairs, pounding on something at his worktable. She walked to the calendar and put her finger on yesterday's date. She slid her finger to Feb. 7, when her next period should start. Two-and-a-half weeks, then, to see if she'd bleed or not.

Mary shuffled to the phone and leaned her upper body on the counter, eyes closed. She waited a moment, then lifted the receiver and listened to the dial tone. She didn't have to call. She'd find out soon enough. But if she called, she'd find out now, direct and honest. She dialed, moved to the table, and sat. She pushed the bowl of soup away and leaned her forearm on the tabletop.

Kathleen's brother answered. He claimed he couldn't understand what she'd said and would she please speak up.

"Just—" Mary closed her eyes. "Just give me Kathleen."

"I—" he said. Then she heard muffled voices in the background followed by grappling of the phone.

"Hello?" Kathleen said.

She cleared her throat. "This is Mary."

"Mary!"

Mrs. McCarthy said something in the background. More confusion and rustling followed.

"Mary?" Mrs. McCarthy said, her tone up close, loud. "Oh lord, Mary. We were so worried about you, honey. Are you all right?"

So worried about you, honey. Not mad, not disgusted, not disappointed. She didn't know what had happened then, which meant Kathleen didn't, either. Mary pressed the palm of her hand into her eye, but the pressure wasn't enough to stop the tears. She cried without a sound, her mouth stretched wide so no one would hear how she choked on her spit, her stupidity, her pathetic, awful relief.

"Mary?"

"Look," Mary said, "I'm really sorry—"

"Oh good grief, Mary, don't worry about it!" Mrs. McCarthy said. "People get sick. You were delirious, poor honey, did you know that? Do you even remember calling?"

"Not really—"

"We were so scared. You must have called about—Oh, I don't know, about 1:30. You sounded so ill; then all of a sudden you weren't there anymore and all I could hear was yelling and screaming. Then someone hung up, and I couldn't call the police because I didn't know where you were. I was just frantic. I didn't sleep all night. Kathleen has been calling all day, but your brother said you were still sleeping, and we didn't hear."

Mary wiped her eyes. "I didn't mean to worry you."

"Oh, honey, don't be sorry. It's so strange how kids say stuff like that, like their being sick is a terrible burden for you when it's not their fault. Kathleen once came down with this awful stomach bug—had it coming out both ends—" Mary heard Kathleen protesting in the background, but her mother continued, "—and all she could say was, 'I'm sorry, I'm sorry,' when it wasn't her fault at all. Are you feeling better?"

She wiped her nose on her robe. "Yeah, but kind of weak."

Mrs. McCarthy told Mary to eat something and drink a lot

of water and stay home tomorrow. Then Mrs. McCarthy was gone, along with the chance to set her straight. But every once in a while, wasn't it okay to take a break from disappointing people?

Kathleen returned to the phone. "Don't you hate when moms say stuff like that, tell all of your grossest moments to your friends?"

Mary sniffed. "Maybe I would if I had a mom."

"You don't have a mom?"

Mary heard Mrs. McCarthy in the background, hushing Kathleen.

"She died when I was five."

"Oh. I'm really sorry."

"It's okay. I was five, you know?"

"Still." Kathleen paused. "Well, I'm glad you feel better. I guess I'll see you in—"

"Listen," she said, though she had nothing to say. She just couldn't bear the thought of hanging up because if she did, she'd go back to her room and in the darkness, what had happened would slideshow through her mind on a continuous loop along with the remembered look of pain in Danny's eyes. That and the news would be all over school on Monday, meaning that maybe this would be the last time she talked to Kathleen before she heard the rumors. That when she did, she'd run.

Mary picked up the spoon next to the soup bowl. She chipped at a hardened shell of dried food on the table. What was she supposed to say? Something. Anything.

"It's," she said. "I mean—My brother—I told you, he's got this chance to go to the Art Institute, like to study art. If he doesn't get a scholarship—Well, it's pretty expensive and we don't have that kind of money. You seem to know a lot about college, so like, how could he get some money?"

Kathleen answered, but her voice seemed thousands of

miles beyond the boom in Mary's chest, a thump so loud she strained to hear what Kathleen said about student loans and how to apply. The longer she listened, the quieter the drumbeat and the closer Kathleen's voice came. The closer the voice, the closer Mary listened until she realized that what Kathleen said was both interesting and specific, instead of just chit-chat bullshit. Mary asked questions. *How much can you borrow?* And Kathleen answered. *It depends on how much money your parents make.* The two going back and forth. *And the loans come from banks? The government sets up the program, but yeah, banks handle the business.* The more questions she asked, the more her mind flooded with new information that edged her out of the black hole of last night and into the light of a possibility. Until she knew enough information that she began to see—actually *see*—herself doing what needed to be done, like filling out a student loan application and stamping the envelope. Though she would have to wait for a reply, there seemed no question she'd qualify for student aid if what Kathleen said was true. And how cool to think colleges will give you money to change your life. To help you purge your present life—reputation, bad habits, everything stupid you'd ever done—and refill your head with whatever you need to finally win. To be someone who earns the benefit of the doubt rather than always getting thrown into the same cage as other fuckups.

"Mary! My gosh! Don't get so discombobulated!" Kathleen said. "It's not like I know everything. Go talk to your counselor. Geez. What time is it, anyway? Oh my gosh! We've been on the phone for an hour. I've got to finish writing up a lab."

Kathleen said goodbye and hung up. Mary sat with the phone in hand. The steady dial tone led into a redial message followed by the pulsing off-the-hook screech of *Eh-eh-eh-eh-eh-eh.* She hung up the phone and sat at the table. She picked up the spoon and twirled. To finally see a way out, yet discover how far she had to go to dig herself out from under. Where to start? She stared at the bowl. At first she didn't see the soup, but then she did. Because what you start with is the soup, which makes you stronger. She pulled the bowl toward her. The soup had cooled, leaving dots of fat floating on the surface, but she ate every noodle. She lifted the glass of water and drank to the bottom.

Danny came up the stairs and leaned against the counter. "I'll call you in sick tomorrow."

"No."

"You can hardly walk—"

"You got a bag I can have?"

"A nickel bag?"

"No." She winced with the violence with which she pushed away even the suggestion of drugs. "A school bag, like for books."

Danny found a backpack crammed into the corner of a closet, a green canvas job with a partly-rusted zipper. She set her alarm, took three aspirin, and laid herself out on her bed with the intention of not moving again for the night. The phone rang, but far away. Just as she fell asleep, someone knocked. The door creaked open. She kept her eyes closed.

"Mar?" Danny whispered. "If you're awake, Chuck just called. Russell's in the hospital."

Chapter 13

Mon., Jan. 22

Mary didn't talk on the way to school. She appreciated the ride from Marco, one of Danny's oldest friends, but kept her face turned to the window. Eyes narrowed, images streamed by in a smooth flow of blended colors and shapes, and how you wish you can slide away into that kind of oblivion.

But then the car turned, leaning her sideways, her cracked rib a Jack the Ripper slash that reminded her how she'd fucked up. For a moment her face flushed with an overwhelming heat and left her unsure if she'd throw up or not. The moment passed. The heat drained from her face.

She opened her eyes just as Marco pulled his 1972 Vega Coupe alongside the curb in front of the entrance and shifted to park. He leaned both forearms on the steering wheel and squinted up through the windshield at the red brick building. Like this was the haunted house where she's agreed to sleep for a night. Marco, who she'd known her whole remembered life. A blond, brown-eyed Italian-American boy Danny had buddied with since second grade. Most striking about Marco—more than his male model looks—was his method of joking with the guys and whispering shit like *Ciao, bambina,* to the girls. But today he had no joke and no smile.

"Are you sure you want to do this?" he said, eyes moving from the school to the students walking toward the front entrance. "Because you don't have to. You've got the best excuse of anybody to lay low. I could turn around and take you home. Or if you didn't want to be there with the old man, I could take you to my house. You could hang out until my mom gets home. Really. You know she likes you. She'd come home from work just to feed you homemade minestrone. She always wanted a daughter. Three boys, man, we've nearly done her in, but you—You could take my bed. Use my tooth-brush if you want to." He shot his eyes to her. "You just look so tired. And you're a complete ghost. Like a vampire clamped onto your neck and sucked out all the blood."

Which was just what a girl wanted to hear.

"I'll be all right," she said. Yet sweat prickled her forehead and she felt nauseous, her every breath like that Hitchcock movie where the black birds used their sharp beaks to pluck out people's insides.

"What if you pass out?" Marco said. "You could hit your head or bust your lip open again. If my mom found out I drove you to school instead of tying you to your bed, she'd thump me on the head, not to mention what Danny—"

"Just—"

"He'd be—"

"God, Marco, would you just open my fucking door?" And she closed her eyes, the urge to vomit sudden and violent. The time hadn't even hit eight a.m. and already she was exhausted from a hellish night tangled in a rage of pain and a nightmare of sleep. She felt the pressure of a hand on her arm. She opened her eyes.

"You don't have to do this," Marco said.

"Yeah, I do," she said. If she didn't show up today, people would think she'd lost to a weak-assed pizza-faced jock, and fuck that and fuck Russell and fuck anybody who thought she was trash. Let them stare and whisper and act like assholes. If James didn't really know what had happened and nobody had actually witnessed any rape, then as far as she was concerned, nothing had happened other than that Russell had gotten handsy and as a result, gotten the shit kicked out of him. People could think and say what they wanted, but that didn't make those suspicions true.

Besides, if you've been raped, you're supposed to bring charges. But she hadn't gone to the hospital, had she? Without evidence—without even a clear memory of what had happened—the situation would be her word against Russell's. A trouble-making burnout against an apparently honest, middle-class, church-going boy. Then again, if there was no evidence, Russell could claim he'd been attacked without cause and so could bring charges against his attackers. If he did, she'd have to speak up to get her friends off of the hook. But if she did, no jury would think a kid taking liberties deserved such a beating. And oh god, what a fucking nightmare, one that leaves you with few options other than to go to class and write down the homework and dress out for gym.

She knuckled a tear from her cheek.

"Ah, shit, now I made you cry," Marco said. "Danny's going to kill me—"

Mary reached for the door handle. Marco hopped out of the car, ran around the front, and opened her door. By the time she edged herself out of the car, she'd shed a fresh coat of sweat, her face flaming despite the freezing air. She pulled the backpack over her left shoulder and kept her eyes locked on the front door, an almost impossible distance away.

"You want me to—" Marco said.

"No." She took one small step at a time, trying not to hunch over or hold an arm against her chest to keep her broken rib from jiggling. She walked behind a freshman guy. Somebody she'd seen at a few parties. A kid low on the social hierarchy but working his way up. He winged open the door and as he did, glanced back. When he saw her, he did a double take and with Scooby-Doo eyes—*ruh-roh!*—stepped back and held the door. She walked through like he didn't exist, which is what you do when you have seniority, and what you do, too, to show people you don't give a shit what they think.

She walked through the halls, face as close to neutral as she could manage. She stopped in the office to make an appointment with her counselor, Mrs. Barnao, and continued to home economics. With every minute, every step, she could see the news spread before her, a wind that blasted people from behind, whirling them around to stare as she passed. Their eyes bright with curiosity, disgust, fascination, disbelief. They whispered what she couldn't hear but could imagine.

If she was raped, what's she doing here?

I heard she led him on.

Wasn't there a gun involved?

Bing appeared beside her and carefully slipped an arm around her waist.

"Mary Berry," he said, though without a smile. "You all right?"

Instead of telling him to let her go, that he was hurting her, she clenched her teeth. "Yup."

"Way to go." He split from her side and walked down an adjacent hall.

Three football players walking in front of her drifted right and stopped outside of a classroom. One of them saw her, leaned toward the others, and said something. They stepped back, out of her way, and watched her pass, their guilt apparent, but guilt about what? That one of their own fucked up, or because they fucked up one of their own?

Mary went to classes. She tried to pay attention, but she couldn't breathe without leaning back in her desk. Her stomach growled, but the thought of eating made her sick.

The throb of her cracked bone matched the throb in her head while her lips grew dry in the radiator heat and split her lip open again, then again, so she had to stop in the bathroom between classes for more toilet paper to blot the blood.

The lunch bell rang. She made her slow way to the office. Her whole body hurt now. Her shoulder and neck from hoisting the pack. Her right thigh from walking weird to keep her left side from moving. The worst, though, was the weariness that kept her close to tears, and what the hell? She'd been tired most of her life—tired from working and from fighting with her dad and from waiting for others to stop being idiots—and had never before felt like bawling, and now look at her. One thought of how James had abandoned her, one memory of fingers inside of her or how she'd kissed him—kissed her attacker, for Christ sake—and her face flushed and eyes flooded.

When she arrived at her counselor's office, Mrs. Barnao signaled to wait a moment outside of her door while she finished a phone call. Mary leaned against the wall. She could hear Mr. Hoggarty in his office two doors down, talking to a man with a voice deep as the deejay Wolfman Jack. Mrs. Barnao hung up and called Mary in.

Though Mrs. Barnao stood, she barely changed in height. A middle-aged woman five feet tall in heels, maybe, Mrs. Barnao carried extra pounds on her hips like two bowls of Jell-O. She sat again and gestured for Mary to do the same. But when you want something, you stand and look down at the other person to convince her you'll get what you want, one way or the other.

"A friend of mine—" Mary said.

"What happened to your lip?"

"Nothing. The cold. It makes my lips split. A friend of mine said I can request to get into honors classes."

Mrs. Barnao stared at the lip a moment longer, then readjusted her glasses with a thumb and index finger. "And?"

"So that's what I'm doing. I'm requesting," she said. "I want to be in honors English and math and whatever else I can. And I want to change out of home ec. And maybe take a foreign language. Or that Latin roots class."

Mrs. Barnao cocked her head to the side. "Mary—"

"What do I have to do, fill out forms or something?"

"Mary, you cut school—"

"Not anymore."

"—and you never do homework—"

"I've started—"

"You get Cs and Ds."

On the verge again, of flooding. She swallowed the curses and argument and forced her tone to sound at least civil. "I got a B on my last math test and I got an A on an essay about ethnocentrism, which is if you think a whole group of people are inferior for no good reason. Is that what's going on here?"

"Mary!"

"I'm smart enough, right?"

Mrs. Barnao frowned, and yet smiled, too. What a counselor did, apparently, when she couldn't believe the crazy she was hearing.

"If you're asking if intelligence is a limiting factor for you, the answer is no," Mrs. Barnao said. "Your test scores prove you've got plenty of smarts, but that's not what counts in this life. It's what you *do*, and what *you* do is below-average work. If you've got a problem, it's a lack of motivation. So when you come in here, into *my* office, and demand to be put in as many honors classes as possible, forgive me if I show surprise, *capisci?*"

Mary wiped the sweat from her forehead with the edge of her hand.

"Are you all right?" Mrs. Barnao said.

But she didn't answer, the urge terrible, to go smart-ass, pissing off adults better than having them laugh at you. But Mrs. Barnao didn't blink. Or smile. Or smirk.

"I just," she said. "I was thinking, you know, I might want to go to college."

Mrs. Barnao leaned forward and tilted her chin down so her eyes peered up at Mary from above glass frames. "Why?"

She licked her lips. "I just—I don't want to work at Ben Franklin all my life."

Mrs. Barnao stared, then said, "College is a lot of work."

When she didn't move, didn't blink, Mrs. Barnao smacked her hands together with such force the clap echoed off of the white walls. She pointed at the chair opposite her desk. "Sit."

"No."

"We've got work to do. Sit."

Mary lowered herself into the chair. Pain made her heart race and breath sharpen. But Mrs. Barnao didn't notice. She walked back and forth behind her desk, scritch-scratching her nyloned thighs together while pulling out forms from one filing cabinet and another. She leaned over her desk and wrote notes. She put together a stack of pamphlets into a folder she handed to Mary, telling her to read through everything and come back next week. Mrs. Barnao said she'd have to convince a few teachers of Mary's sudden academic sincerity, so she'd better not change her mind. When Mrs. Barnao encouraged Mary to eat her lunch, she said she hadn't had time to buy anything. Mrs. Barnao handed Mary a baggied banana nut muffin.

"I shouldn't eat it anyway," Mrs. Barnao said. "It's not part of my diet plan." She lowered her voice to the level of secrecy. "I'm doing Weight Watchers."

Mary looked from the muffin to her counselor. First Lillette and now Mrs. Barnao, alien abductions apparently as common as the *National Enquirer* claimed because really, what happened to the real Mrs. Barnao? The one who never before had gotten out of her chair, never smiled, never showed an ounce of enthusiasm for Mary?

"I'll throw in a few forms about financial aid, but don't worry about that now," Mrs. Barnao said. She smiled. "See you next week."

The signal to leave. As she pushed herself out of the chair, she turned her face to the ceiling to hide the wince. She opened the door. She turned back to Mrs. Barnao.

"What?" the counselor said.

"Well. Thanks—"

"My pleasure."

"—but."

"Yes?"

"How come you never told me any of this before?"

Mrs. Barnao threw her arms and eyes to heaven. Then she dropped both and stared at Mary with an open mouth. "You were barely getting through high school and I'm going to tell you about college? Not to mention I hold college-prep seminars all the time. I practically wallpaper the school with flyers. Have you ever seen them? Have you ever come? Uh-uh." She shook her head and wagged a squat finger. "Twenty-seven years I've been doing this, and you know what I've learned? You can't make people hear things before they're ready. You're just lucky you heard before it was too late."

She smiled. "Gosh, Mrs. Barnao, you don't have to get so discombobulated." To which Mrs. Barnao popped a, *Ha!* Mary turned and walked out into the hall.

"Miss Donahue," said a man behind her.

She turned. Mr. Hoggarty leaned out of his office door, a hand on the doorframe. "I was planning on calling you out of class, but Mrs. Donofsky told me you were already here. Considering the convenience of the situation, can you come in and talk a moment now?"

"Class is going to start."

"Mrs. Donofsky will give you a pass."

Why would he want to see her? Yet she was too tired to

care about an answer. All she wanted was to go to the nurse's office, say she had bad cramps, and lay down for a while, because she had a whole day to get through. And then she had to work. She couldn't afford another day off, yet the thought of working, of pricing and stacking while trying not to remember and remember and remember, made her want to fall down, just melt into the floor and never get up.

"I'm not feeling too good," she said.

"I'm sorry to hear that," he said, "but this is important."

Mary walked into his office. A gray-haired man in a black overcoat and navy suit stood to the left of Mr. Hoggarty. With the broad chest and drooping cowboy mustache, the man looked like the evil twin of Dennis Weaver's *McCloud, PI* character.

Mr. Hoggarty introduced the man as Detective Janich. And uh-oh, a real detective, rather than a Hollywood hack who played at investigating crimes. The man stretched out his hand to shake. She paused, then extended her own. As she did, her backpack slid off her shoulder and dropped to her arm, the motion jerking her sideways and causing a wave of pain that made her squeeze her eyes shut and pant. She heard Mr. Hoggarty, though far away. "Mary, are you all right?" She nodded, swallowed, and opened her eyes, barely able to see the two men for the white dots that pocked her vision.

"Just, you know, girl problems," she said.

And how they looked at her. Detective Janich's eyes lingered on her split lip, while Mr. Hoggarty's expression was a mix of vice-principal serious, fatherly concern, and Navy SEAL hard-ass.

"A student named Russell Zemaitis was badly beaten Saturday night, apparently during a party at another student's home," Mr. Hoggarty said. "Detective Janich would like to ask a few questions to find out what might have happened."

"Were you at the party," Detective Janich said, "and if so, did you witness the assault and who took part?"

Mary looked from Mr. Hoggarty to Detective Janich, the men almost shoulder to shoulder. Two men against a girl, and what the hell? Mr. Hoggarty, who'd said he didn't want her to drown, yet here he was, introducing her to a shark.

"Are you asking students at random, whoever happens to walk into the office?" she said.

"No," Mr. Hoggarty said. "Only students we think might know what happened."

"What makes you think I do?"

Detective Janich said, "Apparently you associate with a number of young men who have juvenile records for assault."

She looked at Mr. Hoggarty. "Is this legal? I mean, I'm a minor and my guess is most of the people you're going to drag in here are minors. We don't necessarily know our rights. I don't. What if a kid admitted to something he didn't know was illegal and wound up in juvie? Why don't you ask this kid Russell what happened?"

"We plan to," Detective Janich said, "if he ever comes out of his coma."

Mary kept her eyes on the detective. A coma. Jesus. Why hadn't anybody kept her informed? James, Chuck, Bing? But maybe they hadn't known. Maybe the good detective had kept the information close, wanting to surprise those he interviewed. To see how they'd react. To see if they'd get red in the face or laugh or cry. To see if they'd get scared and blame others or get mad and curse him out, this Russell, this twisted asshole wrapped in his blankie of respectability who'd had the audacity—the fucking *audacity*—to take what wasn't his. This chicken-shit jock who'd gained entry into her dreams, her thoughts, making him everywhere in her life, her head, when he was nothing, *nothing!* So much of nothing, in fact, that he wasn't worth even one mention, much less an outpouring of emotion that could incriminate those who'd defended her. So she kept her mouth shut.

The detective used the tip of his tongue to brush the underside of his mustache. "Understandably, Russell's parents want us to find out what happened. If you have any information that might help, we'd appreciate it."

If you have any information that might help. A nice way to say he was hunting for evidence that Russell's parents could use to press charges against someone, anyone.

But Jesus, a coma.

"Did you injure yourself?" Detective Janich said and pointed at her.

She looked down, realizing she was no longer standing upright, but rather hunching. And she was holding an arm under her rib and sweating. She dropped her arm, straightened, and with a last look at Mr. Hoggarty—Mr. I'm-So-Concerned-About-You-Bullshit—walked out.

Mary got that hall pass, and on the way back, made four stops. You knock. You say you need to deliver a note from the office to Student So-and-So, then you deliver that message. And so she spread the word about Russell and Detective Janich.

***

Mary stood in the alcove after school, squinting at the blue afternoon sky. Blue, yet glaring, too. What was there about a winter cold that could suck every speck of dirt from the air so images came sharp, like needles to the eye? She lit her cigarette and pulled smoke into her lungs. Chuck and Lucy stood to her left, while James flanked her right. Tina stood in front of them, bouncing on her toes and shivering.

As hundreds of students streamed away from school, her eyes darted from one to the other. She checked out parked cars for plainclothes cops who might be watching and waiting, just as she and her friends did. Each side watching the other.

"But—" Lucy said.

"They can't do anything if they don't know anything," Mary said, this the fifth time she'd had to explain the obvious, and Jesus, Lucy could be such a dunce. There was something about this whole thing, the party, the coma, the witch hunt. A sense that a limit had been set, a boundary that if crossed couldn't be recrossed. And how the concept felt new, that though you'd squeaked past trouble so far, you may not this time.

She glanced sideways at Chuck, who stood behind Lucy, rubbing her arms. From this angle, the collar of his coat covered the mashed banana-colored bruise on the right side of his throat where Mary had punched him at Duncan's party. She took a drag on her cigarette and exhaled.

"Sorry about your throat," she said.

Chuck didn't look at her. "Don't worry about it." Which was not what he'd wanted to say, not by the way he pressed his lips together. Maybe he was mad at how she'd snapped at Lucy. Well, too bad. Nobody could risk being an airhead who could make things even worse.

James slipped his arm around her waist. "How you doing?"

"Better," she said without looking at him. He pulled her toward him, but she resisted and stepped away, making him stretch his arm to an awkward length. He dropped his arm. She gazed off, like she didn't care if she hurt his feelings, which she didn't. And what a stupid question, *How you doing?* She'd come to school. She'd showed the entire goddamn world she didn't give a shit. And by talking to Mrs. Barnao, she'd started down that yellow brick road to the Emerald City. To the land of money and security and enough Sno Balls in your pantry you can't count them all. Then Mr. Hoggarty had happened, and Detective Mustache and the news of Russell, which is the problem with setting your sights higher. At least when things are constantly screwed up, there isn't a big difference between normal and worse. But when you reach for better and get nothing in return, the disappointment makes you want to strangle someone.

She spotted Kathleen, who walked along, eyes on her feet.

"I got to go." She handed her cigarette to Tina, turned to James, and without blinking, said, "You're coming tonight, right? To give me a ride home?"

"I'll be there," he said.

"Are you sure?"

James dropped his eyes to his feet. He couldn't help being who he was. Then again, neither could she. Gritting her teeth, she picked up her purse and backpack and walked away from them all.

**

Mary cupped her hands around her mouth and called to Kathleen a half-block ahead, but she kept her head down. Mary called loud enough to make her insides scream with pain. Kathleen turned, looked at Mary, then turned and continued up the street. Mary stopped, her scalp tingling and face flushing. She'd just been snubbed by Kathleen. Had she heard what happened? That instead of coming down sick with something legit like the bubonic plague, Mary had been high? The involuntary and therefore worthy of pity, and the other voluntary, which means you deserve what you get.

"Kathleen!"

Kathleen stopped and turned, her eyes a glaring blue.

She kept her arm tight under her ribcage and walked the remaining twenty yards.

When she got to Kathleen, Mary had to catch her breath before saying, "What the hell, man? I've been calling you for the last block."

"I just don't feel like talking today. What happened to your lip?"

"I fell. Why not?"

"What are you talking about?"

"Why don't you want to talk to me?"

Kathleen looked down.

"Look," she said. "If you heard anything, at least have the guts to say it."

Kathleen's mouth drew tighter, then exploded open. "It's my stupid friend!"

"What friend?"

"This girl I know," Kathleen said. "Stacy. She moved here from Cleveland last summer." Kathleen said she'd seen the new arrival sitting alone in the cafeteria and invited her over. From then on Stacy had been one of Kathleen's group. Yet today she found out Stacy had not only excluded Kathleen from a sleepover on Saturday, but that some of Kathleen's friends had gone to the party and not said anything to her.

Kathleen closed her lips and stared at Mary, waiting, maybe, for a reply. But Mary didn't say anything. Motion caught her eye and she lifted her face to the sky. Black birds cut a diagonal across the blue, screeching as they flew.

"A sleepover," Mary said, almost to herself. Then she considered Kathleen. "You're upset about a fucking sleepover."

Kathleen dropped her chin and frowned from beneath dark eyelashes. Angry, upset, humiliated, like Mary couldn't appreciate the seriousness of the situation, which was true. Just as Kathleen couldn't imagine being the reason a kid had been beaten into a coma, maybe never to wake up. Just as she wouldn't know your urge to ask your counselor that along with those college brochures, maybe she can give you a pamphlet about the signs of pregnancy and herpes. Or what it feels like to have people think you deserve to be raped? That you're loose and cheap? When Mary was clean, because there'd been nobody before James. Clean, and now she wasn't.

Mary didn't raise her voice. She didn't have to. The pain and guilt, the shame and anger, all had pressed down into a small, dense quiet within her. "You have no idea, do you? No idea of what you've got. A nice house. Great parents. You do well in school. So what the fuck are you crying for?"

"But they shouldn't have done that to me," Kathleen yelled.

She leaned forward, to within inches of Kathleen's face. "Then tell them they fucked up. Tell them they're assholes and get new friends, but Christ, do you even know what a real problem is?" She turned and walked away.

"You're supposed to be my friend!" Kathleen said.

She turned around fast, but this time the pain—a searing, mind-clearing sting—felt good. "And I am. And as a friend, I'm telling you, you're an idiot. You have no idea how lucky you are. Wise up!"

And you walk away. Because you're so smart, so obviously right all of the time that people follow your example. Of how to wise up and get yourself drugged. Get yourself raped. Get yourself to where you're fifteen and need to start your pathetic life over.

Chapter 14

Wed., Jan. 24

Mrs. Perez stood at the chalkboard writing an equation. Mary watched, and what a pain, this *biconditional* shit. A *conditional* and its *converse*, like a *not* and a *not not*. Two boys in back laughed—again—and Jesus, what was their problem? She looked back. The Two Stooges sat slumped in their desks, hands covering their mouths and shoulders shaking. Their red eyes could have starred in a Visine commercial and how pathetic, to be baked on a Wednesday morning. They obviously hadn't had to stay up late doing homework or answering fifty million phone calls from friends who couldn't keep their goddamn mouths shut.

And how pitiful that she'd told her friends what to say. *Talk to my lawyer*. Just say that, *Talk to my lawyer*, and the cops have to leave you alone. At first her friends had laughed, like they could afford lawyers? And what was this, a rerun of *Perry Mason*? Then she'd gotten mad, gotten bitchy, and told them to shut up and not say anything, or if they couldn't help themselves, to spit it out, *Talk to my lawyer!* Because you don't actually need a lawyer to say it. Now repeat after me, *Talk to my lawyer*, because the cops have a hundred times the smarts and years of experience. So saying nothing is the only hope you have.

But everybody had the willies and shakes. The more nervous they got, the more careless they'd be, which made her more jumpy and irritable by the day, by the hour. The cops had talked to twenty, maybe thirty kids so far. How long before somebody blabbed the truth? Or maybe someone already had. If so, those fingered for beating on Russell would be charged with assault. But that was *if* he lived. If he died, the charge would be murder. One bad, the other disastrous. All she could do was watch, wait, and listen. To rumors. To lies. To any hint that Russell might wake up and claim he'd gotten beat up for no good reason or that she'd been willing.

Yet even so, *If he died...* The thought generated a shiver that snaked from her head down her spine, like the feel of his fingers inside her and of his tongue in her mouth. And how she hated the fucker, and wished he'd die, yet she didn't want him to die, either. Because goddamn, *goddamn*, to think that the life in those fingers, that tongue, could seep away to nothing. How gross. How putrid. To be alive, then dead; young, then snuffed out.

The clowns in back laughed.

"Shut up!" she said.

The class stilled. Mrs. Perez in mid-scribble, the clowns in mid-laugh, life a freeze-tag nightmare. Mary turned her face to her notes, but her eyes jumped around the page and her hand shook, the pencil she held showing her how much.

Someone knocked on the door and came in. A girl Mary knew, though not well. The girl handed Mrs. Perez a note and turned to go. Yet she walked slower, her eyes flying around the room until stopping on Mary. The girl's wide, unblinking stare held a clear warning, that Mary had a target painted on her forehead.

And sure enough, as soon as the messenger left, Mrs. Perez finished reading the note and looked at Mary with a gaze both skeptical and unsympathetic, like she'd hoped Mary would be different, but wasn't surprised to learn otherwise.

"You're wanted in the office," Mrs. Perez said.

She rose.

"Take your things," Mrs. Perez said.

Take your things, which meant she wouldn't be returning to class. Just for today, or forever? While you can't get suspended or prosecuted for being raped, you sure as hell can be charged for withholding information about who'd defended you. She shoved her notebook into her backpack and slung her purse over her shoulder.

With that much adrenaline in her body—her heart a Van Halen trill—she had to force herself not to run, because then she'd be running toward the lion's den. And if she ran out of school and away, they'd only come find her. So you make yourself slow down to think about why Mr. Hoggarty would call you in. To ask more questions? Or to let you know Russell had died.

Mary staggered against the wall, her shoulder the only thing keeping her from sagging to the floor. She gagged. When nothing came out, she touched her shaking fingers to her lips. She couldn't fathom the horror. Of seeing yourself pushed over the boundary into death, and not by nature either, like the cancer that ate your mom. But rather by another person who forced you to fight the fight of your life, the worst part being that even though you fight with everything you have, you might not win. Not this time, which means there will be no next time. Like the girl strangled in the woods. Had she known she was going to die? Had she felt life bleeding from her eyes, leaving only the reflection of her murderer?

The heat, the nausea, no choice but to wait and let both subside and the breathing slow. Then she pushed away from the wall and walked on.

When she got to the office, she handed the note to Mrs. Donofsky. The old woman smiled and said, "Mrs. Barnao wants to see you."

Smiled, so maybe things weren't that bad. Maybe Russell hadn't died. She put a trembling hand on the counter and let out a long, silent breath, as though Armageddon had once again been postponed.

"My goodness, Mary, are you okay?" Mrs. D. said.

"Yeah, I just need—" To eat, to sleep, to collapse. She smiled at Mrs. D. and went to Mrs. Barnao's office.

When she knocked on the open door, Mrs. Barnao popped out of her chair and said, "Okay, Mary, you got what you wanted, a transfer into honors geometry," and she held out a green slip.

Mary just stared at the slip because sometimes the gap between what you'd expected and what has happened is that enormous. From the fear that someone had died to the prospect of a new math class, the first so horrific as to make the other inconsequential.

"You're kidding," she said, watching her hand lift to take the note.

"No sirree," Mrs. Barnao said, smiling. "I can be hell on wheels when I want to be. Now—Mary, look at me."

Yet a moment passed before she lifted her eyes.

"Are you listening?" the counselor said.

Mary nodded.

"I had to sweet talk a few people into this arrangement, especially Mrs. Perez, so you'd better make me proud, *capisci?*" Mrs. Barnao said.

Mary nodded again.

"All right then, off with you," Mrs. Barnao said.

"What do you mean?"

Mrs. Barnao laughed. "Take the note and go to your new class."

"Now?"

"No, in June when summer vacation starts." Then Mrs. Barnao smiled. "Good luck."

The note read, *Rm. 117, Mr. Helpren*, and what was she supposed to do? Just walk in and say, *Hi everybody, I'm Mary and I'm so gosh-darned happy to be here?* Never mind the class was half a year ahead. How was she going to catch up? Though a better question was how could she have asked for this aggravation on top of everything? Which was like somebody with a migraine begging to be slammed in the head with a hammer.

As she passed room 113, she slowed. Maybe she should ditch or back out or ask to wait until next year. You know, to get a fresh start. Then again, Mrs. Barnao had stepped out for Mary, just as Kathleen had, and when people do that—put themselves on the line for you—you don't leave them hanging. And as yet, nobody had died or been arrested, which, when compared to those, made this an insignificant deal. She was just switching classes. There'd be a teacher, kids, a chalkboard. She finished the distance. Mr. Helpren stood in front of the class, explaining something. She knocked twice on the open door and strode in. She handed him the paper. He read the note. The room remained quiet, yet she could feel every eye on her.

Someone snickered. She managed not to flinch, though barely. After a moment of silence came a light smattering of repressed laughter, and goddamn them. Like they could get away with that shit—could make her sweat and flush—anywhere else. Mr. Helpren flicked his eyes to someone, presumably the snickerer. Mr. Helpren neither blinked nor moved. The noise level dropped to nothing but the hum of a fluorescent light rod overhead.

"Yes, I remember," Mr. Helpren said and extended his hand to Mary. "Welcome." He held out his hand to her and they shook.

"After class, let's arrange a time to meet so we can figure out how to catch you up," Mr. Helpren said. "For now, go ahead and find a seat."

Mary headed to the farthest row near the windows, where a seat could always be guaranteed. While she didn't get the back corner desk, she came close. She sat and kept her eyes forward, giving everybody a chance to get a good look. At the same time, she kept an eye on them by using her peripheral vision and tilting her head right, like she was trying to listen closer. She remained still until one by one, people lost interest and turned their attention back to Mr. Helpren. Only then did she glance around the room, looking for Snicker Boy. She found him smiling at her. A real Charles Manson grin. He was a musclehead from the football team, a Jeffrey something. He winked at her. She yawned and while covering her mouth, raised her middle finger. She turned her eyes to the teacher.

"Okey-doke, you cowpokes," Mr. Helpren said, "saddle up for Geo-Matho." The room exploded into a chaos of cheering, laughing, and people moving to new desks. She sat up, hands flat on the desktop, waiting. But no instructions came.

"My turn," yelled a heavy geek who stabbed his hand into the air.

Mr. Helpren pointed at the boy. "All-righty, first up for the Cyclops Isosceles is Cowboy Dave, while from the Outrageous Octagons, Cowgirl Maureen is up to lasso a win. Mary, you're a double-O, too, but for now, just sit and watch."

Like she could do anything else.

Maureen and Dave jogged to the board. Each grabbed a piece of chalk and stood with their backs to the class. Desk legs scraped the floor as students took seats in either of two rows, one aligned behind Maureen and the other behind Dave, leaving Mary alone in her row. Mr. Helpren stood with his back to the competitors at the board. Facing the class, he lifted two large white cards, each the size of a large, square shoebox lid. Each card had a different geometric shape. The first girl on Maureen's team gave an equation. Maureen tapped her chalk on the board fast, apparently thinking, then started to draw what looked like one of the lines from the design on her team's card. And so the game went, the members on each team taking turns giving their competitor a math equation that hinted at the geometric shape he or she was supposed to draw. People laughed or groaned when the drawer made a mistake based on a bad clue.

Mary tried to concentrate on the game, but her thoughts kept veering toward the bizarre contrast between this class and every other one she'd taken. For starters, nobody was sleeping or high. That and everybody seemed to have the required books and homework, not to mention there wasn't one burnout. Even the teacher smiled and laughed, apparently excited about his job instead of ditching class for twenty minutes to smoke in the teachers' lounge. She didn't understand, then she did. The better students got the better teachers. Teachers did more for better students. Those notions so stark the phrase looped through her head. *The better students got the better teachers. Teachers did more for better students.* She'd come upon one of those unwritten rules, the kind no one talks about. A system of favoritism you long suspected but had hoped was untrue. The real surprise was not the discovery of the system, but the rage that rocketed through her, making her hot and violent beneath her skin. Just as fast, she cooled down enough to see the logic. Why waste good teaching on kids who didn't care?

But Jesus, how could she have lived this long and not known a whole other world existed? A planet where the right people were given the advantage without having to ask, success not just a possibility, but a right. How had these kids gotten here? How was she supposed to compete against them in a game she'd never played?

She slumped in her desk. She'd wait. When the bell rang, she'd walk out and never come back, and too bad for Mrs.

Barnao. Didn't she know, as Mrs. Perez apparently did, that you don't invest in a known failure?

On the other hand, she'd no more screw someone who'd helped her than let an asshole businessman cut into line. And she was tired of losing. By coming in here she deserved success, too. So she'd stay. She'd try. She'd mess with people like Snicker Boy, who didn't think someone like her belonged to the club.

After class, she made that appointment with Mr. Helpren. He gave her a list of homework, and she left with her new book. She whizzed through biology on a *fuck-you* adrenaline rush and into gym on the remaining fumes. But by lunchtime, she crashed, the buzz gone. She sat at the end of the long cafeteria table she and her friends had claimed every day during lunch for the last two years. They talked. She didn't. She rested her forehead on her folded forearms.

A hand rubbed her thigh.

"You okay?" James said.

She raised her head to look at James, who sat across the table. He pushed a plate of fries toward her.

"Yeah," she said.

Yeah, though there was no way she could do all of that math homework. And her friends. Why didn't they try harder? And why was she constantly nauseous? Normally by now she would have scarfed down those fries.

Lucy, who sat next to James, leaned across the table toward Mary. "You look so tired," she said. "Can I have a fry?"

Mary pushed the plate to the middle of the table and watched hands reach out. Besides, Tina, who sat next to Mary, and Lucy, James, Chuck, Havermeyer, and Bing, about ten others sat yakking about nothing. Cars, parties, stupid things people had done. Anything but what had happened last weekend because you don't talk about that shit in public where others might be listening. She watched them. How they licked their fingers and talked with their mouths full. How they laughed and shook hair out of their faces. Did she look as old-hag as they did?

Mary slid her eyes across the cafeteria to where Kathleen sat with her friends, all of them girls. Kathleen laughed. She took a bite of sandwich and chewed with her mouth closed. What did she and her friends talk about? If Mary asked them, would they help her with her math?

Just then Kathleen looked and caught Mary's eye across all that distance. Kathleen smiled and lifted a hand chest-high in *hello*.

Mary smiled a little, too, and lifted a hand.

"Hey, isn't that the dweeb from toboganning?" Tina said, chucking her chin in Kathleen's direction.

Mary lifted her head, and in a tired voice said, "Shut up, Tina."

But Tina's eyes held a bright, mean excitement. "You guys. Listen. Do you remember that girl and her brother at the park that time?"

When a rush of air brushed Mary's cheek, she turned her head to the side and saw Steve, the school's quarterback. He squatted beside her, his muscled forearm on the table.

"Did you..." he said in a voice so low Mary couldn't hear above Tina's retelling.

"—was wearing these dweeby boots she called mukluks," Tina said, "but that I called *muck-fucks—*"

Though Mary leaned closer to Steve and said, "What?" she still couldn't hear with Tina yapping with pride about how their ignorant asses surrounded and scared two kids.

Mary straightened and looking straight at Tina said, "Shut up," in a tone so sharp everyone at the table stopped talking.

Still angry and confused and exhausted, she turned back to Steve. "Did I hear what?"

"Russell pulled out of his coma."

Chapter 15

Fri., Jan. 26

Within a minute of delivery, the news of Russell's newly-regained consciousness spread person-to-person down the cafeteria table. After Chuck heard, he pushed up and strode away as a worried Lucy followed at a jog. James lowered his head and with elbows on the table, pressed the bridge of his nose with his thumbs. Everyone else leaned forward to whisper. From then on a global hush descended on Mary's crowd and that of the jocks while the rubberneckers waited for what promised to be a bloody, fiery crash that would leave the bodies of burnouts and jocks strewn everywhere, and who could resist that kind of gossip gore?

She went to her classes. She stayed after school to get help from Mr. Helpren. She went to work. She walked home to her dad and his lowlife friends who sat around the table, laughing and looking at her as they always had, like she was a hooker playing hard to get. Mary opened her new math textbook and tried to work the problems. But her friends called and called and called, everybody talking to everybody, when nobody knew anything. She slept and got up again to yet another day of perpetual dusk and steady nausea. Flurries blew down her neck. Math terms drifted through her mind. All day she felt people watching. Waiting.

But nothing happened. Word spread that though Russell's friends went to visit, he wouldn't let them in the room, and surprise, surprise. You wake up. You're told you've been in a coma. The people who beat you up and almost kill you must be enemies. But wait. Your friends had piled on, too? About then you get a glimpse of yourself in the mirror and see that your pizza face has been turned to hamburger, and the rage, man, that your friends would side with the enemy. A situation like that might be enough to make revenge boil in your soul like Jed Clampett's oil. *And up through the ground came a bubblin' crude.* The question being: will you act on that revenge?

Nobody knew, or would know, until Russell talked, if he talked. She did homework, went to work, cleaned her closet. Thursday rolled into Friday. Though people talked to her and she to them, odd memories shot at her from all sides. Of her face in the mirror, blood a fine mist of red spray paint across her cheek. Of the fluid ribbons of metal that hung above her bed. Of the girl who'd smiled at Mary during a party last July— bashful eyes, lips closed over a mouth of crooked teeth—and how only a week later the kid was found dead in the woods. The lunch bell rang, and Mary walked toward the cafeteria. Toward her table. Toward people who would ask the same questions they'd asked twenty million times already. *What do you think...? What if...? When...?*

Mary stopped, as in couldn't go one more step, her body stranded in the middle of the hall. In the middle, between, undecided, the options these: a cafeteria to her right or an empty art room to her left. Door number one a certainty and door number two a wild card in the reality version of *Let's Make a Deal*. One known, the other unknown. She chose the art room. She ducked inside fast, her back to the wall, and slid sideways, away from the door where her friends might see her. Like she was hiding, when she wasn't. She just needed a rest. Yet her heart, man—Set on automatic fire so furious, so constant you have to tell yourself, *Be calm. Just... be calm*, until finally the beat slows and your head clears.

Mary peered out the door. She watched. When Kathleen approached the cafeteria, Mary whistled. Kathleen glanced up. Mary ticked her head backward, *Come here*. Kathleen frowned but walked toward the art room. Mary pushed away from the wall and backed farther into the room, where she waited by a poster of Van Gogh's *Starry Night* with its butter light and blue water night. The air smelled of paint and ceramic dust. Kathleen walked in with books in her arms and a lunch bag in hand.

"Over here," Mary said.

Kathleen walked over, her eyes moving over Mary's face as though looking for signs of illness. "What's wrong?"

She shrugged. "Nothing."

"Aren't you coming in to eat?"

"Not today."

"How come?"

"I just—" She shrugged. "Sorry I yelled at you. You know, the other day."

Kathleen's eyebrows shot up. "Oh my gosh, I didn't tell you!" She put a hand on Mary's forearm and led her to a paint-spattered table where Kathleen sat on a stool across from Mary. While Kathleen unpacked her lunch—a banana, two gingerbread men, and a sandwich—she said, "It was so funny, Mary! You would have been so proud of me."

"For what?"

Kathleen leaned forward and lowered her voice. "For telling her off, that girl, the one I told you about. Where's your lunch?"

"I—"

Kathleen handed Mary half a turkey and lettuce sandwich. She stared at the food and for the first time all day, maybe all week, her stomach growled. She took a bite of sandwich and replayed the memory of only a moment ago, of a warm hand on her forearm.

"I mean, to tell you the truth," Kathleen said, "I was really mad at you at first. Like if I'd known how to, I would have made a voodoo doll of you and stuck it with pins until you were a sieve."

Though Mary smiled, she kept chewing, the taste filling her, overwhelming her. The mustard, the wheat bread, the deep green leaf lettuce that curled at the edges like in sandwich ads where everything was fresh.

"But then I went home and talked to my mom," Kathleen said.

Mary chewed slower, then stopped and swallowed. "She must have thought I was a bitch."

Kathleen's eyes popped wide and she smiled. "No, no! My mom, she wouldn't think anybody was a—well, you know. Especially not you. She said you were right. That sometimes you've got to stick up for yourself. She's used to doing that because, I mean, I know she doesn't look like it, but she had it kind of tough when she was a kid. Her dad left her and her mom, and they had to live with my grandma. Anyway, I'm really, really bad at sticking up for myself."

Mary raised one eyebrow at Kathleen, a girl who'd stood between her brother and a pack of burnouts. But Kathleen was busy plucking a cinnamon button from a gingerbread man. She tossed the red pill into her mouth and after moving the candy to her cheek where she could suck on the dot, kept talking.

"But I decided I was tired of getting stepped on," Kathleen said. "So the next morning, I walked up to Stacy, and she was standing with all my other friends, and I didn't say hi or anything. I just told her she'd been really mean by leaving me out and that's not how friends are to one another. Not if they're really friends." Kathleen shrugged. "My friends said they were sorry. But the best thing is, Stacy doesn't hang out with us anymore." She leaned forward and smiled. "Thanks."

Mary brushed sandwich crumbs from her palm. "I'm glad it worked out for you."

"Here," Kathleen said and held out the other cookie, its row of cinnamon buttons intact. "Did you hear about the guy who got beat up pretty bad at some party last weekend? They say he might die. Geez. What could he have done to deserve that?"

"Mm," Mary murmured.

Kathleen licked her finger. "So how's it going with you? You seem tired."

Mary stared at the gingerbread man. At his white coat and smile of tiny, silver candy balls. She couldn't remember the last time anyone had smiled at her and said thanks. Just like she couldn't remember the last time she'd done anything for which to be thanked. She reached for the cookie and saw how her hand shook and that Kathleen was watching, seeing, and maybe for the first time. And how you're glad Helen Keller can finally see, but wish she didn't see you, but there it is. Mary took the cookie and lowered her arm to the table, unable to lift her eyes. Again she felt a hand on her forearm.

Mary cleared her throat. "It's just that time of the month. Sometimes I get weird."

"I know what you mean," Kathleen said. "What a pain. Don't you wish guys got a monthly bill too?"

A laugh shot out of Mary's mouth, the sound a smack, a crack, a shock that jumped her mind out of the quicksand as, half-smiling, she stared at Kathleen. "A 'monthly bill'?"

"I know, I know," Kathleen said. "That's what my mom calls it. That or 'your friend.'" She arched her brows, and in an exaggerated but accurate Mrs. McCarthy tone, said, "'Do you have your friend, Kathleen?'"

Mary shook her head. At how *friend* could be applied to something you normally never want, but that now happened to be the very thing you'd pay a million bucks to get. She really shouldn't be laughing, but sometimes there was no other choice.

"I guess I should thank you for telling me about the honors class," Mary said. "I got transferred to honors geometry on Wednesday."

Kathleen's eyes flew open and she made Mary start at the beginning, with how she got called out of Mrs. Perez's class. Generally, you should keep such explanations short because what's there to tell? She got the transfer and went to class. But the longer she talked, the more she blabbed. About how nervous she was while walking from the office to Mr. Helpren's class. About Snicker Boy. About how pissed she'd been at Kathleen for suggesting the idea.

"Me? You're the one who asked for it!" Kathleen said. "And it's not like you can't do it. If you need help, give me a call. It's no big deal."

No big deal, though at this moment, the words felt true, Mary lighter than she'd been all week. Light to the point of *euphoric*, as Mr. O'Brien might say. She bit the head off of her gingerbread man and while chewing, said, "You want to come for a sleepover sometime?"

"I don't know," Kathleen said. "When?"

She stopped chewing. She stared at Kathleen, the moment requiring a rerun. Had Mary really asked Kathleen to sleep over? Yes, though that couldn't be. There are things you think about and things you actually say. Sometimes you say the things you think, and sometimes you don't. You never ever blurt what strikes you as funny because you know the situation will never happen. Unless you get careless.

Mary set down her cookie. "Forget it," she said. "You're probably too busy."

"Not really," Kathleen said. "Things are pretty dead until spring concert. How about Saturday? I'll ask my mom."

The bell rang.

"Oh my gosh," Kathleen said. "I totally wasn't paying attention to the time." She crushed her garbage in one hand and hoisted her books with the other. She walked toward the door, then turned. "By the way, I won't be in English because I've got a dentist appointment. Copy the homework for me, would you?"

She said sure. She went to social studies. She went to English. She stared at her open copy of *1984* by George Orwell and thought, shit. Maybe if she never mentioned the idea again. But Kathleen wasn't the kind to forget. She'd ask and ask and ask. *When?*

"Mary?"

Mr. O'Brien stood over her, his eyebrows lifted.

"I can tell by the pensive expression on your face that you've got a strong opinion about the main character," he said.

"I do," she said. "Winston is a wimp."

People laughed. Mr. O'Brien walked to his desk, turned and sat on the edge. "I assume you have evidence to back that up?"

"He's like this old guy, almost forty, and he's just shuffling along with everybody else," she said. "He feels depressed, but he doesn't know why, even though everything around him is a bombed-out ghetto and everybody's a robot. You'd think he'd look around and say, 'Damn, this sucks. I'm hauling ass out of here.'"

Again students laughed. Like the guy's situation was funny instead of desperate.

"But he's blind to his surroundings, don't you see?" Mr. O'Brien said. "He grew up in this bombed-out ghetto. He doesn't know any better. How can anyone aspire to be better than he is when he doesn't know what better looks like?"

"Check it out," said the fat kid who always sat in back. He'd risen from his seat and pointed out the window at where five cop cars had pulled up alongside the curb in front of school. Six officers dressed in bulky, dark blue winter coats got out and walked fast toward the main entrance, breath steaming from the corners of their clamped mouths. Four officers remained by the vehicles. She stood and stepped to the window. The other students crowded around.

"Somebody's in trouble," said a boy behind Mary. He laughed.

The officers opened the doors and disappeared into the school.

"Well it's not our trouble," Mr. O'Brien said. "Everybody take a seat."

She backed up and sat. She lowered her eyes to her desk, heart pounding. She stared at her hands, so dead in the white light.

"Mary?"

She looked up.

"Do you understand what I mean?" Mr. O'Brien said.

She shook her head, a slow side to side. Mr. O'Brien strolled across the room and called on someone else. Her eyes wandered to the clock. Twenty minutes until school ended. She looked out the window again. Snow had started to fall. Wind made the snowflakes curl and twist on their way down.

The fat boy jumped out of his seat, the chair legs screeching against the floor. "Look!"

The students ran to the window this time. She stood. Without looking at anyone, she pushed her way through the crowd. The officers who'd gone into school now walked toward their vehicles, each gripping the arm of a boy. James, Bing, Chuck, Steve, and two other football players.

"What did they do?" someone said.

"It was that party," someone else said.

"They messed him up, that guy. A real jockstrap."

An officer gripped Chuck beneath his armpit, pulling hard, because he was leaning back. He threw his head to the side and yelled something over his shoulder, toward school, the sound muted through the window. Yet you get the gist of what he's saying, that if they take him, who will watch out for Lucy? The harder the officer pulled the more Chuck leaned back. Then in one motion, he yanked his arm away and spun toward school, shouting this time. Five officers descended on Chuck. They slammed him to the ground, spread his legs, and handcuffed him. They hauled him up and shoved him into the backseat of the lead cop car. Chuck, who if he couldn't make bail—because who had the money for that?—would have to stay in jail overnight, if not longer. Lucy would have no protection against her oldest brother, at least for now, though maybe for good, considering Chuck was eighteen and could be tried as an adult. Leniency not something judges handed to tough-looking former juvenile-delinquent males who crossed over into adult crimes.

"Goddamn," she whispered. The cops drove away.

"Okay, people. Show's over," Mr. O'Brien said. "Sit down."

Students wandered back to their desks. Excited. Whispering. She studied the clock again. Five minutes. Then the bell would ring and everyone would scatter, which meant she'd be five minutes too late. She slipped the book into her backpack and walked to Mr. O'Brien. She leaned toward him, her back to the class.

"It's that time of the month and I'm really nauseous," she whispered. "Can I go to the nurse?"

Mr. O'Brien wrote her a slip. Once out of class, she ran. She came to the hall intersection, looked left, then right and spotted the girl carrying a green slip, the same office messenger who'd delivered the note to Mary's math class.

She ran on the balls of her feet to keep from causing a clomping echo in the quiet hall.

She apparently succeeded because when she caught up to the messenger and said, "Hey," the girl whirled around looking very surprised. Maybe at seeing Mary, and maybe, too, because her casual tone didn't match her heavy breathing.

"Who's it for?" Mary said.

After a pause, the girl read the name on the note.

"Okay if I walk with you?" Mary said.

The girl looked uncomfortable. "I guess." She kept glancing sideways at Mary until they reached the classroom. The girl knocked, entered, and delivered the note. When she came out, she glanced at Mary again and passed by. Soon after, Lucy came out holding the green slip. Clueless, airhead Lucy, who smiled at Mary.

"Listen up, Lucy," Mary said. "I've got some news for you and I can't have you freaking out on me."

Lucy blinked, the smile gone. "What's—"

"I'm not kidding," she hissed.

Lucy nodded.

"They arrested them," she said. "Chuck, James, Bing. Three others. That's why they want to see you in the office. To tell you."

Lucy raised a hand to her mouth. A whine escaped.

Mary grabbed Lucy's upper arm and squeezed hard, turning Lucy's whimper into a yelp. "When school ends, go straight to my house, do you understand?"

Because odds were, that was what Chuck had been yelling. Trying to explain. That Lucy couldn't go home until Chuck was released, and who knew when that would be now that he'd resisted arrest.

"You're going to stay at my house until this is cleared up, got it?" Mary said. "I kid you not, Lucy. If you're not at my house when I get home from work tonight, I'm going to hunt you down and beat you up. Now. Chuck keeps a set of keys on The Beast. Where?"

Lucy's wide, crying eyes wandered. "What?"

Mary shook Lucy. "Keys. Come on, man!"

Lucy sucked in her lower lip, inhaling tears, too. She told Mary about the keys, then said, "What am I going to do?"

"Jesus, Lucy, stop being such an airhead. There's no time

for that shit. Where are you going right now, this minute?"

"The office?"

"Yeah. Then?"

"Your house."

Mary turned and ran to the gym exit, an arm held tight beneath her mending rib. She pushed out the door as the bell rang. When she got to The Beast, she kneeled by the back fender and felt underneath for the film canister, which was attached by duct tape. She used a thumb to flip off the lid and shake the key into her palm. She got into the car and turned the ignition. The Beast exploded with noise and shake, the radio blaring and muffler woofing a heavy beat. She turned off the radio and backed out. Already students streamed into the parking lot, threatening to block her way.

Mary headed west while trying to remember the exact location. She passed a cemetery and glancing over, caught the image of a statue atop a white-pillared monument. Of a robed angel, white wings spread against a gray sky, and Christ, how creepy. She turned left at the next road, came to a busy street and looked in one direction, then in the other. A car honked behind her.

"Fuck you!" She gripped the steering wheel and turned right. After two blocks she saw St. Mary's Hospital on the right.

A woman at the information desk in the lobby gave Mary the room number. She rode up in the elevator with an old black man in a wheelchair and a younger black woman who leaned against the wall. The fourth floor doors opened and she walked out. She passed the nursing station and a steel rack with food trays in the slots. The air smelled of peas, ketchup, disinfectant. She found the room and tapped on the door with her knuckles. Nobody answered. She went in.

The room had a bathroom on the right. Just past that, she could see the foot of a bed. Someone had left a paperback splayed on a wooden chair by the window. She walked past the bathroom and stopped. She peered around the corner and there was Russell, asleep. Several bouquets of flowers crowded the windowsill. A half-deflated *Get Well Soon* balloon floated at the end of a slack pink ribbon tethered to a pot of African violets. She went back to close the door. She turned the lock. She stared at Russell beneath a white sheet, his face smashed. A patch of his dark red hair had been shaved to make room for a row of stitches that arched back from his forehead. Eyes closed, he seemed to be sleeping.

Sometimes, in some situations, there's a moment when you don't feel anything, which leaves you light and floaty. Suddenly you're hit from behind—*bam!*—by a Mack truck filled with horror, rage, and disgust. You and all of that go splat across the pavement. Then you pick yourself up. You face what hit you. And you go after it.

She walked to his bed and stood over him. She pulled her hand from her pocket, made a fist, and with a backhanded tennis swing, smacked the metal rail. Hard enough the bed rolled away a few inches.

Russell's eyes fluttered open. He squinted at her, his teeth bared to show the wires that kept his jaw shut. His eyes focused. Then widened.

"Yeah, Russell. It's me," she said.

"What are you doing here?" *Wha a you doin hea?* he said, his words a slurred mess through the swelled lips and wire. He was mad all right, but worried, too, judging by how his eyes slid around the room, looking for whoever had been reading that paperback. But Mommy or Daddy had stepped out, leaving no one to rescue him. Russell's blue eyes came back to her.

"Get out of here," he said. *Ge ou of hea.*

"Not until we make a deal."

"What are you talking about?" he said.

"The police arrested six guys at school about an hour ago."

"Good," he said with enough power to lift his upper body off of the bed, "because they almost killed me." He blew the words at her, his breath holding the stench of his unbrushed teeth.

Almost killed me, the guys he thought were his friends. The real outrage, rather than what he'd done to her.

"You're going to drop those charges, Russell," she said.

"The hell I am."

"You're going to drop those charges and then maybe I won't tell them you raped me."

Russell of the thin, pale lips. "Raped you?"

"Yes. Rape, you fuck. What do you think those guys were doing, just beating your brains out for fun?"

"I was high," he said.

"So-fucking-what?"

"You enjoyed it."

Mary gripped the bed rail with both hands and shook his cage. Shook until his eyes jellied, the stupid fuck finally coming to understand what he'd done.

"Stop it. God, stop!" Russell said, the veins in his neck popping from the strain of his wired-jaw yell. "I can't just do that, do what you say, get the charges dropped. They said once we filed, that's it, there's no going back."

Mary stopped shaking the bed and in a hard-breathing whisper said, "Well Russell, you'd better think of something then. That you lied or were delirious and didn't know what you were saying or you were too high to know who beat you up. But, goddamn, Russell, god*damn*, you're going to get those charges dropped."

"And what, like if I don't you're going to blab? Like that'd work? Nobody would believe somebody like you." A sneer.

"They will when the kid is born."

Russell swallowed. His eyes narrowed. "There's no way you

could prove it was mine."

Her eyes skinnied to the width of his. "It's called a blood test, you asshole. You used to be an altar boy at St. John's, didn't you? Kind of a shrimp. Skinny, buckteeth. Then you got big. You got tall. You got on the football team. Got the girls. Got to thinking you could take anything you wanted." Her voice dropped further still. "You cracked my rib and split my lip. You do something like that and people notice, *Russell*. My brother noticed. My friends noticed. Mr. Hoggarty and Detective Janich noticed. Not to mention Chuck saw you trying to drag me back upstairs. Eye witnesses, you understand? Those charges are going to get dropped by the time I get to my car. You know why? Because despite all of your muscles and height and letterman jacket shit, you're a coward. You know why else?" She pulled the bed toward her and leaned over the rail and into Russell's face. "Because you picked the wrong girl. Because if those guys get convicted, any of them, I'm going to dog you the rest of your life. I'll be there to fuck up your chance for college. I'll be there to fuck up your wedding. I'll be there to fuck up your job interviews and your chances of promotion. I'll find out where you live, when you sleep. I'll call your wife and claim to be the other woman. And baby, the biggest mistake people have made about me is thinking I won't do what I say. Thinking I'll just roll over and take it. So that's the choice, *Russell*. If you decide to take revenge—Man, you're going to pay for it the rest of your life."

Russell didn't move. Didn't blink. And the sound came, of knocking and the rattle of a door handle. She straightened and wiped her eyes of tears she hadn't felt, but that would now be useful. Tears make you look like a concerned friend, one who maybe wants to be more than just a friend, and who would mess with that disguise? So she lit her eyes to girl-friend gorgeous and her smile to neon. She unlocked the door and opened to a woman dressed in black slacks and a gray sweater. A mother. Whose heart would probably break if she knew what an asshole she'd brought into the world. Just as Mary's mother would if she knew what people thought of her daughter, that she was just a piece of ass, a thing, or a *no thing*. A nothing.

She surged toward the mother, who backed up, out of the way. Mary gushed about Russell. She was sorry to have locked the door, but she needed to tell him something in private. That he was—pause—*special to me*. Then she turned and walked fast to the elevator. The doors opened for her and closed behind her. She gripped her skull. Closed her eyes. And the coffin went down, down.

Chapter 16
Mon. to Fri., Jan. 29 – Feb. 2

Mary walked to work with her eyes on the sky. What was there about January that could so thoroughly, without mercy, wash the Chicago area in gray? The weathermen blamed the lake effect. How freezing air from Canada swept south over the warmer water of Lake Michigan, causing friction, unrest. Opposing currents knocked heads, resulting in enormous, bruised clouds that cloaked the city and suburbs in warfare. Glass-shard winds whistled while the grim sky and brevity of light made every face slack, every encounter a possible attack.

Mary turned her face to the sidewalk. She hunched her shoulders against the cold. Walking from school to work, then work to home, home to school. Five more days of this shit. Her period would either come by Friday or not. Until then, what better distraction can there be than to plan your first sleepover? Christ.

At least when she got home, Lucy wasn't there. She'd been able to go home yesterday. So Mary finished her homework and then, for some reason, she filled a plastic mixing bowl with warm water and scrubbed the kitchen with a sponge and cleanser she'd bought. She started with the counters, moved to the cabinets and even rubbed off the red crayon streak on the refrigerator, a slash that had been there for years. Absent a mop, she got down on hands and knees to scrub the floor, stopping three times to dump the dirty water and refill the bowl. When done, she stood in the hallway looking into the kitchen, eyebrows arched. Because the room did look better. Brighter, when that had seemed impossible.

Frank pushed open the door and lifted his foot to step inside. Mary's hands flew up. "Wait!"

Frank jumped back. "What are you goddamn yelling about?"

"Just stay there."

She ran to the living room and grabbed a newspaper from the floor beside the couch, one she'd plucked from the neighbor's driveway to study for a current-events quiz that morning. She ran back and laid a path of sheets from the hall to the back door. Frank trundled through while muttering about why she all of a sudden felt the need to wash the floor. Was the queen coming?

***

On Tuesday, she hauled the carcass of the Christmas tree to the curb. The ornament box went into the closet under the stairs. The hallway got swept. In the living room, she pulled the couch away from the wall to find dust, cigarette butts, a beer can, a rubber band, and a condom wrapper, and who knew who'd dropped that. The pile of dirt grew to a mound. She picked out two dimes and a quarter from the heap and loaded the rest onto a newspaper to be dumped into the trash can on the back porch. And Jesus, that you can live in such filth without noticing.

Yet how fascinating, the contrast between dirty and clean. And what a surprise, too, that cleaning itself—the movement, the focus on something mindless—can make you feel better. A little.

***

On Wednesday, her day off, she treated herself to a smoke in the alcove. James didn't even try holding her hand or putting his arm around her waist. She inhaled on her cigarette and held the burn in her lungs. The babble all around. Of how they'd lucked out, James, Chuck, the others, the charges just dropped like that. Luck. Chuck the luckiest of all for being suspended until the school administration decided whether his reason for struggling with the cops—mental anguish about his sister's safety—was enough to let him off of the hook. Chuck delighted with the unexpected vacation, despite the fact he might not graduate due to missed class time. Now he had all day to cruise around in The Beast.

Sometimes you reach that point, where you just can't stand it anymore, where you are. So you walk away without a backward glance or a goodbye. You turn your back on those you know and go home.

Mary opened the front door and took off her snowy boots and put them on a piece of newspaper she'd set out last night. Though the house was cold, the sun shone through a side window in the living room. Onto a floor if not smooth, then at least clean. The refrigerator hummed, a dim rattle, while the branches of a tree scraped the roof. She inhaled and held her breath, her face rigid and throat tight because Christ, who cried about a clean house? Yet the place looked so much nicer. Lovely, even, in a barren way. And if you had been raped, and if you're pregnant, maybe a sleepover will make you feel less desolate. Will help you survive the gray. She sniffled, wiped her nose with the back of her hand, nodded. Today she'd do the bathrooms. She'd scrub the black rings from around the bathtub and throw away the toothbrush her middle brother, Johnny, had abandoned when he gave up on life.

***

On Thursday the phone rang. She got up from the dining room card table, littered with social studies papers, and answered the phone in the kitchen. Mrs. McCarthy. "Mary, is that you, honey?" Mary smiled. At the depth of tone, the touch of sun. But as Mrs. McCarthy talked, Mary's smile disappeared.

"Oh, yeah. No problem," she said. "I'll get him."

She cradled the phone to her belly for a moment and tapped her lip. She could be honest. Or she could lie. Say Frank must have gone out. But this was Mrs. McCarthy. The hand-warmer, an arm-twister, a woman who called her *honey*. She set down the phone and bounded upstairs. She stopped at her dad's door and put an ear against the wood. She heard a light snoring and opened the door enough to see her dad curled on his side facing away from her, a whiskey bottle on the floor beside the bed. The lamp was on. She put a hand on Frank's shoulder and shook. He murmured, but didn't stir. She pinched him hard on the flab beneath his armpit. He reared up and snorted. She leapt out of the room and closed the door. She inhaled and exhaled to slow her breathing, then opened the door and walked in.

"There's a call for you," she said.

Frank grimaced. "Char?"

"No. It's the mom of a friend of mine." She handed him his glasses. He put them on and blinked.

"My friend is coming over Saturday night," she said. "Her mom wants to talk to you. To see who'll be supervising."

"What do you mean?"

She hooked her thumbs into the back pockets of her jeans. "Look, Dad—This girl is like... Well, she's a really nice girl, as in really square, like she goes to church every week, and her mom, you know, she just wants to make sure a parent is around, so there won't be any drinking and stuff. But you don't have to stay around or anything. I'm sure she'd be okay if just Danny's around. He's going to be eighteen soon—"

Frank pushed to a sitting position and stared at his sock feet.

Mary tapped her lip. "Come on, Dad. She's waiting."

Frank pulled on his black shoes, the dull ones with the outside corners worn off the heels.

"And Dad, this girl..." She paused. "She doesn't drink, doesn't smoke, so be really—Nice."

Frank stood. When he passed through the doorway, he swayed and put a hand against the frame. She chewed on her lip, watching without blinking. After a moment, he walked down the stairs to the kitchen. He picked up the phone. She faced him and chewed on a thumbnail.

Covering the mouthpiece, Frank whispered to her, "Who is this again?"

"Mrs. McCarthy. She's Irish. And Catholic."

He uncovered the mouthpiece. "Hello, Mrs. McCarthy? This is Frank Donahue, Mary's father." He listened. "Yes, I'll be here." He listened again. "Yes. Thank you for saying so. Goodnight."

Thank you for saying so, which meant Mrs. McCarthy had said something nice about Mary. Frank hung up and turned to go.

"God, Dad," she said. "What did she say?"

Frank threw out a hand. "What do you think she said? You were standing right there."

She followed him down the hall. This asshole who never told her anything. Yet he hadn't sounded drunk or stupid or mean. He'd sounded like—A dad. She reached out to touch his bowed back. But didn't.

"Thanks," she said.

Frank stopped and turned. He glanced at her, a momentary flash of blue. Then he returned his gaze to her feet. "I'm glad you have at least one decent friend. Don't screw it up."

Though a shitty thing to say, his tone this time seemed sadder than mean. Like maybe if his Fiona hadn't passed away, Mary would have turned out more like this Kathleen. Decent. But Fiona had died and left Mary in Frank's care, and who could out-drink that fact? He clumped upstairs in his old shoes.

***

The alarm clock went off. Mary flew out of bed and slammed the buzzer on her dresser. Heart crazy. You wake up day after day, a Rip Van Winkle time slog, then one day, you open your eyes and it's Friday. She stood in the dim light, the cold air leeching the warmth from her T-shirt, her skin. She tiptoed to the bathroom. Normally she peed in the semidarkness, but today she turned on the light, pulled down her underwear, and looked at the crotch. White. She dressed. She went to school and took a math quiz, and that's fascinating, too: how you can act normal, look normal, despite the unreality that surrounds you, that directs you to the bathroom between classes in order to witness the still-white of your cotton pantyliner.

Mary skipped lunch and hung out in the art room reading *The Catcher in the Rye*. Holden, what a wimp. Wandering, wandering, no idea where he was going or what he wanted to do, a kid who had everything and still managed to lose.

And then English.

"Should I bring some albums?" Kathleen said. She whispered. She leaned over and whispered.

"Yeah. Sure."

Mary went to work and hauled boxes from the stock room, slit the packing tape with a utility knife, checked the contents against the invoice, and priced the items. On her third trip into the storage room, she sat behind a boxed artificial Christmas tree and smoked. Her head hurt. Her boobs ached. She felt queasy. Yet when James picked her up, he insisted on taking her for pizza. With money his grandma slipped him because his parents had cut off his allowance, both of them still pissed about the arrest. While they probably suspected he had something to do with the fight, they probably also laid most of the blame on her. *We told you to break up with her. She's trouble.* Which was what James reported they'd said. These people who feel the need to tell you everything, never dreaming you might not want to know.

James popped a crust into his mouth and chewed. A guy pretending he had no worries. He swallowed.

"Maybe he didn't even—" James said. "You had your jeans on, when they got to you. And underwear."

"But that's the thing about not knowing. You don't *know.*"

He rolled his lips together. "Did you get—"

"Nope."

He flicked crumbs off the table with the edge of his hand, the movement sharp, brief. "Okay." He nodded at the table then looked at her. "Well, do you—"

"Yup."

He looked away. Cheeks flushed and jaw muscles tight. "Wh—"

"Wednesday."

"God, Mar," James said. He looked around and leaned forward to whisper. "I can't get the money by then."

She didn't move. She didn't blink. How unfair to expect James to pay for what someone else might have done. Then again, if James had stuck around during that party as she'd requested, that someone wouldn't have had a chance to do anything. How was she supposed to get over that fact?

James looked down and rubbed his forehead. He took her home. She walked to the kitchen and stopped. Frank, Aunt Eileen, and Uncle Harry sat around a table dusted with cigarette ash and filled with beer cans. A half-consumed fruitcake sat on the counter. Crumbs everywhere. Dirty boot prints covered the floor. The counter she'd had scrubbed. The floor she'd swept. The dirt she'd washed away but apparently couldn't get rid of.

"Mary," Aunt Eileen said, slurring while blinking her half-closed eyes. So slowly. She raised a wavering hand in greeting, but Mary kept going. Down the stairs to the basement. To the smell of metal and heat, where two bare bulbs hung from the ceiling, casting light on the old furnace and the tools that hung from a pegboard on the concrete wall. Danny stood in the middle of the room at a table made of two sawhorses and a sheet of plywood, his back to her. Mary walked around the table. Danny looked at her through safety goggles and smiled.

"You're home early," he said.

Mary watched him solder strips to what looked like a metal river of murderous current. Niagara Falls where the water sweeps you over, no hope left. The piece seemed to reflect a brutality that didn't fit Danny's easy flow.

"You going to be done in time?" Mary said.

"I think so."

"When's your appointment?"

"February 17."

"Danny?"

"Yeah?"

He looked at her.

She opened her mouth, wild with the temptation to tell him—tell someone—*I might be*—

"I'm—having a sleepover," she said.

Danny smiled and lowered the soldering iron until his fist rested against the table. "A sleepover? No, shit! Who's coming?"

Mary hooked her hair around an ear. "You don't know her. A girl named Kathleen—"

"The one who kept calling."

"Yeah. Well, she's like…" She shrugged. "She's a prep."

Danny laughed. "A prep?"

"Well, not really. More a wannabe." She took a hand from her coat pocket. To explain. But no words or gestures came. She let her hand rest on the table. "She doesn't drink or smoke and she's almost for sure a virgin."

Danny laughed. "Where'd you find her?"

Mary sighed. "It's kind of a long story."

Danny pointed at her with the soldering iron, smile growing big. "That's what all this is about." He looked up at the ceiling and circled the tool to indicate upstairs. "The sweeping, the cleaning."

Mary looked down and pressed her finger into the wood table like she was squashing a bug.

"It's okay," Danny said. "That's good, Mar. That's good. What do you need?"

"For you to keep Frank away," she said. "If he comes home drunk, Kathleen will freak."

Danny turned his eyes upward. Toward the sound of guffaws and snorting overhead.

"I want you to get him drunk off his ass, my treat," she said, "then strand him at Char's." Frank's girlfriend lived at least two miles away. A long walk for a drunk.

Danny nodded. "What time do you need him gone?"

Mary told him.

Danny considered her. "You don't seem too excited about this."

Mary's eyes drifted to the small ground-level window near the ceiling. With snow packed tight against the glass, she felt buried here with Danny in a chill cement hole. The sensation that of when your heart takes off, not in excitement, but because you can't control the momentum and the speed just increased and increased, your control slipping away. Because she knew James wasn't going to get the money. Not by this Wednesday or the Wednesday two months from now.

"What's the date?" she said.

"Feb. 2. Why?"

"And your appointment's the seventeenth?"

"Yeah—"

Mary cut her eyes to Danny. "Make sure you keep it," she said. "Leave three hours early."

Danny smiled and opened his mouth.

"I'm not kidding," her tone the metal tear of two cars colliding. Shrill. Then still. All onlookers watching, mouths open, no breath here, there, or for anyone.

"Don't rely on friends," she said. "Take the train. I'll pay. And call first. Get directions, like to the office you're supposed to go to, because maybe it's in a different place, like around the back of the building and you don't want to be running. Or I'll call. Give me the number. I'll draw you a map. I'll make you a sandwich. I'll wash your clothes, but goddamn—Just—" She licks her lips. "Make it."

And he looks at you, not understanding he has to escape because you might not.

Chapter 17

Sat., Feb. 3

When Mary woke up on Saturday, she opened her top dresser drawer and pulled out a fuzzy purple sock with a hole in the toe. She withdrew her square bankbook, leaned toward the light from the window, and considered the balance. All she'd saved. All she'd now lose. She'd withdraw the money today. Wednesday would come. Wednesday would go. She slipped the book in her purse.

Though harsh, everything was clear now, including the sky. A thin layer of fresh snow had fallen, making her footprints the first of the day. She kept her head down and chin buried in her coat collar. Even so, the air was so cold her nose hairs froze on every inhalation. When she got to work, she put her frozen hands beneath the electric hand blower in the bathroom.

Mary took her place behind the register. She took her midmorning break, her lunch break, and then her afternoon break. Each time she went to the bathroom. The third time she found three spots of blood on her underwear. She stared at the Christmas red against the white snow. At the fluid made of blood cells, platelets, and plasma, as Mr. Dickey in biology would say. At the brightness of a future restored to possible.

She screamed rock-concert loud, causing her co-worker, Karen, to charge into the two-stall bathroom and ask if Mary was all right.

"Just a spider. I got it," she said, almost singing while dancing her arms overhead, two mesmerized cobras. She boogied her body to the tampon dispenser, back to the stall, to the sink where she washed her dancing hands, the joy squeezing out her throat as a stoked hum of Queen's "We will rock you." Because sometimes you deserve a break. As she did. More than anybody she knew. Maybe she'd never been raped, a possibility she'd never share with Russell. Just as she'd never tell him about getting her *friend*, her *monthly bill*. Let him sweat. Let him pretend to ignore her. Let him fight for those stolen glances at her belly, watching for the swell. And how ripe, that he'd given up his shot at revenge for a now-nonexistent threat. She drifted out of the bathroom. A snowflake that swirled to the black phone in the stockroom. She dialed, spoke, and held the phone away from her ear as James yelled his relief.

The afternoon opened into a world of sun cutting gold ribbons across cars, roads, and snow until closing down to a white sky behind black trees and rooflines. When she got off, she crossed to the grocery store because when Kathleen talked about parties, she always mentioned the junk food. Mary grabbed a bag of on-sale potato chips, on-sale grape pop, and a bag of on-sale Circus Peanuts, the orange ones that tasted like sugar Styrofoam. She also bought a box of almond cookies cut in the shape of windmills. Not on sale, but Mary had always wanted to try them and now seemed as good a time as any to splurge. By the time she left, full dark had descended. She walked fast with her chin down, the iced air in her face. Kathleen would no doubt be on time. Mary jogged the last two blocks and took the front steps three at a time.

"Anyone home?" she yelled. Again with all of the lights on,

yet no one answered. And happy days, baby. The kitchen clock read five minutes to seven. She hid the bottle of pop in the refrigerator behind a carton containing only one egg. She ran upstairs and set the bag of groceries on her dresser before kicking off her boots. She pulled down the plastic bag containing the pink pajamas Danny had given her for Christmas. How cool that your brother wants you to have something pretty and prissy, but Jesus, she hadn't once thought of wearing the PJs. Hadn't once had a reason to, until now, when dorky called for dorky. She laid the pajamas on the bed, but they looked too staged. Too evenly-creased from the packaging. She threw them against the wall where they slid down in a huddle.

She pulled Pink Floyd from her collection, but put the album back in the stack. She'd wait to see what Kathleen brought because that's what you're supposed to do, right? Let your guests have their way. She arranged the snacks in a row on her dresser, but that looked stupid, like they were for sale. She put them on the floor in a group.

She looked around. She looked out the window at the empty street. She looked at the clock. Ten minutes after seven. She brushed her hair with fast strokes. She dug in the back of her dresser drawer for a card deck. If she and Kathleen had nothing in common, they could play something. Go Fish, maybe, or Crazy Eights.

Someone rapped on the glass pane of the front door. She stood still as her mind inexplicably jumped to a worn memory of her first day of kindergarten: holding her mom's hand, wearing a new dress, carrying a daisy lunchbox she got to pick out. Excited, yet ready to puke.

She slipped on her canvas shoes, and on the way downstairs, slowed her pace to casual. She opened the door and there stood Kathleen, an arm around a pink sleeping bag and white pillow while holding a lavender overnight case in her other hand. Though she was smiling, she wasn't smiling fully.

"Sorry I'm late," Kathleen said. "I couldn't get my cat to come inside." She stepped in. Just enough for Mary to close the door. Mrs. McCarthy waved and smiled. When she drove away, Kathleen's eyes followed until the wagon disappeared. Then her eyes flicked to every floor scuff and wall gouge. What made the moment so much worse was the fake bravado of that upright posture and polite, bullshit smile. And what a saint for trying to make you feel better about living in the equivalent of a gas station bathroom.

Yet you know she really is trying to be brave, and kind. So you aim for a jokey tone.

Mary cleared her throat. "I know it's not exactly your house—"

"Oh, no, it's fine," Kathleen said. "Really. Thanks for having me."

"You want to take your stuff upstairs?"

"Where is everybody?"

Mary put her hands in the back pockets of her jeans and shrugged. "My brother had to help my dad with an errand. They'll be back soon. You think that's okay with your mom?"

Kathleen peered down the hall toward the kitchen. "Yeah. She's been leaving me alone since I was thirteen."

Thirteen, when Mary couldn't remember how old she'd been when her dad and brothers started leaving her alone. Six, maybe seven? Mary led Kathleen upstairs in silence, the air cold. No colder than normal for her house, yet suddenly embarrassingly cold for guests. She walked into her room and turned. Kathleen remained on the threshold. She looked around, eyes stopping on the sculpture above the bed.

"What's that?" Kathleen said.

"My brother's an artist. He made it for me. For Christmas."

Kathleen walked closer to study the sculpture. "What's it supposed to be?"

"I don't know," she said. "But it's made of car parts."

"Oh," Kathleen said. Then her eyes widened and she pointed. "That's a gas cap, right?"

She laughed. "Yeah. My brother's weird."

"That is so cool," Kathleen said. She turned in a full circle. She studied the photo on Mary's dresser. "Is that your mom?"

"Yeah."

"How'd she die?"

"Cancer."

"She was really pretty."

"You want to put your stuff down?"

Kathleen got a goofy look on her face. "Geez. I forgot. Here I am holding on to everything—"

"It's all right, just dump it."

Kathleen dropped her sleeping bag, pillow, and overnight case. Her eyes moved to the corner near the closet and again widened. "You have your own stereo?"

"Well, it's a pretty s—It's a crappy system," she said. "What do you want to listen to?"

Kathleen smiled and shrugged. "You'll think it's stupid."

"No I won't."

Kathleen considered Mary. For a heartbeat. Then Kathleen unzipped the overnight case and pulled out five albums. She held up the first one. "Barry Manilow," she said, then held up each cover in turn. "And this one is Jim Croce. I also brought Captain and Tennille, the Bee Gees, and this is really good, too, John Travolta and Olivia Newton-John."

Jesus Christ. Death by Top Forty. But you aren't supposed to make fun of your guest for having terrible taste in music, right? Mary nodded and kind of smiled.

"Which one do you want to hear first?" Kathleen said. "Let's do Barry Manilow." Kathleen handed the album to Mary, who set down the needle. "Mandy" played. Barry Manilow sang a bunch of bullshit about some selfless chick as Mary and Kathleen stared at one another.

"You hungry?" Mary said.

"No, we had fried chicken for dinner. Want to get into our pajamas? Then we can do our nails. I brought everything." She pulled out her pajamas and a pink cosmetic bag. "Where should I change?"

She looked around. "In here, I guess. I'll take the bathroom."

Kathleen looked at the window. "Do you have a shade or something?"

Jesus. "Okay, you take the bathroom. It's just across the hall."

Kathleen walked to the doorway and peeked into the hallway. Apparently looking for anyone who might jump her. When satisfied, she walked out. How many more hours until they could go to sleep?

Mary flipped off the light switch and undressed. She put on the pink pajamas and turned on the light again. She looked at herself in the mirror above her dresser, and Christ, but did she look stupid. The curvy cat across her chest. The cotton-candy color and little ruffles at the wrist.

Kathleen walked in, looked Mary up and down, and smiled. "Those are so cute." *Soooo*.

Mary laughed, Kathleen's sincerity at once outrageous and disarming. Kathleen wore a light blue flannel nightgown with ruffles at the wrist, so that now she and Mary had something in common.

As Kathleen filed down the rough edges of Mary's bitten nails, Kathleen asked questions. About the new math class, which was a lot of work, Mary said, but at least she understood what the teacher was talking about. While talking, she studied Kathleen's downturned face. The long lashes and how she held the tip of her tongue between her lips while concentrating.

"I noticed you never swear," Mary said. "How come?"

Kathleen shrugged without looking up. "My dad would kill me."

"Just for swearing?"

"Yeah. My parents never swear. My mom says it makes people sound like truck drivers."

"What's wrong with truck drivers?"

"Nothing, it's just… Well, truck drivers usually aren't that educated and their manners aren't too good."

"How many truck drivers do you know?"

Kathleen stopped filing and sat up. "Look, I know you swear a lot, but it's like swearing is a low-class thing to do. Like you don't know any better."

She said, "*I* don't know any better?"

Kathleen flushed. "Not *you*, you, but you as in generally." She sighed. "Oh, you know what I'm trying to say. Don't be a pain."

"I'll bet the president swears."

"No, he doesn't."

"Come on, Kat, he's got big shit to worry about. You think he's like, 'Oh gosh, I really shouldn't have started that war.'"

"Why not?"

Mary considered Kathleen. "Have you ever cursed?"

Kathleen didn't look up.

"Not even once? Like when nobody was around?" She smiled. "I'll bet you could. If you tried. Come on, Kat; you can do it. Say 'shit.'"

Kathleen looked up from beneath her brows. "You're just teasing me. You think I'm a dork and don't know anything."

"Come on. Just once. Just imagine you're really mad and nobody's around to hear. Imagine that bitch Stacy insults you in front of all your friends and you say—"

"No—"

"Then tell me off. Say, 'Shit, Mary, will you shut up?'"

"I'm not kidding—"

"You mean, 'I'm not shitting you.'"

Kathleen leaned forward, and with a face red with embarrassment and eyes shining with daring, said, "'Shit, Mary, will you shut up!' There, are you happy?"

She laughed. "Shit, yeah. Are you?"

Kathleen bowed her head low enough to hide her face. Her shoulders shook. Mary stopped laughing. You aren't supposed to make your guest cry. Or maybe Kathleen was worried she'd committed some mortal sin and was going to hell. Mary tried to get a glimpse of Kathleen's face, but she turned away. Mary leaned down a little more. Kathleen turned away a little more. Mary studied the back of Kathleen's head.

Then Mary slowly smiled. "You're so faking it." And she poked Kathleen in the side.

Kathleen flung her head back and exploded with laughter. Mary laughed, too. Barry Manilow crooned in the background.

They opened the potato chips, Circus Peanuts, and grape soda and as they ate and drank, Kathleen told Mary things only a few other people knew. Then she asked Mary if she had any almost-secrets, until Mary caught on. This a game, of how you're supposed to take turns divulging personal information. Once you know your friend's vulnerability and she knows yours, both of you have the power to hurt one another, which means neither of you will.

Kathleen said she was scared of learning how to drive because she'd had a dream about running over her brother.

"Aren't you nervous about learning?" Kathleen said.

Mary shrugged. "I don't think it's as hard as you think."

Later, while they spread a thin layer of glue on their palms, to dry and peel like lizard skins, Mary said, "You mean your parents told you, like when you were in kindergarten, that you were going to college?"

Kathleen tapped her palm, her fingerprint visible in the as-yet soft glue. "Pretty much. You make more money with a college degree."

"How much you think lawyers make?"

"I heard my dad once tell my mom my uncle made ninety thousand a year."

"Dollars?"

"No, pesos."

Mary whistled. Ninety thousand. Which beat the hell out of two extra dollars an hour as a bank teller.

Kathleen kneeled behind Mary, and braiding her hair, said, "Yeah, hard to compare it to a three-dollar-a-week allowance."

"You get an allowance?"

"Yeah."

"Three dollars a week to do nothing?"

"Not nothing. I have to clean a bathroom and keep my own room nice."

"That's nothing," Mary said.

"That's not nothing."

"I work almost thirty-six hours a week."

Kathleen crawled around to face Mary and still on hands and knees, gaped. Then Kathleen sat and asked one question after another. *How come you work so much? When do you do your homework? Don't you get tired?* Questions Mary never realized she wanted to answer until now. And with every answer, she could see the reflection of wonder in Kathleen's eyes. And maybe admiration, too, like if she was dropped into the same circumstances, she wouldn't survive.

Mary and Kathleen moved on to a spitball contest, then to boys.

Mary leaned forward and lowered her voice. "Have you ever even kissed a guy?"

"What, so now you're going to make fun of me?" Kathleen said.

She threw up her hands. "No, no. It's, you know, nice. Do you want to?"

"Do I want to what?"

"Kiss a guy."

"Eventually," Kathleen said. She lowered her eyes to the bedspread. "What's it like?"

"Just lips, or tongue?"

Kathleen covered her ears, screamed, and pummeled the bed with her feet.

A loud bang sounded downstairs. Mary jumped off the bed where she'd been sitting across from Kathleen and stood, listening.

"What's wrong," Kathleen said.

Male voices and laughter rocked off of the bare walls downstairs.

"It's probably just my brother," she said. Casual. She walked out of the room. When out of Kathleen's sight, Mary jogged down five stairs and peered over the banister. There stood Danny and his friends Dennis, Allen, and crazy-boy driver Marco. Danny looked up at Mary and smiled.

"Dad with you?" she said, keeping her voice down.

"No, ma'am," Danny said.

She looked up the stairs to where Kathleen stood, peeking out from behind the wall.

"It's just my brother and his goon friends," she said. She turned her face to the boys. "You scared the shit out of us."

"Hey," Danny said, smiling, "you've all met my charming sister, right?"

"Mary baby," Marco said.

"Won't you be mine?" Dennis sang.

"Hey, cutie pie," Allen said.

"Yeah, yeah." Mary opened her mouth to say more, then smiled. "I've got a friend over tonight. Want to meet her?"

Cheers rose, the sound male. Deep, rich, virile. Mary considered Kathleen, who waved a hand of *no-no-no* so fast it looked ready to fly off. When the boys started up the stairs, Kathleen disappeared. Mary ran up the stairs and into her room where Kathleen jumped up and down, eyes excited, but serious.

"I can't talk to them like this," Kathleen said.

"Like what?"

"In my nightgown."

Mary threw Kathleen's sleeping bag at her. Then Mary put on her teal robe because she looked pretty stupid, too.

"Come on," Mary said. "These are the best-looking guys in school. Other than James. Maybe I can fix you up."

Kathleen's face went from a frown to slack jaw when Danny walked in followed by Danny's boyhood friends and fellow senior heartthrobs, the Gorgeous Three. Italian-American Marco with his olive skin. Allen and his wavy, dark brown hair, dimpled cheeks, and shoulders so broad you can't see beyond them when standing behind him. And Dennis, the Midwestern surfer boy of sand-blond hair, blue eyes, and an easy gait. The four so different from Kathleen in terms of academics and social life that she'd never otherwise cross their paths, much less get a chance to talk to them. And what did she do? She stood there, the sleeping bag snug around her, and the hem of her nightgown shaking above her small, bare feet, the toes curled under. No wonder Miss Modest hadn't kissed a boy yet.

Danny looked down at Kathleen and smiled. He extended his hand, forcing Kathleen to produce her hand without uncovering any other body parts. They shook.

"Hey," Danny said, "I've seen you before. It's Kathleen, right?"

Like he'd noticed her at school and asked around. What a good brother. Marco and Allen played gentlemen, too, while Dennis lifted Kathleen's hand and kissed her fair skin. Kathleen looked from one face to the other. With fear and delight. Delightful fear.

When Marco turned to Mary, he looked her up and down. A man looking at a woman.

"My, my, but what fancy PJs you're wearing tonight," Marco said.

"Shut up," Mary said. "I've been told they're cute."

"They're cute on you," Dennis said and raised his eyebrows

into two lecherous arches.

"Kathleen loves the sculpture you did for me," Mary said to Danny. Then she looked at Kathleen. "Want to see his workshop?"

Marco threw up a clenched fist. "Yeah! Let's go fire up the blowtorch. I'll get the beer."

"Come on, Kathleen," Mary said and led the way.

Kathleen followed so closely, the guys' gorilla hoots and laughter just behind her, that she kept stepping on Mary's heels. Once in the basement, Danny gave Kathleen the grand tour of his tools and box of scrap metal. Kathleen listened as Danny talked about the river sculpture on the worktable.

Allen leaned over Mary's shoulder and whispered, "Where'd you find her?"

Mary turned her head sideways, lips an inch from his. "Not your biz. Just be nice."

Another bang upstairs. Of somebody opening and closing the front door. Mary's eyes shot to the ceiling and followed the sound of unsteady footsteps in the hall, moving toward the kitchen overhead.

Mary looked at Danny, who'd heard, too. He jogged to the stairs and took them two at a time until he disappeared.

Kathleen looked at Mary. "What's wrong?"

"Nothing," she said. "It's just my dad."

Danny would take care of Frank. Would wrestle him to his bedroom or, better yet, shove him back out the door.

"—the fuck you do—" Frank yelled. Though stretched to sloppy and slow, his words sounded clear. Kathleen and the boys shut up and stared at the ceiling.

Mary caught Dennis's eye and nodded toward Kathleen.

"Hey Kathleen, you want to see what Danny made his freshman year," Dennis said, voice loud to cover some of the yelling now coming from the kitchen. "It almost got him—"

But Frank's voice rose. "Don't you tell me that. I'm her

father and I said I'd be here." A chair crashed to the floor. Kathleen flinched. She stood with one hand up, like trying to ward off oncoming danger. The hem of her nightgown shook.

Mary leaned over and whispered into Marco's ear, and he nodded.

"The party's going upstairs to Danny's room," Marco said as though emceeing a wedding party. He knocked his head sideways, signaling for Allen and Dennis to follow up the stairs. The advance guard that would lead Mary and Kathleen safely past Attila.

Mary looked over her shoulder at Kathleen. "Just ignore my dad. He's just mad, probably about something stupid."

When she got to the top of the stairs, she stopped, Kathleen behind her. Mary peered in the gaps between Marco, Allen, and Dennis, who'd lined up to form a shoulder-to-shoulder barrier in front of Frank so Mary and Kathleen could slip past.

"You had no right to just leave me there," Frank yelled.

Char swayed nearby, a hand to the back of her neck. "Now Frank," she said, barely able to lift her eyes. What Mary's mom used to say to Frank when he tried to swat Mary—*now Frank*—or when Mary took a swipe at him—*now Mary*. A father and daughter taking shots at one another, even then.

"I had to get Char to drive me home," Frank said.

Dennis and Allen made a line Kathleen and Mary could pass behind. She started through the kitchen, Kathleen close behind. Frank lunged between Allen and Dennis and grabbed Mary's wrist.

"You!" he said. "Did you tell him to do that, to leave me like that?"

Mary yanked her arm away. "Come on, Kathleen."

But Kathleen froze long enough for Frank to grab her wrist. Kathleen reared back. The sleeping bag fell from her shoulders. She weighed so little that Frank, even though drunk, pulled her toward him with apparent ease. Allen put both hands on Frank's chest, shoving him back, while Dennis tried to pull Frank's hand off of Kathleen.

But Frank held on, saying, "Your mother called. She said she wanted me—"

Mary punched Frank in the shoulder. "Let her go!"

Kathleen wrenched her wrist free. Frank stumbled backward, yelling, "Don't you goddamn hit me!"

Mary grabbed the sleeping bag and pulled Kathleen into the hall. Mary stuffed the bag into Kathleen's arms and said, "Go to my room. I'll be right up."

Kathleen turned and ran. Face white.

Mary went back into the kitchen and lunged at Frank, her fist connecting with his jaw.

"You stupid, fucking asshole," she said. Frank, drunk Frank, so drunk, so slow of mind and dim of brain he couldn't do anything but put his arms up to block the blows, Mary threw punches until Dennis and Marco pulled her back. The air, the light, her own voice. All became a whirlpool of knives that cut her with each revolution. Her head pounded for lack of oxygen.

"You always ruin everything," she said. "You dickhead. You shit. You goddamn motherfucking craphead—"

She ran out of breath and bent over, hands on her thighs, everything over. The moment, the night. The glimpse of ease and loveliness that life could be. Even though she'd thought of everything. How to make her guest comfortable. How to get rid of Frank. The need to stash drug paraphernalia and lie to her friends about feeling sick so they wouldn't drop by. Her body one of those kids' toys, the little skeleton with limbs joined by elastic so when you push the button on the base, the corpse falls, limp. Broken.

She straightened, body hot and shaking. Her father had collapsed onto a chair, his back bowed and head in his hands.

She turned and walked upstairs. She stood in front of her room and turned the knob, but Kathleen had locked the door. She knocked three times, gently.

"Kathleen," she said. "Everything's okay now. Nobody's going to hurt you." She pressed her ear to the door and heard nothing but her own heart. "Come on, Kat. It's over. Let me in."

The lock turned. The door opened and there was Kathleen, dressed in her jeans, boots, coat, and hat. She held her rolled sleeping bag in her arms. Her eyes were red.

"I have a really bad stomachache," Kathleen said. "Sometimes I get that. Like on the first sleepover I ever went on—"

"It's okay."

"Could you call my mom?"

Mary did. Then she escorted Kathleen downstairs. Rather than wait in the hall, Kathleen wanted to wait outside, even though the temperature outside hovered only a few degrees above zero. Mary followed.

"You shouldn't be out here without a coat," Kathleen said.

She tucked her arms under her armpits in the still, breakable cold. Her body shook. Her toes grew numb. She didn't care.

"I'm really sorry," Kathleen said.

Mrs. McCarthy drove up.

"Bye," Kathleen said. She was down the stairs before the car stopped. She got in. They drove away.

She stood awhile longer. No hurry now. She turned and went inside. She walked past the living room where Allen, Dennis, and Marco were splayed on the couch. They spoke to her, but she ignored them and continued to the kitchen where Char handed Frank a rag filled with ice cubes for his swollen cheek. Danny stood, leaning on the table, sorry all over his face like tar. Thick, heavy, burning.

She opened the pantry door and took Frank's bottle of

brandy from the top shelf. The bottle she and Danny kept on hand for Frank when he ran out of liquor so he wouldn't go Tasmanian Devil on them. She turned and stood, bottle in hand, and waited. Frank lifted his eyes. To her and what she held. He said nothing, though. She turned and walked upstairs. She closed and locked her door then turned off the light and set the bottle on her dresser. She took off the robe, the pajamas. Naked, she walked to the window and looked down. At the frozen, empty street. And you shiver, the first stage of hypothermia, according to your science teacher. Then after awhile, you get so cold you feel hot and pull off all your clothes. From there you lose consciousness and freeze. Mary put the bottle to her lips and drank.

Chapter 18

Mon., Feb. 5

You can calculate almost everything, if you take the time. If you care enough. How many jellybeans fill a jar of a certain size. How much you have left over from a paycheck after buying groceries and paying bills. How slow you have to walk to arrive at English class just as the bell rings, and not a moment sooner or there will be that awkward moment in which you have to ignore someone and she has to ignore you. Or worse, she may feel the need to chitchat. Polite bullshit to bury a nasty incident that can't be covered. Though who could blame Kathleen for running away? She'd expected good, clean fun and instead been scared shitless.

The bell rang. Mary walked into class and crossed the room and sat at her desk without acknowledging Kathleen in the next seat over.

"Okay," Mr. O'Brien said, "so Holden is in deep trouble by this point, do we agree?"

She opened her copy of *The Catcher in the Rye*. From the corner of her eye, she could see Kathleen waving a little. How people do that sometimes, hold their hand close to their chest and wave, trying to say hi without drawing attention. She looked out the window, the clouds tall, thick, and moldering. Piles of whipped cream gone bad.

When Mr. O'Brien called on Mary, she answered. When he collected homework, she turned in the assignment, which she'd finished last night after working a full shift while hung over. Because next year she'd take that goddamned honors English class.

Mr. O'Brien called for quiet so people could think about the topic of their next book report. She wrote in her notebook. As she wrote, a hand—Kathleen's petite paw—crept into view, set down a baggie, then withdrew. Mary stared at the baggie. At the two chocolate chip cookies inside. Her body warmed to a burn just from looking at the treats. How thoughtful. How gentle. How screwed-up because, Jesus, didn't Kathleen understand yet? You can't be friends with someone unless you can handle who they are and where they're from.

The bell rang. Mary shoved her notebook into her backpack. She strode out, leaving Kathleen and the cookies behind.

**

Mary stopped by her locker, then headed to the alcove. She shifted from foot to foot and took a drag on her cigarette, the cold wind whipping the smoke away. Chuck drove up to the curb in The Beast, followed by Bob in his lime green Dodge Charger, its hind lifted and roof black. Bob leaned across the front seat, opened the passenger side door, and stared at Mary, nothing between them but ten yards of sidewalk. Him and his stringy blond hair, rounded shoulders, and eyes that never blinked. She looked away.

Lucy walked toward The Beast. "Who's coming?"

"Where?" Havermeyer said.

"To hang out at my house," Lucy said. "You coming, Mar?" She didn't look at Bob or his open door. "I got to work."

James caught her around the waist and kissed her. A guy who'd returned to a carefree, boyhood James Dean now that his worries had vanished. A kiss on the mouth, with tongue, warm, playful, like nothing had ever happened. And Jesus, with Bob watching. She wedged her hand between her and James and shoved him away. He smiled into her eyes anyway.

"I'll pick you up tonight," he said. Then he bounded toward The Beast.

Chuck called to her through the open passenger door of his car. "Havermeyer's having that party on Saturday. You think Danny could buy for us?"

"How do I know? Ask him."

The loaded cars pulled away.

She dropped her cigarette. She ground the stub beneath the ball of her foot, angry at James for kissing her like that in front of creepy Bob. Giving him ideas, maybe, dreams of what he'd do to her if he could. She picked up her purse and backpack and walked to work with eyes cast down. Only two days had passed since the end of the possible rape-and-pregnancy scare. And two days, too, since Frank—poor, pathetic Frank—had tried to live up to the one responsibility anyone had given him in a long time. Not to mention Kathleen and her stomachache, which, if she'd decided to lie like a coward, should have gone bold. *I have to go. I have a brain tumor. Sometimes I get that.* Running away, running away fast as she could, that look in her eyes. Of horror.

A shot rang out. She stopped, shoulders hunched and one hand flung to the side. If she didn't move, maybe she wouldn't fall. But nothing happened. A man down the street walked from his parked car to his house. He'd been driving. He stopped. He got out. He slammed the door. A door slam that had sounded like a shot, but wasn't. She lowered her arm. The man disappeared into the house. This, a residential neighborhood, one she had walked through almost every day. Yet everything seemed different. So fucking quiet. How does that happen, that you wind up somewhere without noticing how you got there?

The wind dislodged bundles of snow from the tree limbs that creaked overhead. She looked behind her, but no one was there. No one running to catch up. Or explain. Or ask. She walked on, her steps slower, more hesitant.

Chapter 19

Tues., Feb. 20

Mary stared at the fucking social studies quiz. What the hell was that country, anyway? The one north of the Democratic Republic of Congo? Africa such a pain in the ass. She closed her eyes and pictured the map she'd studied last night. Someone came into the quiet room, the footsteps quick and quiet, yet plucking at her attention. Step, step, step. Three words. The country's name had three words.

The dark behind her eyelids dropped a notch blacker. She opened her eyes. Mrs. Dariano leaned over Mary with a note in hand.

"You're wanted in the office," Mrs. Dariano whispered.

"Hang on." She turned her eyes to the paper. What was that trick she'd used? *You got a ticket if you were caught drunk driving a—*CAR. Mary wrote *Central African Republic.*

"Mary," Mrs. Dariano said.

She glanced up. "But I'm not done yet," she whispered.

The teacher leaned lower and put one hand on the desk while holding out the note with the other, her black eyes on Mary.

"You'd better go," Mrs. Dariano said. "The note says to take your things. I'll give you time after school to finish."

"I got to work."

"I'll give you time during class tomorrow."

Now she'd have to remember this shit for another day, on top of everything else like waiting for a response from the Art Academy, Danny having turned in his application five days ago. But she exchanged the quiz for the note, stood, and hauled her backpack and purse over her shoulder. She walked out. Maybe they'd let her out early, whoever wanted her in the office. Then she'd have time to buy a cake mix for Danny's birthday, which was just two days from now. Though she couldn't make the cake until tomorrow after work. Hopefully James would manage to borrow his parents' car on Thursday like he promised, because if he didn't, she'd be screwed. There was no way she could haul Danny's present home on foot. Four sheets of light-gauge aluminum for his next project. Then they had to wait another week to find out if he'd gotten into the art program, but three of the four people who'd interviewed him had been women, and women loved Danny.

She opened the door to the office. "Hi, Mrs. D."

"Hello Mary." Mrs. Donofsky rose from her seat behind the counter. She rolled her lips together, then said, "Dr. Greene wants to see you."

"The principal?" she leaned an elbow on the counter and stared at the principal's closed door. She looked at Mrs. D. and in a lowered voice said, "You know what it's about? I mean, I haven't done anything."

Mrs. Donofsky shook her head. They stood a moment. Mary looked over her shoulder. At Dr. Greene's door. She patted the counter twice, walked over, and knocked.

Mr. Hoggarty opened and stepped back so Mary could enter. He didn't smile or try to shake her hand. Dr. Greene stood behind his desk and came around to meet her. From the corner of her eye, she saw someone else and glanced to her left. What the hell was Mrs. McCarthy doing here? She hadn't even taken off her black wool coat. Her hair was messed up and a cuff of her navy pants had caught on her ankle-high rubber boots. Her eyes were red. What really gave her away, though, was the way she cradled her purse to her chest. Like a baby. Mary walked to Mrs. McCarthy.

"Did something happen to Kathleen?" Mary whispered.

"No, honey," Mrs. McCarthy said, her dark blue eyes on Mary.

"Mary," Dr. Greene said, "Mrs. McCarthy has—"

Mrs. McCarthy lifted a hand without taking her eyes from Mary. Dr. Greene stopped talking. Mrs. McCarthy reached for Mary, and in doing so, dropped her worn purse. Instead of picking up the leather bag, she took Mary's hands. Mary looked down at the purse, the contents splayed on the floor. Keys, wallet, half a roll of peppermint Life Savers. When normally if you drop your purse, you get down and gather up what's spilled before anybody can swipe anything or see something embarrassing.

"Mary, I need you to listen to me. Are you listening?" Mrs. McCarthy said, her tone quiet. Firm.

She pulled her hands away and stepped back. Mrs. McCarthy stepped forward and again took Mary's hands. She tried to pull away, but Mrs. McCarthy gripped tighter. The room seemed to expand, the men moving outward, farther away, while Mrs. McCarthy and Mary drew together without taking a step. So close she couldn't breathe for the lack of space, of air.

"Did Kathleen tell you I work part-time as an ambulance dispatcher?" Mrs. McCarthy said.

"Yeah."

"Well today I got a call. About an hour ago."

Mary yanked her hands out of Mrs. McCarthy's grasp and stepped far back. Out of reach. "So?"

"There was an accident. A car accident," Mrs. McCarthy

said. She rolled her lips together. "A car ran a red light at the intersection of 47th and Willow and broadsided a truck."

Mary's fingertips tingled. She lowered her voice. "And?"

"Your brother was a passenger in the car."

"Which brother?"

Mrs. McCarthy blinked. Like she hadn't known Mary had three.

"Danny," Mrs. McCarthy said.

Mary stepped forward and stopped. "Goddamn. Is he hurt?"

"He's at the hospital," Mrs. McCarthy said. "I'll drive you to see him."

"I didn't ask that," Mary said. Eyes narrowing. "How bad is he?"

"I don't know." But a tear. Slipping from her eye.

"You're lying."

Mrs. McCarthy shook her head, voice webbed with phlegm. "No—We don't know anything for sure. Nobody's been able to reach your father. We need to get to the hospital."

"Shut up!" Mary said, hands flying out. To fend them off, anybody who came toward her, though no one did. "Just— let me—" She looked into Mrs. McCarthy's eyes and for the first time saw where Kathleen had gotten her inability to hide what she felt, what she knew. And wasn't that just the bitch of honesty, that couldn't lie for shit.

"Now," Mary said, tone quivering, but holding, "I know you're trying to help, and, it's just, you know, sometimes— Adults, they don't—" she licked her lips. "Adults have fucked me over my whole life. And Kathleen said you had it kind of tough when you were a kid, so you know. You know how it is. So don't bullshit me here, all right? If I go and I'm expecting him to be alive, even if only a little bit, and I find out other-wise—and you didn't tell me—Mrs. McCarthy don't bullshit me. Please. Is he dead?"

Mrs. McCarthy said nothing. Mouth crumpling. Eyes streaming.

Mary could feel the light more than she could see it, how the room dimmed to a uniform shroud of gray. There wasn't a sound, not even a breath.

"Who was driving?" Mary heard herself say.

No one said anything. Then Mr. Hoggarty said, "Chuck Gorski."

Mary staggered back a step. Everyone rushed toward her, but she put up a hand—felt it float upward—and they stopped.

"I just," she said, or thought she said, though maybe someone else had. Someone who sounded ancient. "I got to go... to the bathroom. I'll be—I'll come—Then you'll—"

She felt her hand on the doorknob. The door opened. Air rushed over her. She walked through the lobby with hands in front of her so she wouldn't run into anything, the world a wave of watery images. Her shoulder smashed against a doorframe and then she was outside. Pins of cold struck her from every angle, the world snowing. They would try to follow. They might even send the police. Now that she was outside the building without permission, she was truant. She couldn't remain in the open. She looked both ways and ran across the street toward the hole. She climbed the bank of plowed snow, her bare hands clawing the graveled ice. Once atop the bank, she jumped down on the other side and into the wooded lot. Snow up to her thighs. Coat open. Backpack and purse swinging against her hip. She lifted one leg and plunged her foot down, shattering the crust. She took another step and another until she was well into the woods, a nothing plot of land between neighborhoods, but that makes you feel like the only person in the world. A place she'd walked count-less times. Where a girl had been murdered and no one cared. But today the hole was a different world: the buildings gone, the people gone, the colors reduced to black and white, the contrast simple. Stark. Like the fact that when she got there, to the hospital, she was going to kill Chuck if he wasn't already dead. No one would be expecting anything. She'd slip in, kill him, and leave because that's what you do to people who kill your best brother. And maybe on the way there, on the way to murder the murderer of your brother, you happen to trip and fall, your bare hands disappearing up to your armpits in snow because you finally understand what happened, and you scream. And scream. And scream. And when your throat burns out, you turn over onto your back, arms flung out, and you looked up. And what you see the white sky and the snow drifting down. And you know now, as you didn't before—as you suspected but couldn't take in—that there's no need to hurry anymore.

Chapter 20

Mary lay on her back, face to the sky, long enough that snow collected on her coat, eyelashes, and hands. Her fingers grew numb in their nests of white, her mind wandering, wondering. Would it really be so bad, having someone squeeze her neck until the sudden, vast emptiness of a Danny-less world ended? Or maybe she could just fall asleep, the cold seeping in until her heart slowed, stopped, and froze.

But then there would be no one to take care of Danny. So she pushed herself to a sit. Tufts of snow fell from her forehead. Then she reached for a nearby branch and pulled to a stand. She found her purse, her backpack. She trudged out the other side of the woods and through a park to a sidewalk where she walked, her mind empty, her eyes on the gray sky, knowing he could only be in heaven. Because he'd raised her up. He'd done good, and you deserve heaven if you'd done good.

By the time she got to the hospital, Mr. Hoggarty and Mrs. McCarthy had arrived. They came toward her, but she'd become a ghost now, untouchable, and they saw this and stopped. Her world silent, despite the images and sounds that surrounded her. Of people moving and voices over an intercom. Of her voice asking *Mrs. M, can you call my work? Tell my manager I can't come.* Of a business-suited man who takes you to his office. *Are you sure there's no one else? Your mother, your father?* And she said, *No.* Yes, but no, the others elsewhere, who knew where, yet she'd make a few calls anyway, leave a few messages. The man talked more, of death certificates and funeral-home shit and, *Right this way,* to see her brother. And she stared at him, thinking, *Okay.* And, *All right.* And, *We're done here.* She'd been shivering, but now didn't. The next stage of hypothermia, according to Mr. Dickey, is that you grow hot with cold. Then get sleepy. Then drift off.

We're done here.

And then Frank showed up. Drunk. Nuts. He came at her in the lobby. All this her fault. Security guards swooped in, followed by cops, and how you watch and when you can, request they haul Frank away, and they do. For a night, maybe, because that was all she needed.

Someone asked if she had someone to call. Someone who could drive her home. She said no. But Mrs. McCarthy said yes, and how you'd forgotten about her. She drove. She talked. Mary heard the voice but didn't listen. She stared out the window. The snow fell. The world had gone dark.

She stopped at the curb. *Come home with me, honey. Stay with us. Or I'll stay with you.* But she said nothing. Mrs. M insisted, then pleaded. She put her hand on Mary's arm. But Mary got out anyway. She walked the front steps and went inside. She closed the door and stood in darkness sliced by the dim light of a streetlight shining through the living room window. She walked upstairs and stood at the threshold of her brother's room and stared at the messy bed. Where he'd slept last night. From which he got up this morning. Weariness— finally, the weariness—descended on her. How you stagger forward through a blizzard that whispers for you to sleep. Your eyes grow heavy. Your backpack and purse slide from your shoulder. You wade toward the bed and sit. You lean sideways until your cheek rests on his pillow. You pull up the covers. You blink slowly, then slower, your last thought a prayer. That you never wake up.

But then you do. You goddamn do.

Chapter 21

Fri., Feb. 23

On this gray funeral day, Mary stared at the angel a few graves from Danny's. While all of the other angels in this cemetery stood with their wings folded and eyes down in the victim way of *I deserved to be shit upon*, this one didn't. She stood white and clean atop a tall monument with her wings spread wide for flight. Leaning forward, she reached her arms forward, her empty palms facing skyward. Not just welcoming transformation, but desperate for deliverance—*finally*—from all of this earthly bullshit.

Though Mary stood at the edge of her brother's grave, she kept her eyes on the angel. Why look down at a coffin that held nothing but a body? Because Danny's spirit was no doubt long gone. He partied with the angels now, or at least the fun ones like the chick atop the monument. If he'd been able to stop by, he'd apologize for the hassle of dying and encourage everyone to get out of this blowing, sleeting day. *Go home*, he'd say. *Pop a beer. Sit in front of the fire.*

He'd tell her to do the same. But there would be no warmth there, or maybe ever again. With a near-zero wind whipping her cheeks, the raw within her felt as bare and clear. Everything and everyone here was bullshit. All of them, these

people who circled the hole. Frank on her right, in his black
overcoat and suit, probably the same he'd worn at his wife's
funeral. And on the left, her oldest brother, Mike, a porker
twenty pounds heavier than when she'd seen him last July;
six months in which neither had probably thought about the
other. And Johnny, nowhere to be found. Not to mention
the huddles of Danny's weepy former girlfriends and packs
of buddies, from the Allen-Dennis-Marco trio to those who'd
ever benefited from Danny's beer runs. James, Bing, Julie
V. , Havermeyer. Aunt Eileen clutched the arm of her pimp
husband. Darby stood nearby, the official representative of
her absent politician husband. The McCarthys, a fortress of
four, with Kathleen and her brother in the middle, protected
on either side by a parental guard tower. And Lucy. Stupid
Lucy, who'd exiled herself to a spot beneath a bare tree.
Crying, wringing her hands, probably still not sure what had
happened. Apparently Chuck would survive, though with
what kind of brain damage, nobody knew. Maybe he'd be a
vegetable his long, long life. If so, the humane thing would be
to kill him. The reason she'd decided not to.

These people and all the others, too. The kids who'd gone
to school, this just another day for them. And the mothers,
all the good mothers out shopping for Friday night dinners to
set on checked tablecloths. And don't forget those who'd ever
loved and tried. Who'd ever failed and wailed and bitched and
moaned and laughed, their hands warmed and hearts frozen,
humanity nothing but a collective weakness, a spreading
plague.

She leaned over to Mike and whispered about how she felt
sick and would wait by the car. She didn't bother with a slow
pace to confirm her agony for all of the eyes that followed her.
Instead, she lit out at a fast stride—away, away. She reached
the narrow cemetery road and instead of heading left toward
the parked cars, turned right, knowing the road led to an exit

on the other side of the cemetery. She and Danny and the angel, all out of here, to somewhere else.

She followed the road down a small hill and around a curve. She heard a shout. She looked up, but didn't see anyone. Another shout. She turned. Kathleen trotted down the hill in her dark green overcoat and white mittens. Mary turned away and walked faster.

"Come on, Mary, stop!"

But she didn't. If Kathleen had called since the accident, Mary didn't know. She hadn't been answering the phone, which rang without end. Maybe Kathleen had gone with Mrs. McCarthy the two times she'd knocked on Mary's front door, yelling for her to open up. Maybe Kathleen had even prayed for Mary and Danny, but what the hell good was that? Would God bring Danny back to life? Not a fucking chance. So that now all she wanted was to be left alone. She and her bank book with the zero balance, she and Mike having pooled their money to pay for the funeral home, coffin, and rectangular granite plaque so small there was no space for anything but a tragedy in shorthand: Daniel Andrew Donahue. Feb. 22, 1961 – Feb. 20, 1979. There hadn't even been room for *born* or *died*, much less what she had wanted: *I'll save a piece of cake for you.*

A snowball exploded against the back of her head, snow spraying off to either side. She spun around. Kathleen stood about twenty feet away. Guilty, but resolute. She apparently had something to say because she was Kathleen, who knew so much about the goddamned world.

Everything within her clenched. Teeth, fists, heart. "Son of a—" she whispered. She took off after Kathleen.

Kathleen's eyes widened. She put her hands out in front and backed up. "No, Mary, I—"

When she didn't stop, Kathleen turned and ran, a scream climbing in her throat, from a *Maaar* to an *ahhhh*. Soon she was within five feet of Mary's hands. One lunge—

But then Kathleen jumped off of the road and into the snow. Though Mary was a faster runner, Kathleen's boots had more traction. Mary fell, got up, fell again, but got up again. She followed Kathleen's crazy, panicked pattern around gravestones until Kathleen dodged behind a wide, chest-high slab.

"Stop," Kathleen screamed.

But she didn't. Kathleen bombarded Mary with snowballs, hitting her in the face, the throat, the shoulder. When Mary got close enough, she chased Kathleen around the gravestone three times before faking a reverse and dodging right again. She caught the hem of Kathleen's coat. Kathleen fell forward, pulling Mary down, too.

Kathleen tried to crawl away on her belly while glancing over her shoulder. "Mary!" she screamed. "Stop it. I didn't do anything. I didn't kill your brother."

She got onto her knees and sprang forward. Kathleen raised her foot and smashed Mary in the nose. She fell on her ass so hard she bit her lip, the taste of salt instant. The world dissolved into the white snow of off-the-air TV stations.

"Oh my gosh," Kathleen said.

She opened her eyes and with her fingers, touched her lip, then wiped a hand under her nose. She pulled her hand away and stared at the blood.

"I'm so sorry," Kathleen said. She got onto hands and knees and crawled toward Mary, but stopped at a distance that kept her out of reach. "Are you all right?"

Mary raised a handful of snow to her swelling lip. She rolled over onto her hands and knees and let her head hang. Her throbbing nose dripped. Her tears fell into the snow. She pushed to a stand, turned and looked down on Kathleen.

"See, that's what I don't get," she said. "You have so much and I don't have shit. To even things out, you'd think God would take your brother. But no, Danny dies, and I don't understand. I don't get how some people are born and it's like they get this good life handed to them, and other people are born and right from the start, things are fucked up, when they didn't even do anything." She turned and slogged through the snow to the road. She stamped her feet.

She turned to Kathleen and walking backward, yelled, "That's what I want to know, Kat. What am I supposed to do now? Where am I supposed to go? When you know that, give me a call. But you won't. You want to know why? Because you don't know. You'll never know."

She turned and walked away.

Chapter 22

Wed., March 14

Mary lay with her cheek against the desk, staring into the winter dusk. At the black tree limbs dripping with snowmelt, the temperature almost forty degrees today.

"And what do you think, Mary?" Mr. O'Brien said.

She lifted her head off of the desk. She stretched her arms overhead. She yawned. "I don't know. What are you talking about?"

Someone in class laughed. Mr. O'Brien didn't. He cocked his head to the right. Considering her for a moment, it would seem. He leaned down and wrote. She sighed and stood. She slung her purse over her shoulder and walked to Mr. O'Brien's desk. She didn't look at Kathleen now or much at all anymore, or talk to her or think of her because what was there to talk or think about? Your world. Her world. There no overlap between them, something Kathleen had apparently gotten through her head because she didn't call anymore. Or bring cookies. Or try to catch up when walking home.

Mr. O'Brien tore a sheet from the notepad, but instead of handing her the note, said, "Let's talk in the hall."

She followed Mr. O'Brien into the hall and stood, hands in coat pockets, eyes almost closed.

"I know you've had a tough break, Mary, but I can't allow this behavior to continue," Mr. O'Brien said. "As a teacher, it's frustrating to watch. As a parent, it's excruciating. You're sinking and I apparently can't help, and I just can't watch anymore."

She stared at him.

He shook his head. He handed her the note. She walked away. She stopped in the bathroom and lit a cigarette with Danny's lighter. A cheap yellow Bic she always kept in her pocket now. She used one hand to smoke. With the other, she turned the lighter over and over within her pocket. The same lighter with which she'd set the letter on fire, the one saying Danny had been accepted to the art school. She stared into the bleeding glow of the afternoon sun through the frosted-glass window. When she got to the office, she nodded at Mrs. D. and continued to Mr. Hoggarty's room. She ignored his outstretched hand, tossed the note on the desk, and slumped in the chair.

"It's been three weeks since your brother died," he said. "I can't imagine the grief you're experiencing. As far as I know, your teachers have been very sympathetic. But there comes a point when such treatment only hastens failure. This is the fourth time you've been sent to the office. You've been truant twice and have started cutting classes again. You're no longer turning in assignments. You're failing tests. This has got to stop."

She blinked. Full of slowness and sleep. "You're not going to make that whole floating in the ocean speech again, are you?"

Mr. Hoggarty didn't speak for a long moment. Then he said, "I'm going to have Mrs. Barnao set up an appointment for you with the school district's psychologist. At your convenience."

Like she would go.

The bell rang. She got up and left.

Chapter 23

Sat., March 17

Mary pushed her way through the crowded living room. Havermeyer had talked her and James into coming to this party, claiming good times had by all. But she didn't know anyone and was bored and drunk. She hadn't meant to get shit-faced—hadn't even felt like drinking tonight—but she'd been thirsty, and stupid her had thought the cherry Kool-Aid was just cherry Kool-Aid, so cold and simple. She drank down a full cup without stopping. But she should have known. Nobody served anything straight at parties, especially a kids' drink. If Kool-Aid tasted like the watery, sugary delight, you can be sure someone spiked the drink with colorless, tasteless grain alcohol, probably Everclear, a hundred-and-ninety proof. Within ten minutes of draining her cup, the room started to spin. Now she felt dizzy, hot, and pissed off, the stereo blaring some punk shit. Jesus, but what she wouldn't give to be home right now and sleeping, the feeling desperate, like she'd never get there. To get home, she had to find James.

The apartment was over a guitar shop in a row of old, brick storefronts along a busy street in Brookfield, an older suburb more rundown and closer to the city than her town. She worked her way toward the back door and pushed out onto a small second-story porch crowded with people laughing and smoking. She made her way to the railing, leaned over the edge, and scanned the gravel parking lot below, the height making her dizzier and more nauseous. She shouldered her way past people on her way down the stairs and when she reached the bottom, walked out another ten or twenty feet. Until clear of everyone, because everything swam with suffocation. People and people and people. She looked up at the full moon and inhaled, the air mild, like everything else in her life. Mildly amusing, mildly tragic, mildly boring, this a *sort of* land where she was sort of awake and kind of alive.

Her eyes wandered the lot. Slower this time.

"I saw him leave," someone said.

She looked sideways. To Bob. He stood beside her, a few feet away, hands in the pockets of his jeans. Shoulders rounded. T-shirt rippling in the mild night wind. She hadn't seen him in the apartment, so where he'd been all night, she didn't know. Psycho Bob. Yet this time, for the first time, she didn't shiver or want to turn away. Maybe because this time, for the first time, he didn't strike her as psycho. Instead he seemed quiet, even normal, and how weird.

"You know where he went?" she said.

Bob shrugged. "He was with Havermeyer."

With Havermeyer, which was believable. While James would never strand her permanently, he would, if the need arose, do a liquor run without telling her, especially now that he possessed Danny's fake ID, a funeral present from her. Now James would be gone for who knew how long, leaving her here. With Bob.

"Want a ride home?" he said.

With the freak stoner. The blinkless creep. When maybe he'd never been either. Maybe he was just another fucked-up soul trying to get by. Somebody who, by virtue of the life he led—had been made to live—now behaved more like a feral dog than a human. And Bob was here, whereas James was not.

"Yeah," she said.

Bob tilted his head left, indicating the way. She checked for any feelings of hesitancy or regret, but didn't locate any, not that she would, though, considering she didn't feel anything anymore. She followed Bob to the green Charger parked between an askew black Camaro and a red Pacer. Bob opened the passenger side door for her, and Jesus. Bob the Gentleman. She slid in and set her purse between her feet. The car's interior was white and clean. Angel white, angel clean, not a crumb anywhere. Rather than reek of cigarettes, the air smelled lemony. Furniture polish, though less obnoxious.

Bob got in and started the car, the engine quiet and smooth and the radio off. He backed up and pulled out. He didn't say anything and rather than feel strained, the silence descended on her like a sleeping potion, a thousand years wanting to slip from her being.

"Mind if I open a window?" she said.

"No."

She rolled down the window and leaned her head out, cheek resting against the window frame. The wind sharp, the kind that blew only on the cusp between winter and spring, the latter still weeks away, maybe years, maybe never; your life an endless winter. She watched the flicker of headlights in the windows of darkened storefronts. The hour late and road empty.

"You want to go to a party?" Bob said in a pillow voice, so soft.

"Where?" she said, the sound drawing out.

"My brother's in the city. Not too far. He's got a lot of shit."

Not too far. Then again, what's too far? Could there be a *too far* when no one knows or cares where you are? *Which begged the question,* as Mr. O'Brien might say, of why pass up the chance to score some shit that can help you forget you don't exist?

"Sure," she said.

Bob turned at the next street. He didn't careen around the corner like Marco or Chuck, but kept to a responsible speed. He took a ramp onto the raised highway that lifted them above old neighborhoods of tall brick walkups and narrow city roads. Of shining neon bar signs and billboards advertising toothpaste and Scotch. She lifted her eyes to the moon, a piss-colored sphere for a piss night, a piss life. Though the air streamed over her face, her eyes closed. The car rocked. Her weariness a blanket, warm and heavy. Willing you to disappear for a while. Yeah, just a while.

Chapter 24

Sun., March 18

Mary's cheekbone bumped the car's window frame hard enough she lifted her head, eyes half-closed. She blinked, for a moment the world a movie screen of unreal images that passed too quickly. Triple X-rated movie theaters, check-cashing stores, bail bond shops and drunks who clutched brown-bagged bottles by the neck. She sat up. She didn't know this part of Chicago. They were south of the stadium, but where? *Not far*, Bob had said. But the time had to be well past midnight, which meant they'd been driving for a while. She thought of asking Bob where they were, but then she'd have to keep the edge out of her voice, something telling her that to keep Bob acting like a gentleman, she couldn't show any fear. That if she did, he'd circle, his senses heightened by the scent of blood in the water. She'd have to wait, then. To see what happened, and in the meantime, stay sharp, stay ready. And Jesus, the tingle rampant through her body, from a heart that for the first time in weeks had picked up to a pace faster than a lope.

Bob turned left and drove toward high-rise apartment buildings that reared against the black sky. Most of the small, prison-narrow windows were dark while others glowed. The buildings were surrounded by a blast zone, no trees in sight, or fences, either. Yet the desolation crawled with human shapes. Walking, dancing, their hands a rhythm of fight. Cars didn't drive by; they cruised, slow and steady. Women in platform boots shifted from foot to foot. Guys strolled up to cars, making an exchange then backing off. Though she'd never been here, she knew this place by reputation. The projects, a sinking raft of dark faces through which two white tourists drifted. Yet Bob didn't drive faster. She rolled up her window. Slowly, like she'd gotten cold even though she was sweating.

Within blocks, the projects disappeared from view, replaced by old, brick two-stories built right to the sidewalk, shops below and apartments above. A Brookfield, except a lot more rundown. A street of vacant shops and boarded windows where the glass had been smashed. Where bars and roll-down metal doors covered the storefronts that remained. All entries and exits blocked.

Bob had slowed the car to a walking pace. He headed toward a dented garbage can on its side in the middle of the street. But before reaching the can, he pulled alongside a curb and parked. Though other vehicles lined the narrow street, the sidewalks were deserted. Bob got out and walked around the front of the Charger in his hunched, springing step against the yellow of a weak, distant streetlight. And Christ, his movement. Easy, light. A cheetah waiting to spring. Bob, who was the only one who knew where she was.

Bob opened her door and she got out, her senses, so long dormant, fired with the smell of oily snowmelt and garbage. Every image cut her, sharp and without sentiment. The street signs and windows, all dark. She could refuse to go inside wherever he was headed, but good luck getting home without getting raped or killed, this not the place to hitch a ride or ask directions, if you find anyone to ask. She could demand he take her home, but what if he refused? She'd have to play along—stay cool, stay sharp—until she got to a phone. But who would come get her?

She kept her hands in her pockets and followed Bob across the street to a door beside a closed pawn shop. He pushed through into a narrow entryway. They went up the stairs to a second-floor hallway lit by a single light bulb. There were three unmarked doors on the right and three on the left. Six apartments in all. At least a few tenants had to be home, which meant she could yell for help if she had to. But would they call the police?

Bob used the side of his fist to bang on the first door on the right. He stepped back and stood still. A kid getting his picture taken. She followed his gaze to a peephole in the door, somebody there, on the other side, looking out that pin of darkness.

The door opened, and an all-bass rhythmic beat poured out, the sound that of bodies dropping to the floor over and over. A woman peered out, her movements a bird-like quick and sharp. Her white skin and short, black hair matched her eyeliner and lipstick. She looked from Bob to Mary and stepped back. Bob walked in. For a moment, Mary didn't move. She narrowed her eyes to the width of boredom and followed into the purple semi-darkness. The door closed behind her.

A brick wall of a man stepped in front of Mary. Biceps like two rocks, the guard slid his hands beneath her armpits and with a flick of his wrists, popped her arms out to either side. He patted her down.

"What the fuck, Bob?" Mary yelled over the music.

"Be calm," Bob said.

Be calm from a guy nobody moved to frisk. The advantages of having your brother own the place, apparently.

The guard squatted and rode his hands from the inside of her crotch down to her ankles, then rose.

"Bob," she yelled, staring at the man's shoulder holster.

"This guy is wearing a gun."

"Calm," Bob said.

But the guy had a gun, when she'd never seen a gun up close before.

Bob took her hand, his touch light, gentle. She wanted to pull away. But that would be a wrong move. This was some kind of performance. How things turned out seemed to depend on following a script she didn't know.

He led her through a room so big the space couldn't be just one apartment. The walls of all three apartments must have been knocked down to make one room. Butcher paper covered the windows. People lay on mattresses and cushions, cigarette smoke curling in the purple light. Nobody danced, ate, or talked. A drug den, then, and Jesus.

Bob led her toward the back of the room and pushed through a curtained doorway into a rundown kitchen. The bright overhead light shone on the blond head of a boy who sat at a white metal table. A boy wearing jeans and a T-shirt with the name of a muffler shop across the back. A kid maybe her age. Maybe. He inserted a needle into his left arm and pressed the plunger with his thumb. Then he melted. Head to his chest, chest to the table, arms spread wide. A puddle.

The kitchen had two doorways. After leading her in through one, Bob now walked her out through the second. They continued through a short passage with a bathroom to the left. The passage opened to a second huge room, so that now she understood. Forget the six apartments. They'd all been turned into this, an entire floor dedicated to drug addicts. No tenants lived nearby. No one would call the cops.

The light in this second room shown orange. A creepy-clown tint bright enough to illuminate the three doors that led to the exterior hall, all of them barricaded by two-by-fours. Bright enough, too, to show the contour of Bob's arm muscles. Long, lean, strong. When she had only ever seen scrawny, and that you can be so blind. She glanced around. Caught the face of a woman leaning against the wall on her forearm. The woman lifted a cigarette to her mouth and inhaled, the tip flaring, offering enough light for her to see what she hadn't before. Of a man who stood behind the woman, hands on her hips. Thrusting himself into her bared ass.

And how your eyes drift away from something like that. Shock makes you appear casual, though your heart sprints, your legs hum, and your mind quivers with the image following you. Of a man fucking a woman. Out in the open. The woman smoking, watching strangers pass, no big deal. The shock that Bob didn't seem to notice. Or if he did, that he didn't care. Which meant he was used to the sight. Used to that.

She leaned back, making him drag her a little. Maybe he'd stop. Ask what was wrong. She could say she felt ready to throw up. But Bob didn't stop. He tightened his grip on her hand and pulled her toward a corner office made of three-quarters-high walls. Light blasted out the top of the room, UFO bright and white.

Bob knocked and waited. Though she didn't hear anyone inside invite him to enter, Bob opened the door and led her in. He dropped her hand, closed the door, and stood with his back against the wall. Like, *Here you go. Package delivered.*

A man sat behind an olive green metal desk, a crook-necked lamp shining down on his head. He stared at her, his face ten years older than Bob's and eyes a deader shade of hazel, though just as watchful. Bob's brother then, his hair businessman short and mouth a line. And with the white dress shirt opened at the collar and the rolled-up cuffs, he could be a banker who'd just gotten home from work. A banker who lived alone, ate alone, slept alone.

"This her?" Bob's brother said.

"Yeah," Bob said.

"She have money?"

"My treat," Bob said.

"What's your pleasure?" Bob's brother asked her.

You should respond. But your mind is still caught on the, *This her?* She licked her lips. "Haven't really thought about it."

"Needles?"

"No."

"Smoke?"

"Depends."

"Pills." Bob's brother opened a bottom drawer and pulled out a plastic, pill-filled box like the one Duncan's cousin had used. She slipped her hands into her coat pockets. So he wouldn't see them. Wouldn't see how they shook. She scanned the pills, aiming to appear interested, but only somewhat. As though there wasn't a white guy standing six feet away to the right, a gun holstered beneath his armpit. As though the doors to the hall weren't nailed shut. As though this place had a phone she could use. The thought outrageous and at the same time hard-edged and possible, that she might not get out of this. That maybe Bob had planned this moment. Her. Here. Now. Seen this in his head, then lain in wait and when ready, would drug her and fuck her, because what else could it mean, what he'd said? *This her?*

Bob's brother held out a small white pill. She felt her hand pull out of her pocket. She watched the hand stretch forward. She noted how the pill dropped through the air, from the brother's fingers to her hand.

"What is it?" she said.

"A surprise," Bob's brother said.

"Real thoughtful," she said, "but what is it?"

Brother kept his mouth closed. Eyes not mad, not curious, not lustful. Not anything but empty. Completely. The numb she felt after Danny died, the ambivalence about breathing and eating, the straightjacket isolation that kept her heart bound. None of these could compare to the void she saw in Bob's brother's eyes. Two rooms that could echo sound, but not originate it.

She looked at Bob. "Gosh, Bob, this is turning out to be such a special date."

Bob didn't even shrug. Just waited. His eyes empty, too. And what will you do with so much emptiness? Whatever you want. Eat a burger. Steal a car. Drug a girl. Because no matter what you do, one action is the same as another, no more- nor less- interesting, your soul nonexistent, your days a flatline.

A person like that can, without a thought, make you disappear.

She stared at the pill, her mouth open, because if she closed her lips, she wouldn't get enough air for a still-beating heart.

"What," she said, "you're not taking anything, Bob?"

Bob shook his head. She smiled. The irony. "You at least going to allow a girl to pee, big guy?"

Bob held out his hand, indicating that she should lead the way. She opened the door of the small office and walked out. She slipped the pill into her coat pocket. She passed the woman, who now sat slumped against the wall, head back, eyes closed, jeans around her ankles. She continued to the bathroom along the corridor connecting one large room to the other. She turned in, but before she could close the door, felt Bob's hand on her wrist. Tight. She stopped without turning.

"Give me the pill," he said.

She remained still. Then turned and looked at him. Bob extended his hand, palm up. She retrieved the pill, extended her arm toward Bob, and dropped the pill on the floor. Bob didn't even blink. He kept his eyes on her as he bent down and picked up the pill. He slipped both hands into his jeans pockets and leaned back against the wall. To wait for her.

She stepped into the bathroom and closed the door. She ran

her hands through her hair, all of this a repeat of Duncan's party, but on a lethal level. She'd allowed herself to sink and sink, instead of taking Kathleen's hand, or anyone else's, for help. Refusing salvation in favor of, *Poor Mary*, so that now she might become the victim angel, *I deserved this*, instead of the one that got free. Allowing her bitterness to bleed her almost dry. Almost.

She turned in a circle, around and around, because goddamn, there had to be some way out, something she could do. But the bathroom was bare. The medicine cabinet didn't have a mirrored door, so forget breaking a shard to use as a weapon. Maybe she had something in her purse. But when she grabbed for her bag—No bag. She must have left the purse on the floor of Bob's car. Tears filled her eyes. When everything depended on seeing clearly, thinking straight. She shook her head and slapped her cheeks. She could fight him. But there were too many people around. People more motivated to help Bob and earn Brother's favor than to help her. Which left only one option. She wiped the sweat off of her forehead. She stood straight. She inhaled and exhaled three times, then opened the door.

"Bob," she said. "Even though you've been very kind—bringing me to this lovely neighborhood, introducing me to your family, and paying for my drugs—I'd like to go home now."

"No."

"Even though you said you'd take me home?"

"Right."

"Which makes you a liar."

Bob shrugged and pushed himself off of the wall. Rather than look her up and down like other guys, he gazed into her eyes.

"This doesn't have to be like that other time," he said.

Like that other time. Duncan's party. When someone has to

take you by force, or try. *Doesn't have to be*, though would be if you don't do what he said. What argument could she cough up to counter that threat? That she'd scream? That her brother would find Bob and kick his ass? She couldn't even say people were waiting for her at home and would get worried if she didn't turn up.

So you think *Jesus* and make yourself hold out your hand, all while hating yourself as you watch the pill drop into your palm.

You place the pill on your tongue. And because you know he'll check, you swallow.

"I need water," she said.

He told her to open her mouth. She did. He held her chin—just two fingers, his touch light—and made her move her tongue, from one side of her mouth to the other. She closed her mouth. He dropped his hand and gestured for her to lead the way.

She walked to the sink in the little kitchen. She gathered her hair to one side, turned on the faucet and bent to drink. How long before the drug took hold? Ten minutes, maybe? She was beyond crying now, or shaking or arguing or sweating, everything within her having stilled to the simplicity of a world reduced in time and scope to minutes and inches.

She turned, eyes falling on the boy pooled atop the table. He had a quarter-sized birthmark on the left side of his neck. Proof that he'd been born, clean and new, and not that many years ago. Yet here he was on the down slope of life. Maybe that was Bob's goal, to make her like the boy. To dope her regularly. Until she didn't care about anything but her next fix. Bob's obedient bitch.

She lifted her eyes to Bob. "How did this happen?"

"How did what happen?"

"That you wound up here."

Bob shrugged. "Born in Chicago. Parents divorced. Mom took me to the 'burbs."

"What did she do to you?" she said. "Did she beat you? Call you names? Burn you with her cigarette?"

"She's dead."

Dead. Not a surprise, yet she shivered anyway, her eyelids already growing heavy. The room began turning at the edges. She pushed off of the counter and walked into the big room. To let her eyes adjust to the dark. The volume of the music was lower now, but the rhythm as insistent. She stopped, hissed, and clutched at her heart, her shoulders rounding. She massaged her chest with her palm.

"Christ." She winced again, this one bigger and longer. She squeezed her eyes shut and through gritted teeth, said, "What was in it?"

"I don't know," Bob said.

She bent forward, the whole room fun-housing. "Well go find out. Oh, fuck!"

Bob signaled to the guard. To watch her. The man nodded. Bob turned and left.

She felt someone take her arm. She looked up to see the woman with the white face, the black lips.

"I need air," she whispered, sweat falling from her face. The woman held Mary beneath the arm. She tried to walk, her steps lopsided, the world a nightmare to navigate when spinning at this speed.

When they neared the door, the guard said, "Bob doesn't want her to leave."

Mary fell to her knees, stuck her finger down her throat, and threw up on the guy's shoes. He swore and jumped to the side. She reached up for the doorknob and twisted. She opened the door a few inches, but her body blocked the way. A shoe kicked the door shut. She turned and fell on her ass with her back against the wall. She punched hard at crotch level. The guard grunted. She got onto her knees, opened the door, and crawled out. She pushed to a stand, lightheaded and nauseous. She leaned her shoulder against the wall while stepping down the stairs, the distance long, then short, then long again.

She pushed through the glass door. The night cool. Good. Though the doorways lined the street, they were all too shallow to hide her. Whereas the Cadillac parked on the street. Wide, solid, a barrier. She dragged her stumbling feet to the front and crouched so she couldn't be seen by anyone walking out of Brother's building. She leaned a forearm on the fender. So she wouldn't fall on her face.

Footsteps came. Measured, unhurried. Coming her way. She lowered to her knees and crawled around the Cadillac toward the street, to keep the car between her and Bob. She stopped near the overturned metal garbage can that blocked the road. She got to her feet, but remained in a crouch. She listened. Nothing. Then footsteps bulleted toward her. She shot up. To Run. But Bob caught her in a hug that pinned her arms to her sides, his chest to hers.

She yelled obscenities while jumping up and down. She worked one arm loose and beat Bob on the head with her fist. He let go, but only long enough to pin her arms to her sides again, and goddamn, she hated that feeling of being imprisoned. She twisted right and left, her heel backing into the garbage can. She yanked an arm free, arched backward, and grabbed the can's handle. She heaved the can, swinging with her whole body. The can missed Bob and landed on the hood of the Cadillac. A smashing clatter.

"Rape, rape, rape!" Mary yelled in an almost-scream. She held onto the can and kept banging. A second-story window of the walk-up next to Brother's opened and a black man leaned out.

"What the fuck, you motherfucker!" the man said. "That's my automobile."

Bob hit Mary in the bicep with his fist. Pain shot to her brain. Her muscle lost power, causing her hand to open. The can fell to the ground. Bob spun her away from him and grabbed her from behind. He dragged her backward, toward the sidewalk, toward his brother's den. Bob let go for a moment so fast she noted the absence only after it was gone. Only after she felt the thin cord slip around her neck. She clawed to get her fingers between the cord and her throat. But too late. The cord pulled tight and she could no longer breathe. The girl. The silent woods. And how you kid yourself, thinking you know how these things happened. But you don't. Until the moment comes. Then you think, *I'm dying.*

The owner of the Cadillac walked out the front door of the building in bare feet and sweats, his chest naked. She reached a shaking hand toward him. He lifted a gun and pointed the barrel at her. Though not at her. Instead he looked through her like she wasn't there, dying before his eyes.

"You planning to smash my automobile and walk away, motherfucker?" the man said.

"Send the bill to Richard," Bob said, the sound tight, controlled.

"You Richard's little brother?" The man lowered his gun. Laughed. "Need help taming your bitch?"

Her body convulsed. She had a second, maybe two, before she blacked out. She thrust her hips back into Bob's crotch. He grunted and loosened his grip. The rope slackened and she gasped. The urge incredible, to run. But maybe the strangled girl had tried to run, too. So instead, she twisted toward Bob. Her chest to his, she wrapped an arm around his neck and still out of breath, kissed him hard. His mouth opened to hers and as he kissed her in return—an odd, hard caressing of lip and tongue—she slipped her hand into her pocket. For what she'd forgotten. Danny's lighter. Their mouths together, her hands where he couldn't see them, she pulled the back of his T-shirt away from his body and set the cloth on fire. One thousand one, one thousand two, one thousand—

Bob arched his back and yelled.

She ran down the block in a heavy, side-to-side motion, while trying to keep the world in front of her. She wanted to vomit, but there was no time because how long could it take to pull off a burning T-shirt or roll on the ground to extinguish the flames? Five seconds? She passed the doorway to the drug den and when she reached the corner, turned. She ran toward a church and stumbled, then crawled, up the broad, shallow steps to a black corner of the deep doorway. She pulled her knees to her chest, throat throbbing. Bob ran by, his stride light and fast. Assuming she'd be nearby, he'd come back from the other direction, in which case the streetlight would be in his favor. Instead of being hidden in black, she would be outlined against the white stone. She tottered down the steps and turned the corner. She ran another block, turned right, and stopped. People milling halfway down the block. Fifteen? Twenty? She raised her arms. But they all looked male.

"Yo, baby," a man yelled. Some of the figures walked toward her, then broke into a jog.

She ran to the next block. One sideways glance and she saw it: a phone booth at the end of the street. She ran toward the booth. But Bob would see her before she had a chance to call. There was an alley. But she'd be an idiot to risk heading into what might be a dead-end. Then again, she was an idiot, right?

She turned into the alley and heaved open one of two lids atop a metal dumpster. She hauled herself up onto the edge and fell in, head first. She closed the lid and burrowed through the half-filled bin to the far corner where she sat in liquid that soaked through her coat and jeans. She pulled bags over her head. She heard people run by, laughing. A car door slammed, the sound muffled through the bags. Another car gunned down the street. After a while, a third car came, this one cruising. She imagined Bob's calm face behind the wheel of the Charger. Those watching eyes. The sound slid by.

Silence came, and with it, the smell. Of garbage thrown in without bags, the pieces falling between her knees along with the feel of slime on her ass and in her hair. And to think that before dawn came, she could be dead and decaying, too, among the wads of toilet paper, used diapers, cans, and bottles. Just another piece of trash. She threw up on herself. And when she couldn't hold her pee any longer, pissed.

Lots of shit, Bob had said.

Sure, she'd said.

And he'd almost given her what she'd prayed for, and oh Christ, that she could have hailed death. *Hey, over here. Come get me!* She belonged in a dumpster. Surrounded by the goneness of Danny, the absence of Kathleen, and a loneliness that leaves you bound, mangled, deserted. She cried without sound, her mouth stretched wide. For herself and the poor, stupid, idiot of a girl who'd died in horror, eyes bulging as the last images of her world faded.

Time passed. But how long? Too much, maybe, or not enough. The minutes, the hours, the years. No time enough to cry for such loss. Yet the phone booth. The loss, and yet the phone booth, too, out there, waiting. If she waited for morning, he'd see her, because the time for illusions had ended. He'd look until he found her.

She picked up bags and set them aside as quietly as possible. Then she rose and pushed open the lid and peered out. Nothing moved. She listened. Nothing again. Still she waited, remembering the silence before Bob rushed at her. Though her legs cramped and her body shook, she climbed out.

She must have thrown up most of the drug because the world was only a little dizzy now. She tiptoed to the alley's entrance and looked up one side of the empty street and down the other. She swallowed, and sticking close to the buildings, bounded on the balls of her feet to the street sign. Then she ran to the phone and closed the booth door. The light didn't go on. She squinted, but the booth was too dark to read the digits for the police. She pushed zero and twisted around one way, then the other.

"Come on," she whispered.

The operator answered, and Mary's aching throat opened, spilling everything. An emergency. Somebody tried to strangle her. Still after her. Send somebody. She gave the intersection.

Mary hung up and ran back to the alley. She squatted behind the garbage bin. She bit her lower lip, tearing pieces of skin off with her teeth until tasting blood. Her thighs shook and her teeth chattered. She heard the engine, the familiar purr, there no time to climb back into the bin, so she remained still. The Charger moved past.

At almost the same moment, the cop car cruised by going the other way. If Mary waited until the Charger was gone, the police car might disappear, too. Door Number One or Two? She ran into the street after the police car, which was at the far end of the street, ready to turn the corner.

"Over here!" she yelled, voice hoarse.

The wheels of the Charger squealed behind her. A car door opened. She glanced behind her to see Bob running toward her. The police car stopped. Bob stopped. He turned and ran back to his car. He'd get in and drive away from her. From what he'd done to her. And how you know you're supposed to run toward safety and away from your attacker. But the rage, the *rage*. Rocket fuel in your blood, making you run against all reason into the blinding glare of the explosion.

"You fucking asshole!" she screamed.

Bob leapt into his car. Light. Easy.

"You think you can do that to me?"

He slammed his door.

"You think I'll take that shit?"

The Charger shot forward.

Mary glanced over her shoulder at the cops, who were out of their car now, jogging her way. Jogging, when they should be running.

"That's him. That's the fuck!" she said.

She turned back. Bob's taillights disappeared around the corner.

She shot her fists up and screamed, "No!" until it became a note that stretched out as she arched her back and fell to her knees, crying.

***

Mary sat in a wood chair in the lobby of the old police station. She stared at the door that opened onto the street. She'd done everything the police officers had asked. Given information for the police report. Let them take pictures of her neck. And when they brought Bob in, she'd picked him out of a lineup. Even then he seemed to stare at her, despite the one-way glass. Bob, who'd shown her what true nothing really meant. Then a female officer asked Mary if she had anyone who could come get her. And did she? Have anyone to pick her up, take her home, no matter the time of day or night, no questions asked?

And how you realize you do. That though you told yourself you don't, you now know you've been lying. So you make the call. A short one. About where you are and that you need a way home. *Can you come?* A short answer followed. And then Mary waited for what she hadn't believed existed. Good Samaritans. Guardian angels. People just waiting to jump out of nowhere to do good deeds. That they can be there for you, even when you don't deserve them.

The officer had asked Mary if she wanted to wait in another room. Because of how bad she looked and how she stank. But she said no. She sat facing the door. To see if it would open for her. Because this time she'd go through this door and let it fall shut behind her, never to open again.

The door opened. Mary leaned forward. Cold air swirled in with someone dressed in a parka. A man, a stranger. She dropped her eyes to her grimy hands. Because that's what you do when you look and smell like shit. When you are shit. *When I am shit.*

The stranger walked past and got buzzed through the locked door beside her. Warm air blew on her head from a vent in the ceiling. A female police officer at the front counter talked on the phone. Yellow light shone down from two over-head-hanging lamps. The sky through the tall windows had lightened. Her eyes crawled across the worn stone floor, then up the flagpole by the door. Past the limp flag to the gold eagle on top, wings spread for flight. Yet the bird couldn't fly, could it? The eagle, a symbol of freedom, yet forever impris-oned in a perpetual state of readiness. Like the angel in the cemetery. Like the car buckle in Danny's sculpture. Every-thing reminding her of what Danny had made. The eagle, the angel, a heart-shaped box of candy, the way somebody turned away, the reflection of light in a mirror. Maybe that was the point, what Danny wanted her to know. How something could be anything, as in nothing or everything.

The front door opened. Light shone, a rose of imminent sunrise. Someone entered, head down. Someone with a puff of short brown hair. Someone who wore a black wool coat and navy pants that caught on her ankle-high rubber boots. Mrs. McCarthy looked up. Mary stood, her body shaking. And the tears, always the goddamned tears. But she didn't care. Not anymore. She took a step forward, her arms out and empty palms facing skyward.

Acknowledgements

Winter Light, along with everything I've ever written, came to be through the contributions of everyone I've ever interacted with and every experience I've had in life. I'd like to send a special thanks to childhood through high school friends and teachers, especially those at Lyons Township High School in La Grange, IL.

I'd specifically like to thank every member of my Monday Night Writers group who offered astute comments and suggestions on this manuscript through many revisions. I'd also like to thank my good writing friends Dennis Sides, Alan Tracey, and Catherine Thrush.

I'm indebted to Peter Snell for lifting my manuscript to the top of the pile, and to Amie McCracken and Jessica Bell at Vine Leaves Press for their organizational and artistic help in making this book happen. Melissa Slayton provided a marvelously sensitive touch during the editing process.

Lastly, I'd like to thank my husband, Mike, for giving me the time and space to let my imagination run and run and run.

Vine Leaves Press

Enjoyed this book?
Go to *vineleavespress.com* to find more.

9 781925 965445